The STOLEN SCIENCE

DR SANJAY PARVA

Timeless wisdom and remarkable parallels between ancient Vedic knowledge and contemporary science

BLUEROSE PUBLISHERS
India | U.K.

Copyright © Dr Sanjay Parva 2025

All rights reserved by author. No part of this publication may be reproduced, stored in a retrieval system or transmitted in any form or by any means, electronic, mechanical, photocopying, recording or otherwise, without the prior permission of the author. Although every precaution has been taken to verify the accuracy of the information contained herein, the publisher assumes no responsibility for any errors or omissions. No liability is assumed for damages that may result from the use of information contained within.

BlueRose Publishers takes no responsibility for any damages, losses, or liabilities that may arise from the use or misuse of the information, products, or services provided in this publication.

For permissions requests or inquiries regarding this publication, please contact:

BLUEROSE PUBLISHERS
www.BlueRoseONE.com
info@bluerosepublishers.com
+91 8882 898 898
+4407342408967

ISBN: 978-93-7018-409-1

Cover design: Shubham Verma
Typesetting: Sagar

First Edition: February 2025

विद्या सर्वस्य भूषणम्

(Vidya Sarvasya Bhushanam)

Knowledge is the Ornament of All

— *The Panchtantra*

Dedication

– to my **Late Mother** for teaching me the power of selflessness

– to my friend and guide at **Spiritual Veda** for the awakening

– to **Dharmakshetra Foundation** for my inner transformation

– to the **Seekers of Truth**, past and present

By the Same Author

- Unseen Beauty of Kargil
- Words About To Fall
- Disability Is This Ability
- Home Management of Work-Related Pains
- If You Are a Hindu Your Children Must Know This
- Kheer Bhawani: The Divine Presence of Mata Ragnya

Contents

Preface 1

200 Ancient Practices in the Modern World 3

Chapter 1: Introduction 61
   Setting the Stage for the Exploration of Vedic Insights and Scientific Discoveries 61
   The Historical Context of Vedic Wisdom: Echoes of Ancient Realms 68
   Quantum Physics and Vedanta: Exploring the Correlation 81
   Neuroscience and Vedic Perspectives on Consciousness: A Symbiotic Correlation 85
   The Historical Context of Vedic Wisdom and the Evolution of Modern Scientific Thought 96

Chapter 2: The Nature of Reality 99
   Vedic Perspectives 99
   Insights from Ancient Texts on the Illusory Nature of the Material World 100
   Scientific Understanding 102
   Establishing Parallels Between Quantum Mechanics and Vedic Maya 106
   Theories on the Nature of Matter, Energy, and the Fabric of Reality 110
   Drawing Parallels Between Multiverse Hypothesis and Existence of Lokas as Mentioned in Vedas 119

Chapter 3: Consciousness and Self-awareness 124
   Vedic Insights 124

The Role of Consciousness in Vedic Philosophy:
Piloting the Cosmos Within 129

Scientific Exploration... 137

Neuroscientific Perspectives on Consciousness
and the Mind... 137

The Mystery of Self-awareness and its Scientific
Examination 141

Chapter 4: Cosmology and the Universe 148

Vedic Cosmology and Cycles of Creation and
Destruction (Yugas) 148

The Cosmic Dance of Shiva and the Eternal Nature
of the Universe... 152

Scientific Theories 155

Current Cosmological Models and Scientific
Understanding of the Cosmos....................................... 160

Do Vedic Theories of Creation Overlap with Modern
Theories of Creation?... 164

Chapter 5: Time and Space 168

Vedic Concepts... 168

Time as a Cyclical Phenomenon (Kalachakra)............... 168

Kalachakra in Vedic Hymns... 170

The Eternal Nature of Space and the Interplay
of Time... 172

Scientific Theories 175

Einstein's Theory of Relativity and the Concept of
Spacetime 175

Impact on Cosmology and Astrophysics........................ 177

Modern Physics' Exploration of the Nature of Time 179

Similarities Between Vedic Kalachakra and Modern
Theories of Time and Space... 182

Chapter 6: Healing and Wellness 186
   Ayurveda and Vedic Approaches 186
   The Mind-Body Connection in Vedic Healing
   Practices... 191
   Integration with Modern Medicine............................... 197
   The Potential Synergy Between Traditional and
   Modern Approaches in Medicine and Healing.............. 203

Chapter 7: Meditation and Mind-Body Connection.......211
   Vedic Meditation Practices.. 211
   The Impact of Meditation on Mental and Physical
   Well-being.. 215
   Scientific Research 218
   The Growing Recognition of Meditation in
   Mainstream Healthcare... 221

Chapter 8: Environmental Wisdom...............................225
   Vedic Teachings on Nature.. 225
   Sacred Environmental Practices in Vedic Traditions 230
   Scientific Perspectives 233
   Environmental Science and the Urgent Need for
   Sustainability... 233
   The Alignment of Vedic Principles with Modern Ecological
   Concerns 237

Chapter 9: Common Threads and Divergences..............240
   Identifying Commonalities... 240
   Shared Goals and Values in Understanding the
   World... 243
   Exploring Divergences.. 247
   Areas Where Vedic Insights and Scientific Discoveries May
   Differ... 247

    Steering Through Conflicting Perspectives and
Fostering Dialogue..250

Chapter 10: Future Directions 254
    Integration Opportunities...254
    The Potential for Interdisciplinary Collaboration...........257
    Encouraging Dialogue 264
    Building Bridges Between Traditional Wisdom and
Cutting-edge Science 264
    The Role of Open-minded Exploration in Shaping
the Future...267

Chapter 11: Case Studies: Vedic Wisdom in Modern Context..271
    Real-World Examples of Vedic Principles Influencing
Scientific Practices 271
    Instances of Successfully Applying Ancient Insights in
Contemporary Settings..274

Chapter 12: Conclusion 278

Preface

In the boundless expanse of human inquiry, where the shores of knowledge meet the horizons of wisdom, we find ourselves on a sacred journey – a journey that transcends the confines of disciplines and cultures, weaving together the threads of scientific exploration and ancient philosophical insights.

This book is the culmination of a quest – a quest for understanding that has led us through the corridors of time and wisdom, guided by the twin flames of curiosity and reverence. As we embark upon this odyssey, let us pause for a moment to reflect on the path that has brought us to this moment.

In the opening chapters, we delve into the enigmatic realm of quantum mechanics, where particles dance in a symphony of uncertainty, and the observer is inseparable from the observed. Drawing inspiration from ancient Vedic texts, we glimpse the interconnectedness of all existence and the illusory nature of the material world.

From the celestial dance of galaxies to the intricate rhythms of the cosmos, we traverse the vast expanse of the universe, contemplating the mysteries of creation and the eternal cycle of birth and dissolution. Along the way, we encounter parallel realities and diverse realms of existence, each woven into the fabric of creation like threads in a cosmic prayer rosary.

Turning our gaze inward, we explore the mysteries of consciousness – the quantum mind that gives rise to thoughts, perceptions, and realities. In the healing power of nature and the wisdom of ancient healing traditions, we find solace and inspiration, embracing a holistic approach to health and well-being.

As we journey through the pages of this book, we bridge the realms of science and spirituality, forging a path of synthesis that honors the wisdom of the ancients while embracing the insights of modern inquiry. We uncover the timeless truths that lie at the heart of existence, transcending the limitations of time and space.

In the stillness of meditation and contemplation, we heed the call to consciousness – a call to awaken to the deeper truths that lie beyond the veil of appearances. As we bid farewell to these pages, let us carry with us the wisdom gleaned from our explorations, knowing that the journey is never truly over, but rather a continuous unfolding of the mysteries of existence.

With gratitude for the opportunity to embark on this sacred journey together, I invite you, dear reader, to join me as we explore the realms of knowledge and wisdom with clarity and insight. May this book serve as a beacon of light on your own journey of discovery, illuminating your path with the timeless wisdom that resides within us all.

In peace and reverence for this eternal universe.

Dr Sanjay Parva
Ancient Anand Bhairva Temple
Village Malmoh, Tehsil Pattan,
District Baramulla, 193401 - Kashmir
May 13, 2024 – Sukla Paksha Shashthi, Vaisakha 5, 2081

200 Ancient Practices in the Modern World

Several ideas and discoveries from ancient Indian texts, especially in the realms of mathematics, medicine, astronomy, and metallurgy, have been incorporated or re-explored in the modern scientific world, though not always with direct attribution to their Indian origins. Here's a list of some of the concepts and inventions that have parallels in ancient Indian knowledge and texts:

1. Zero and the Decimal System

- **Ancient India**: The concept of zero (śūnya) as a number and its incorporation into the decimal system was formalized in ancient Indian texts like the *Brahmagupta's Brāhmasphutasiddhānta* (7th century CE).

- **Modern Adoption**: European mathematicians used the Indian-Arabic numeral system, but often its origins were credited indirectly. The concept of zero revolutionized mathematics globally.

2. Pythagorean Theorem

- **Ancient India**: The *Śulbasūtras* (8th–6th century BCE), which are part of the Vedic texts, describe a geometric principle equivalent to the Pythagorean theorem, centuries before Pythagoras (6th century BCE).

- **Modern Attribution**: In Western history, this theorem is named after Pythagoras, though the Indian connection is rarely mentioned.

3. Ayurveda and Medicine

- **Ancient India:** Ayurveda, particularly the works like the *Charaka Samhita* and *Sushruta Samhita*, contained detailed knowledge of surgery, pharmacology, and general medicine. Sushruta, known as the "Father of Surgery," described surgical procedures, including rhinoplasty (plastic surgery).

- **Modern Rediscovery:** Techniques from these texts influenced later developments in surgery and medicine, although Ayurveda itself was marginalized in favor of Western medicine.

4. Metallurgy (Iron and Steel)

- **Ancient India:** Ancient Indians excelled in metallurgy, with examples like the *Delhi Iron Pillar* (built around 400 CE), which has resisted corrosion for over 1,600 years. They also developed high-quality steel, known as *Wootz* steel.

- **Modern Metallurgy:** Western metallurgists were inspired by Wootz steel in the development of Damascus steel and other advanced metalworking techniques, but often did not credit its Indian origins.

5. Yoga and Meditation

- **Ancient India:** The practices of yoga, pranayama (breathing techniques), and meditation were outlined in texts like the *Patanjali's Yoga Sutras* (circa 400 BCE) and *Bhagavad Gita*.

- **Modern Wellness:** Though yoga is now a global phenomenon, much of its ancient Indian philosophical and spiritual context is often stripped away in its modern commercialization.

6. Atomic Theory

- **Ancient India:** Indian philosopher *Kanada* (circa 600 BCE) proposed the idea of "anu" (atom) as an indivisible entity in his philosophy of Vaisheshika, predating Greek atomic theory.

- **Modern Science:** Western atomic theory developed much later, with Democritus being credited as the father of atomic theory in the West, despite Kanada's earlier contributions.

7. Heliocentrism

- **Ancient India:** Indian astronomers like *Aryabhata* (5th century CE) posited that the Earth rotates on its axis and revolves around the Sun, well before Copernicus' heliocentric model (16th century CE).

- **Modern Astronomy:** The Western world acknowledges Copernicus for heliocentrism, but Aryabhata's earlier work is rarely credited.

8. Cosmology (Time and Universe Cycles)

- **Ancient India:** Vedic and Puranic texts describe the universe's creation and destruction in cycles, with a timescale that extends to billions of years, comparable to modern astrophysical theories about the age of the universe.

- **Modern Parallel:** The idea of cyclical time and the vast timescales of cosmology in Indian texts parallels modern scientific ideas about the Big Bang, the age of the universe, and cosmic cycles.

9. Cataract Surgery

- **Ancient India:** The *Sushruta Samhita* describes cataract surgery and other advanced medical procedures.
- **Modern Surgery:** Although cataract surgery techniques evolved significantly, Sushruta's early methods laid the groundwork for future advancements, though his contributions are not always credited.

10. Trigonometry and Mathematics

- **Ancient India:** Indian mathematicians like *Aryabhata* and *Bhaskara II* (12th century CE) made significant contributions to trigonometry, including sine and cosine functions.
- **Modern Trigonometry:** These concepts were later absorbed into European mathematical traditions but often without due acknowledgment of their Indian origins.

11. Pi (π) Approximation

- **Ancient India:** The mathematician *Madhava* (circa 14th century CE) and the Kerala school of astronomy calculated Pi with remarkable accuracy, predating European developments.
- **Modern Calculations:** The formula for Pi is often associated with European mathematicians, but the Kerala school's advancements were groundbreaking for their time.

12. Quantum Mechanics Parallels

- **Ancient India:** Some scholars find philosophical parallels between the concept of wave-particle duality in quantum physics and certain ideas from Indian texts like Vedanta and Buddhist thought, which discuss the nature of reality, impermanence, and observer-influenced phenomena.

- **Modern Physics:** These parallels are speculative but suggest ancient Indian philosophy offered frameworks that resonate with modern quantum theories.

13. Binomial Theorem and Pascal's Triangle

- **Ancient India:** Indian mathematician *Pingala* (3rd century BCE) worked on combinatorics and binomial coefficients, leading to the early form of what we now call Pascal's Triangle. Later, *Bhaskara II* (12th century CE) expanded upon these ideas.

- **Modern Mathematics:** The binomial theorem is widely attributed to Western mathematicians like Isaac Newton, but Pingala and Bhaskara's work predated these discoveries by centuries.

14. Concept of Relativity (Time Dilation)

- **Ancient India:** In the *Mahabharata*, the story of *Kakudmi* and *Brahma* presents an idea similar to time dilation: Kakudmi visits Brahma in a higher dimension, and upon his return, many years have passed on Earth. Similarly, Vedic texts discuss varying perceptions of time in different realms.

- **Modern Physics:** Albert Einstein's theory of relativity (1905) introduced time dilation, where time passes at different rates depending on the speed and gravitational field. While not scientific, ancient Indian cosmology hinted at this concept through stories and metaphysical discussions.

15. Gravitational Concepts

- **Ancient India:** *Brahmagupta* (7th century CE) proposed that Earth attracts objects, a concept of gravity. This is often cited as an early idea of gravitational force long before Isaac Newton formulated the universal law of gravitation in the 17th century.

- **Modern Physics:** Newton's discovery of gravity is a major milestone in science, but Brahmagupta's insight was an earlier attempt at understanding this phenomenon.

16. Vaccination and Inoculation (Smallpox)

- **Ancient India:** India had a traditional practice of *variolation* or inoculation for smallpox as early as 1000 CE. This was a precursor to modern vaccination. The practice involved taking material from smallpox sores and introducing it to healthy individuals to build immunity.

- **Modern Medicine:** Edward Jenner is credited with creating the smallpox vaccine in 1796, but the practice of inoculation existed in India and China long before that.

17. Levitation and Magnetic Fields

- **Ancient India:** Ancient texts like the *Samarangana Sutradhara* describe *Vimanas* (flying machines) and the concept of levitation through magnetic fields.

While these descriptions are often considered mythological, they evoke ideas about anti-gravity and propulsion.

- **Modern Science:** Magnetic levitation (Maglev technology) and ion propulsion are modern technologies, though their link to ancient texts remains speculative.

18. Linguistics and Formal Grammar (Panini)

- **Ancient India:** *Panini* (circa 5th century BCE) developed an advanced system of grammar and linguistics in his text *Ashtadhyayi*, which laid out rules for Sanskrit syntax, morphology, and phonetics. His system is considered highly structured, almost algorithmic.

- **Modern Linguistics:** Panini's work influenced modern linguistics, including the development of formal language theory, computational linguistics, and even modern computer science principles like formal grammars and programming languages.

19. Hydraulic Engineering and Water Management

- **Ancient India:** Ancient Indian civilizations like the Indus Valley (circa 2500 BCE) developed advanced systems of urban planning, including intricate drainage systems, water reservoirs, and wells. The *Arthashastra* (3rd century BCE) also discusses irrigation and water management practices.

- **Modern Engineering:** The concepts of urban planning and sustainable water management used by the Indus Valley are comparable to modern civil engineering, and ancient Indian methods of water storage are still influential in sustainable development projects.

20. Fibonacci Sequence

- **Ancient India:** *Acharya Hemachandra* (12th century CE) described the sequence that later became known as the Fibonacci series, in his study of Sanskrit poetry meter. The Fibonacci sequence is a series where each number is the sum of the two preceding ones.

- **Modern Mathematics:** This sequence is usually credited to Leonardo Fibonacci, who introduced it to Europe in 1202, but Hemachandra had already documented it.

21. Botany and Plant Science

- **Ancient India:** Texts like the *Vrikshayurveda* (Ayurveda for plants), attributed to *Surapala* (circa 10th century CE), detail knowledge of plant life, agriculture, and botany, including plant diseases and treatments.

- **Modern Botany:** Much of what was known in ancient Indian botany is aligned with modern plant science, although the early Indian understanding of plant physiology and treatments is often overlooked.

22. Spherical Shape of the Earth

- **Ancient India:** Indian astronomers like *Aryabhata* and *Varahamihira* (6th century CE) discussed the spherical shape of the Earth and its axial rotation, long before such ideas were widely accepted in Europe.

- **Modern Geography:** This idea became central to European Renaissance astronomy, yet Indian contributions to this knowledge are often understated in the West.

23. Ancient Cryptography

- **Ancient India:** In *Kautilya's Arthashastra* (3rd century BCE), there are references to coded messages and cryptography for military purposes. These involved complex methods of encoding and decoding information.

- **Modern Cryptography:** The principles of cryptography, now a fundamental aspect of cybersecurity, were hinted at in ancient Indian military and administrative strategies.

24. Astronomical Measurements and Solar/Lunar Eclipses

- **Ancient India:** Indian astronomers like *Aryabhata* made accurate measurements of celestial bodies, calculated the solar and lunar eclipses, and even posited that the moon shines by reflected sunlight.

- **Modern Astronomy:** Much of this knowledge was confirmed by modern astronomical methods, but Indian contributions were either lost or overlooked during colonial times when Western astronomy took the lead.

25. Acoustic and Sonic Energy (Mantra Science)

- **Ancient India:** Indian texts such as the *Vedas* and the *Upanishads* explore the concept of sound (nāda) and its relation to energy and the cosmos. The power of sound, as found in mantras, was believed to influence mental states and even material reality.

- **Modern Science:** Studies in sonic energy, vibrational frequencies, and their impact on matter (as seen in cymatics) and psychology reflect these ancient Indian ideas about sound energy and its effects.

26. Theory of Light (Wave-Particle Duality)

- **Ancient India:** The *Nyaya* and *Vaisheshika* schools of philosophy (around 6th century BCE) discussed light as both a particle and a wave, with elements of emission and reflection.

- **Modern Physics:** The wave-particle duality of light was developed by scientists like Albert Einstein and Louis de Broglie in the 20th century, but ancient Indian philosophers hinted at these ideas long ago.

27. Sound Frequency and Music (Indian Classical Ragas)

- **Ancient India:** The *Sama Veda* and texts on Indian classical music extensively deal with the mathematical and therapeutic effects of sound and ragas on the human body and mind.

- **Modern Music Therapy:** Modern studies show that specific frequencies and musical patterns can affect mental and emotional states, similar to what ancient Indian texts proposed.

28. Ether as a Medium

- **Ancient India:** Ancient Indian philosophy described *Akasha* (ether) as one of the five fundamental elements, considered a medium for sound and vibration.

- **Modern Physics:** While ether as a medium for light waves was dismissed after Einstein's theory of relativity, it was long considered in physics and reappears in speculative theories regarding quantum fields.

29. Solar Calendar

- **Ancient India**: India developed highly accurate solar calendars based on astronomical observations, such as the *Surya Siddhanta* (circa 400 CE), which laid down rules for the solar and lunar cycles.

- **Modern Calendar Systems**: The Western Gregorian calendar evolved later but was preceded by Indian systems of time measurement, which were often more precise.

30. Chess (Chaturanga)

- **Ancient India**: The game *Chaturanga* originated in India around the 6th century CE. It later evolved into the game of chess as it spread to Persia and Europe.

- **Modern Chess**: While chess is widely popular today, its roots in India are often downplayed or forgotten.

31. Medicine for Diabetes (Madhumeha)

- **Ancient India**: Ayurveda texts like the *Charaka Samhita* and *Sushruta Samhita* describe treatments for diabetes (called *Madhumeha*), including dietary control and herbal remedies.

- **Modern Diabetes Treatment**: The treatment of diabetes with lifestyle changes and natural remedies in ancient India predated modern medical approaches to managing the condition.

32. Atomic Energy Concepts in Vedic Texts

- **Ancient India**: The concept of immense energy locked within matter appears in Vedic hymns and stories, such as those discussing Brahmastras (weapons with the power of atomic destruction).
- **Modern Nuclear Energy**: Although mythological, these ideas echo modern nuclear physics, where immense energy is released from the splitting or fusion of atomic nuclei.

33. Antibiotics and Antibacterial Herbs

- **Ancient India**: Ayurvedic texts describe the use of natural antibacterial substances like turmeric, neem, and honey for treating infections and wounds.
- **Modern Medicine**: These substances have been scientifically proven to possess antimicrobial properties and are used in modern natural therapies and medicines.

34. Theory of Karma and Quantum Physics

- **Ancient India**: The principle of *Karma* describes actions and their inevitable consequences, similar to the cause-and-effect law. It reflects an understanding of the interconnectedness of events.
- **Modern Quantum Physics**: The quantum realm's principle of causality and observer effect resonates with this ancient concept, suggesting that observers can influence outcomes.

35. Vedic Mathematics (Mental Calculation Techniques)

- **Ancient India:** The *Vedic Mathematics* sutras, passed down orally, contained mental shortcuts and rapid techniques for complex calculations.
- **Modern Mental Math:** Techniques from Vedic Mathematics are now taught globally for quick mental math, especially in competitive exams.

36. Magnetic Compass and Navigation

- **Ancient India:** *Rigveda* (circa 1500 BCE) refers to the use of lodestone for navigation, and the *Vastu Shastra* describes directions based on magnetic poles.
- **Modern Navigation:** The magnetic compass became common much later, but early references to magnetic materials and directional guidance are found in Indian texts.

37. Artificial Intelligence (AI) Philosophical Roots

- **Ancient India:** Indian texts explore the nature of consciousness and intelligence, questioning whether machines or entities without consciousness can possess knowledge or perform intelligent actions.
- **Modern AI:** These ancient philosophical inquiries align with current debates in artificial intelligence, particularly regarding consciousness in machines.

38. Torsion Physics and Cosmic Forces

- **Ancient India:** Ancient Indian cosmology talks about forces like *Prana* (life force) and its role in creating motion and stability in the cosmos.
- **Modern Physics:** While speculative, the role of torsion fields and twisting forces in modern

theoretical physics echoes ancient Indian ideas about cosmic dynamics.

39. Conception of Evolution (Dashavatara)

- **Ancient India**: The *Dashavatara* (Ten Avatars of Vishnu) describes an evolutionary sequence of life from aquatic creatures to mammals and humans.

- **Modern Evolutionary Theory**: Though symbolic, this sequence bears some resemblance to modern evolutionary theory, which traces life's progression from simple to complex forms.

40. Color Theory and Perception

- **Ancient India**: Indian art and philosophy explored the psychology of colors in texts like the *Shilpa Shastra*, which tied specific colors to emotions and states of mind.

- **Modern Color Psychology**: Modern research in color psychology echoes many of the principles explored in ancient Indian texts regarding how colors influence perception and mood.

41. Mind-Body Connection in Health

- **Ancient India**: Ayurveda and Yoga both emphasize the deep connection between mental and physical health. Mindful breathing, posture, and thought were believed to directly impact physical well-being.

- **Modern Medicine**: The mind-body connection is now a well-researched field, particularly in areas like psychosomatic medicine, stress management, and holistic health practices.

42. Environmental Sustainability

- **Ancient India:** The concept of *Rta* (cosmic order) emphasized living in harmony with nature, and texts like *Arthashastra* advocated for forest conservation and water management.

- **Modern Environmentalism:** The principles of sustainable development and environmental conservation align with ancient Indian views on ecological balance.

43. Iron Suspension Bridges

- **Ancient India:** Indian engineers built suspension bridges using iron chains as early as 4th century CE in regions like Kashmir and Ladakh.

- **Modern Engineering:** The technology of suspension bridges, using similar principles, became prominent much later in the West.

44. Plastic Surgery

- **Ancient India:** As detailed in the *Sushruta Samhita*, ancient Indian surgeons performed reconstructive surgery, particularly rhinoplasty (nose jobs), using techniques that are still applied today.

- **Modern Plastic Surgery:** Reconstructive surgery techniques developed by Sushruta influenced the modern field of plastic surgery.

45. Non-Euclidean Geometry

- **Ancient India:** Indian mathematicians like *Bharata* explored non-standard geometrical concepts, including circular and elliptical space.

- **Modern Geometry:** Non-Euclidean geometry became a fundamental aspect of modern mathematics, but its ancient Indian roots are often overlooked.

46. Spinning Wheel (Charkha)

- **Ancient India:** The spinning wheel (Charkha) was a key technological innovation in medieval India, used for turning cotton into thread.
- **Modern Industrialization:** The mechanization of thread production during the Industrial Revolution was influenced by earlier textile technologies, though Indian contributions are often forgotten.

47. Time Zones and Measurement of Time

- **Ancient India:** The *Surya Siddhanta* contained precise calculations of time based on the movement of celestial bodies, with detailed subdivisions of time like *nimesha* (seconds) and *kalpa* (epochs).
- **Modern Time Measurement:** Indian timekeeping systems were incredibly advanced and contributed to the development of accurate time zones and modern timekeeping.

48. Magnetism and Electricity

- **Ancient India:** Texts like the *Samarangana Sutradhara* describe the properties of natural magnets and electrical phenomena, such as static electricity.
- **Modern Physics:** Magnetism and electricity became central topics in physics centuries later, but Indian thinkers had speculated on these forces long before.

49. Parthenogenesis (Asexual Reproduction)

- **Ancient India**: Ancient Indian mythology and Ayurvedic texts mention asexual reproduction or parthenogenesis in certain species, especially among plants and lower animals.

- **Modern Biology**: The phenomenon of parthenogenesis, where offspring are produced without fertilization, has been scientifically proven and observed in some species.

50. Martial Arts (Kalaripayattu)

- **Ancient India**: Kalaripayattu, one of the oldest fighting systems in existence, originated in southern India and influenced martial arts forms like kung fu.

- **Modern Equivalent**: Mixed Martial Arts (MMA), which combines striking, grappling, and submission techniques from different martial arts, making it similar in its versatility to Kalaripayattu. MMA also includes punches, kicks, joint locks, and weapon skills, much like the varied techniques seen in Kalaripayattu.

51. Heliocentric Theory

- **Ancient India**: *Aryabhata* (5th century CE) proposed that the Earth rotates on its axis and that planets revolve around the Sun, a precursor to the heliocentric theory.

- **Modern Astronomy**: Nicolaus Copernicus (16th century) is credited with developing the heliocentric model, but Aryabhata's work predated this by more than a millennium.

52. Quantum Consciousness (Mind as Quantum Entity)

- **Ancient India**: In Vedanta and Yoga philosophy, consciousness is considered a fundamental entity of the universe, suggesting that mind and matter are interconnected at the deepest levels.

- **Modern Quantum Physics**: Theories in quantum mechanics exploring consciousness (e.g., the observer effect) echo the ancient Indian understanding of the mind's role in the physical world.

53. Centripetal Force

- **Ancient India**: In the *Surya Siddhanta*, the concept of a force keeping celestial bodies in their orbits (similar to gravity) is discussed. This is an early notion of centripetal force.

- **Modern Physics**: Isaac Newton formally introduced the idea of centripetal force in the context of planetary motion in the 17th century.

54. Fractals and Infinite Patterns in Nature

- **Ancient India**: The concept of infinitely repeating patterns, as seen in the designs of Indian temples, mandalas, and yantras, is akin to fractals.

- **Modern Mathematics**: Fractals were formally described by Benoit Mandelbrot in the 20th century, but Indian art and philosophy had long embraced the concept of infinite recursion in nature.

55. Numeral System and the Concept of Zero

- **Ancient India**: Indian mathematician *Brahmagupta* (7th century CE) is credited with formalizing the use of zero as both a number and a placeholder in positional numeral systems.

- **Modern Mathematics:** The Indian numeral system, including the concept of zero, was later adopted by the Arab world and Europe, profoundly influencing global mathematics.

56. Seismic Science (Earthquake Prediction)

- **Ancient India:** Ancient Indian texts, like the *Brihat Samhita* by *Varahamihira* (6th century CE), discuss the causes and signs of earthquakes, attempting to predict seismic activity.

- **Modern Seismology:** Seismic science advanced significantly in the 19th century, but ancient Indian thinkers had explored earthquake causes centuries earlier.

57. The Use of Mercury in Medicine

- **Ancient India:** In Ayurveda and Rasashastra (Indian alchemy), mercury and mercury compounds were used for treating ailments and preparing therapeutic elixirs.

- **Modern Medicine:** Although now carefully regulated due to toxicity, mercury was used in traditional medicine and was also a key ingredient in Western medicine (e.g., for treating syphilis) until the 20th century.

58. Theory of the Universe as Cyclic (Kalpa)

- **Ancient India:** The cyclical theory of the universe's creation, destruction, and rebirth (Kalpa in Hindu cosmology) suggests that time is not linear but circular.

- **Modern Cosmology:** Cyclic models of the universe, including the Big Bounce theory, echo this ancient understanding of cosmic cycles.

59. Proto-Quantum Field Theory (Vedic Concepts of Vibration)

- **Ancient India:** The Vedic concept of *Nada* (sound as the origin of creation) emphasizes that everything in the universe is a form of vibration, resonating with modern quantum field theory.

- **Modern Physics:** Quantum field theory suggests that particles are excitations of underlying fields, similar to the idea of vibrations as fundamental elements.

60. Astronomical Distance Measurement

- **Ancient India:** Ancient Indian astronomers like *Bhaskara II* and *Aryabhata* made accurate calculations of the size of Earth, the distances between celestial bodies, and the duration of eclipses.

- **Modern Astronomy:** Today's astronomical calculations, though more precise due to modern technology, follow many of the foundational ideas set by these early astronomers.

61. Herbal Birth Control

- **Ancient India:** Ayurvedic texts mention herbs and natural substances used for contraception and managing fertility, such as the use of neem and other plant extracts.

- **Modern Contraception:** Herbal contraception in traditional medicine foreshadowed the development of modern birth control methods.

62. Fermion and Boson Concepts in Philosophy

- **Ancient India:** Concepts of *Purusha* (consciousness) and *Prakriti* (matter) in Samkhya philosophy resemble the idea of fundamental forces and particles in physics, with dual aspects like fermions (matter) and bosons (force carriers).
- **Modern Physics:** These dual aspects of nature reflect modern particle physics, where fermions make up matter and bosons mediate forces.

63. Magnetotherapy and Healing with Magnetic Fields

- **Ancient India:** Ancient Indian texts describe the use of magnetic stones and magnetic fields for healing purposes, aligning with the body's bio-magnetic energy.
- **Modern Magnetotherapy:** The use of magnetic fields for medical treatment is a growing field in alternative and modern medicine.

64. Agriculture and Soil Science

- **Ancient India:** The *Krishi-Parashara* (agriculture manual by *Parashara*), written around the 6th century BCE, provided detailed knowledge on crop rotation, soil quality, and irrigation.
- **Modern Agriculture:** Today's agricultural science relies on similar principles of soil management and sustainable practices, but much of this knowledge was already in practice in ancient India.

65. Erosion and Geological Change

- **Ancient India**: Ancient texts like the *Vayu Purana* mention the slow changes in Earth's landforms due to erosion and the action of water and wind, suggesting an understanding of geological processes.

- **Modern Geology**: Modern geological studies confirm that these natural forces shape the Earth's surface over time, a concept already present in ancient Indian writings.

66. Metal Extraction and Metallurgy

- **Ancient India**: The extraction of metals like iron, copper, and zinc was highly advanced in ancient India. The *Rasaratnakara* (9th century CE) describes detailed methods of smelting and alloy creation.

- **Modern Metallurgy**: Modern methods of metal extraction owe much to ancient traditions, with India's knowledge of metallurgy preceding many later discoveries.

67. Light Therapy and Sun Salutation (Surya Namaskar)

- **Ancient India**: Practices like *Surya Namaskar* (Sun Salutation) were designed not just for physical health but also to absorb and benefit from the sun's energy for healing.

- **Modern Light Therapy**: Sunlight is now used in therapies to treat conditions like seasonal affective disorder (SAD) and vitamin D deficiency, a practice echoed in ancient health traditions.

68. Particle-Wave Duality in Sound (Nada Brahma)

- **Ancient India:** The Vedic notion of *Nada Brahma* (the universe is sound) suggests a duality of sound as both particle-like (discrete vibrations) and wave-like (continuous energy).

- **Modern Physics:** The duality of particles and waves in quantum mechanics reflects this ancient understanding of sound and energy.

69. Precise Surgical Instruments

- **Ancient India:** Sushruta (circa 600 BCE) describes over 100 types of surgical instruments made from metals, used for intricate procedures like cataract surgery and suturing.

- **Modern Surgery:** The precision of surgical tools today echoes the ancient knowledge of fine instruments for medical operations.

70. Ancient Aviation (Vimanas)

- **Ancient India:** The *Vimana* texts describe flying machines (Vimanas) with advanced technologies for propulsion, navigation, and aerial warfare.

- **Modern Aviation:** While mythological, these descriptions of aircraft in ancient texts hint at early conceptualizations of flight, predating modern aerodynamics.

71. Health Benefits of Fasting

- **Ancient India:** Fasting, as described in Ayurveda and Yoga, is prescribed for detoxification, healing, and spiritual growth, with specific techniques for different body types and conditions.

- **Modern Science:** Intermittent fasting and calorie restriction have been shown to have numerous health benefits, reflecting the ancient practice.

72. Sanskrit and Computer Algorithms

- **Ancient India:** The grammatical system of *Panini* (5th century BCE) in his *Ashtadhyayi* resembles a highly structured algorithmic system, which modern computer scientists acknowledge as one of the earliest forms of structured language.

- **Modern Computing:** Panini's work influenced the development of formal languages in computer science, proving the deep roots of algorithmic thinking in ancient India.

73. Yogic Breath Control (Pranayama)

- **Ancient India:** The science of *Pranayama* (controlled breathing) in Yoga was practiced to regulate the body's vital forces, balance the mind, and promote longevity.

- **Modern Respiratory Science:** Techniques like diaphragmatic breathing, used in modern medicine to manage stress and respiratory conditions, have parallels in these ancient practices.

74. Nonlinear Dynamics in Poetry

- **Ancient India:** Sanskrit poetry and texts often employed complex, nonlinear structures with layers of meaning and intertextual references, similar to modern nonlinear dynamics and systems theory.

- **Modern Literature:** Postmodern and contemporary literature often uses nonlinear narrative techniques, a practice that can be traced back to ancient Indian poetics.

75. Sexual Health and Wellness (Kama Sutra)

- **Ancient India**: The *Kama Sutra* provides not only advice on physical intimacy but also explores mental and emotional well-being through balanced relationships.

- **Modern Sexual Health**: Today's holistic approach to sexual health often mirrors the balanced, wellness-focused advice found in the ancient text.

76. Gravitational Lensing Concepts

- **Ancient India**: Indian astronomers like *Bhaskara II* suggested that light and celestial objects could be affected by gravity, indicating an early understanding of what we now call gravitational lensing.

- **Modern Physics**: Gravitational lensing, a concept in Einstein's theory of general relativity, echoes these ancient ideas.

77. Biofeedback and Meditation

- **Ancient India**: Yogic meditation techniques included biofeedback principles, using mental focus and awareness to regulate bodily functions such as heart rate and breathing.

- **Modern Biofeedback**: This method is now a recognized therapeutic technique used to control stress and manage pain.

78. Boiling and Purification of Water

- **Ancient India:** The *Sushruta Samhita* advises boiling water to make it safe for drinking, a method widely practiced in ancient India.
- **Modern Water Purification:** Boiling remains one of the most effective ways to purify water, and this ancient technique is still used worldwide today.

79. Use of Pulleys and Levers

- **Ancient India:** Ancient Indian engineers used pulleys, levers, and counterweights in construction, particularly in temple-building techniques.
- **Modern Engineering:** These simple machines are fundamental to modern engineering, reflecting ancient India's sophisticated knowledge of mechanics.

80. Acoustic Science (Nada Yoga)

- **Ancient India:** The practice of *Nada Yoga* emphasized sound frequencies and their effects on the human body and mind, particularly through chanting and vibrations.
- **Modern Acoustics:** The study of sound waves and their impact on the brain, seen in modern acoustics, is closely related to the ancient Indian knowledge of sound's healing power.

81. Genetic Mutations in Mythology

- **Ancient India:** Indian mythology, such as stories of *Hiranyaksha* or *Hanuman*, contains descriptions of beings with altered abilities, perhaps reflecting an understanding of genetic variation or mutation.

- **Modern Genetics:** Genetic mutation and engineering, now foundational to modern biology, resonate with these ancient tales of altered or enhanced capabilities.

82. Water Harvesting and Conservation

- **Ancient India:** Water conservation techniques such as step wells, tanks, and irrigation systems were used extensively, especially in semi-arid regions like Rajasthan.
- **Modern Water Management:** These ancient methods are still studied and used today in arid regions to manage water efficiently.

83. Speech and Linguistics (Shiksha Vedanga)

- **Ancient India:** The *Shiksha Vedanga* (a part of the Vedas) provides a detailed account of phonetics, accent, and speech production, anticipating modern linguistics.
- **Modern Linguistics:** The detailed phonetic analysis in this ancient text is mirrored in the way modern linguistics studies sound and language structure.

84. Atomic Nature of Matter (Paramanu)

- **Ancient India:** Indian philosopher *Kanada* (around 600 BCE) proposed that all matter is composed of minute, indivisible particles called *Parmanu*, an early concept of the atom.
- **Modern Atomic Theory:** This aligns with the later development of atomic theory in modern physics, beginning with Dalton's model in the 19th century.

85. Vaccination and Inoculation (Smallpox)

- **Ancient India:** Inoculation practices against smallpox were carried out in India long before the development of modern vaccination, using methods like variolation.
- **Modern Vaccination:** The discovery of vaccines in the 18th century by Edward Jenner echoes earlier practices in India to prevent diseases like smallpox.

86. Mental Health and Psychiatry

- **Ancient India:** Ayurveda and other ancient Indian texts described various mental disorders and their treatments, with a holistic approach combining diet, meditation, and herbal remedies.
- **Modern Psychiatry:** The treatment of mental health conditions now acknowledges the mind-body connection and the role of holistic therapies, reflecting ancient Indian approaches.

87. Subconscious and Dreams (Yoga Nidra)

- **Ancient India:** The practice of *Yoga Nidra* is a form of deep relaxation and exploration of the subconscious mind, leading to altered states of consciousness.
- **Modern Psychology:** The study of the subconscious in psychoanalysis (Freud, Jung) shares similarities with the ancient practice of Yoga Nidra.

88. Non-Linear Time (Buddhist Concept of Time)

- **Ancient India:** Buddhist philosophy speaks of non-linear time, suggesting that past, present, and future can exist simultaneously or in interdependent cycles.

- **Modern Physics:** Theories of time in relativity and quantum mechanics challenge the linear perception of time, resonating with ancient Indian philosophical views.

89. Architectural Acoustics

- **Ancient India:** Temples and ancient Indian buildings were designed to amplify sound, creating echo effects for chanting and rituals. This was especially prominent in Dravidian architecture.
- **Modern Architectural Acoustics:** Today's design of auditoriums and concert halls incorporates similar principles of sound amplification and echo management.

90. Invisibility and Camouflage in Mythology

- **Ancient India:** Stories from Indian epics, like those involving *Maya* (illusion) and the powers of deities to become invisible, reflect a fascination with invisibility and camouflage.
- **Modern Science:** Research into optical camouflage and invisibility cloaks using metamaterials reflects a similar desire to manipulate light, akin to these mythological stories.

91. Weather Prediction Techniques

- **Ancient India:** Ancient Indian texts provided meteorological knowledge based on cloud formations, winds, and celestial patterns to predict monsoons and other weather changes.
- **Modern Meteorology:** Today's advanced weather prediction systems use technology, but many

fundamental observations were made long ago in ancient India.

92. Cryptography and Steganography

- **Ancient India**: Ancient texts such as the *Arthashastra* mention the use of coded messages, invisible ink, and methods for secret communication in warfare and espionage.

- **Modern Cryptography**: Techniques of cryptography and data encryption in cybersecurity reflect these ancient methods of encoding information.

93. Surgical Suturing with Ant Heads

- **Ancient India**: Sushruta described the use of large ant heads to clamp wounds, allowing the natural jaws of ants to hold tissue together as an early form of suturing.

- **Modern Surgery**: Today's sutures use various materials, but the concept of wound closure with natural or synthetic clamps echoes these ancient methods.

94. Water-Based Cooling Systems

- **Ancient India**: The use of water channels, stepwells, and evaporative cooling methods in architecture kept buildings cool in hot climates, especially in Rajasthan.

- **Modern Air Conditioning**: The principles of evaporative cooling in modern air conditioning reflect these ancient architectural innovations.

95. Antioxidant Properties of Spices

- **Ancient India:** Spices like turmeric, pepper, and cloves were used in Ayurveda not only for flavor but for their medicinal properties, including antioxidant effects.

- **Modern Nutrition:** The health benefits of these spices, particularly their antioxidant properties, have been scientifically validated in recent research.

96. Optics and Vision Correction

- **Ancient India:** Ancient Indian texts discuss the use of natural lenses made from quartz or glass for correcting vision and enhancing optical clarity.

- **Modern Optics:** The development of eyeglasses and corrective lenses in modern times follows these early explorations of vision correction.

97. Acupuncture and Marma Therapy

- **Ancient India:** *Marma Chikitsa* (a part of Ayurveda) involves stimulating energy points on the body, much like acupuncture, to heal and restore balance.

- **Modern Acupuncture:** Marma therapy shares many similarities with acupuncture, which is now widely practiced worldwide for pain relief and health management.

98. Biorhythms and Circadian Cycles

- **Ancient India:** Ayurvedic and yogic teachings emphasized living in harmony with natural biorhythms, including daily and seasonal cycles, to maintain health.

- **Modern Chronobiology:** Research into circadian rhythms confirms the importance of aligning our activities with biological clocks, a principle known in Ayurveda for millennia.

99. Space-Time and Consciousness

- **Ancient India:** The concept of space and time being interconnected, along with consciousness being a field that permeates the universe, is reflected in texts like the Upanishads.

- **Modern Physics:** The theory of relativity and quantum field theory describe a similar interplay between space, time, and energy, echoing ancient Indian metaphysical ideas.

100. Nanotechnology (Bhasma in Rasashastra)

- **Ancient India:** Rasashastra texts discuss creating fine, molecular-sized particles (bhasma) for therapeutic use, resembling nanotechnology.

- **Modern Nanotechnology:** The creation of nanoparticles for drug delivery and materials science today finds an echo in the ancient practice of producing bhasma for medicinal purposes.

101. Parabolic Reflectors (Temple Architecture)

- **Ancient India:** Certain temple designs, such as the *Konark Sun Temple*, utilized parabolic structures that naturally focused sound waves or light, acting as acoustic amplifiers.

- **Modern Acoustics and Optics:** Parabolic reflectors are now used in telescopes, microphones, and antennas to focus waves, a principle that echoes these ancient architectural designs.

102. Concept of the Ether (Akasha)

- **Ancient India**: The Vedas and Upanishads discuss *Akasha* as a subtle medium that permeates the universe, through which vibrations like sound propagate.

- **Modern Physics**: While the concept of "ether" was eventually dismissed in favor of the theory of relativity, the idea of a fundamental field or medium, as seen in quantum fields, has some parallels with *Akasha*.

103. Forensic Science in Criminal Justice

- **Ancient India**: The *Arthashastra* by *Kautilya* (around 300 BCE) describes detailed methods for criminal investigation, including the use of fingerprints and autopsies.

- **Modern Forensics**: The use of fingerprints, body evidence, and forensic science in criminal investigations today can be traced back to early Indian legal practices.

104. Mercury Purification in Alchemy

- **Ancient India**: Indian alchemists, especially in Rasashastra, had detailed methods for purifying mercury and using it in medicinal preparations.

- **Modern Chemistry**: Mercury purification and chemical manipulation are significant in modern chemistry and medicine, though controlled due to toxicity concerns.

105. Yoga and Neuroplasticity

- **Ancient India**: Practices like *Asana*, *Pranayama*, and *Dhyana* (meditation) were designed to alter brain function and mental states.
- **Modern Neuroscience**: Research into neuroplasticity shows that meditation and controlled breathing can rewire brain circuits, confirming what ancient yogis practiced for mental transformation.

106. Solar Energy in Rituals

- **Ancient India**: The Vedic fire rituals (*Yajnas*) and *Surya Namaskar* practices were designed to harness the energy of the sun for physical, mental, and spiritual benefits.
- **Modern Solar Energy**: The scientific harnessing of solar power today is an advanced technology, though the reverence and utilization of solar energy were integral to ancient Indian culture.

107. Psychosomatic Medicine

- **Ancient India**: Ayurveda emphasizes the mind-body connection, noting that emotional states can directly affect physical health, and vice versa.
- **Modern Psychosomatic Medicine**: This is now a growing field, studying how psychological factors contribute to physical health conditions, a concept long known in Ayurveda.

108. Golden Ratio in Art and Architecture

- **Ancient India**: The use of proportion and symmetry in temple construction, including ratios like the golden ratio, was a hallmark of Indian architecture.

- **Modern Mathematics and Design:** The golden ratio is celebrated in modern mathematics, art, and architecture for its aesthetically pleasing properties, reflecting the balance seen in ancient Indian structures.

109. Ayurvedic Immunotherapy

- **Ancient India:** *Rasayana* therapy in Ayurveda focused on rejuvenating the body and boosting immunity through herbal formulations and diet.
- **Modern Immunotherapy:** Contemporary treatments designed to boost the immune system for fighting diseases mirror the rejuvenation and immunity-building practices of Ayurveda.

110. Concept of Antimatter (Duality)

- **Ancient India:** The concept of duality – *Purusha* (consciousness) and *Prakriti* (matter) – in Samkhya philosophy hints at the existence of opposing forces or forms of energy.
- **Modern Physics:** The discovery of antimatter, which pairs with regular matter to form dual systems, resonates with the ancient philosophical notion of cosmic duality.

111. Fluoride for Dental Care

- **Ancient India:** Ayurveda recommended the use of neem and other herbal sticks, which naturally contain fluoride, for maintaining dental hygiene.
- **Modern Dentistry:** The use of fluoride in modern dental care to prevent cavities has a parallel in the traditional Ayurvedic practices of dental care.

112. Ecological Conservation Practices

- **Ancient India:** The *Arthashastra* and Vedic texts emphasized protecting forests, water bodies, and wildlife, with specific guidelines for sustainable resource management.

- **Modern Environmentalism:** Today's environmental conservation efforts often echo these ancient principles of living harmoniously with nature.

113. Genetics and Hereditary Diseases

- **Ancient India:** Ayurveda's understanding of *Beeja Dosha* suggested that certain health issues were inherited and could be passed down through generations.

- **Modern Genetics:** The modern understanding of genetics, hereditary diseases, and DNA closely aligns with the ancient Indian concept of inherited tendencies or predispositions.

114. Acid-Base Chemistry (Alkali Treatments)

- **Ancient India:** Ayurvedic and Rasashastra texts include detailed descriptions of alkaline and acidic treatments for balancing the body's internal chemistry.

- **Modern Chemistry:** Acid-base reactions are fundamental to modern chemical and medicinal processes, a concept clearly present in ancient Indian alchemical practices.

115. Concept of Inertia in Motion

- **Ancient India:** The *Nyaya-Vaisheshika* school of philosophy discusses motion, positing that objects remain in their state of rest or uniform motion unless acted upon by an external force, a precursor to the concept of inertia.

- **Modern Physics:** This idea of inertia, formally described by Isaac Newton in his first law of motion, reflects these ancient Indian principles of motion.

116. Magnetic Levitation and Floating Stones

- **Ancient India:** Legends and myths, such as the floating stones in the Ram Setu (Adam's Bridge), suggest knowledge of materials with unusual buoyancy or magnetic properties.
- **Modern Magnetic Levitation:** The development of maglev trains and hover technologies today reflects the ancient fascination with levitation and defying gravity.

117. Vitiligo Treatment

- **Ancient India:** Ayurvedic texts mention herbal treatments for vitiligo, a condition that causes depigmentation of the skin.
- **Modern Dermatology:** Treatments for vitiligo, including herbal remedies, are still being researched and developed, with some modern therapies reflecting ancient Ayurvedic approaches.

118. Hydraulic Engineering in Stepwells

- **Ancient India:** The construction of stepwells, like the famous *Rani ki Vav* in Gujarat, involved advanced hydraulic engineering to manage water levels and storage in arid regions.

- **Modern Water Engineering:** These ancient methods of water conservation and hydraulic control are studied in modern environmental and civil engineering.

119. Neutron Stars and Dense Matter

- **Ancient India:** Vedic cosmology speaks of "extremely dense" objects in the cosmos, which could be interpreted as an early concept of neutron stars or black holes.
- **Modern Astrophysics:** The discovery of neutron stars and the study of extremely dense matter by modern astrophysicists echo these ancient ideas of dense celestial bodies.

120. Electroplating and Metal Coating

- **Ancient India:** Ancient metallurgists in India used techniques to coat metals with other substances, such as the gilding of statues and metal utensils.
- **Modern Electroplating:** Electroplating, the process of coating one metal with another using an electric current, resembles these ancient metallurgical practices.

121. Stress Management and Cortisol Control

- **Ancient India:** Ayurvedic practices for managing stress, such as meditation and breathing exercises, were designed to reduce the body's stress response.
- **Modern Endocrinology:** Research shows that meditation reduces cortisol, the stress hormone, confirming the benefits of ancient techniques.

122. Precision Machining (Iron Pillar of Delhi)

- **Ancient India:** The Iron Pillar of Delhi (erected in 4th century CE) is a marvel of ancient metallurgy, showing resistance to rusting due to a high-quality iron forging technique.

- **Modern Metallurgy:** This ancient ability to create rust-resistant iron is still being studied for its technological and engineering precision.

123. Gemstone Therapy

- **Ancient India:** Jyotish (Vedic astrology) prescribed the use of specific gemstones to align with planetary energies and improve health, wealth, and spiritual well-being.

- **Modern Crystal Healing:** While still considered alternative, the use of gemstones for healing purposes has seen a resurgence, drawing from ancient Indian traditions.

124. Panchagavya for Agriculture

- **Ancient India:** Panchagavya, a mixture of cow dung, cow urine, milk, curd, and ghee, was used in Ayurveda for health and agriculture to promote plant growth and protect crops.

- **Modern Organic Farming:** The use of natural fertilizers and pesticides in organic farming reflects this ancient practice of sustainable agriculture.

125. Sulphur Compounds in Medicine

- **Ancient India:** Rasashastra texts described the use of sulfur compounds (such as *Gandhaka Rasayana*) for treating skin diseases and other conditions.

- **Modern Pharmacology**: Sulfur-based drugs, such as sulfonamides, are still used today in modern medicine for treating bacterial infections and other ailments.

126. Agricultural Crop Rotation

- **Ancient India**: Vedic texts described crop rotation to maintain soil fertility and avoid exhausting nutrients.
- **Modern Agriculture**: Crop rotation is now a fundamental practice in sustainable agriculture to maintain soil health and productivity.

127. Intuitive Astronomy (Nakshatras)

- **Ancient India**: The Vedic system of *Nakshatras* (lunar constellations) was used to track the movement of celestial bodies and determine auspicious times.
- **Modern Astronomy**: Modern astronomical systems of tracking celestial bodies rely on similarly detailed observations, reflecting ancient methods.

128. Mercurial Medicines (Rasa Therapy)

- **Ancient India**: Rasashastra texts used mercury in medicines for longevity and healing, with strict purification methods to remove toxicity.
- **Modern Pharmacology**: While mercury is largely avoided due to toxicity concerns, it was once widely used in Western medicine as well, particularly in the treatment of syphilis.

129. Herbal Antibiotics (Neem, Turmeric)

- **Ancient India**: Herbs like neem, turmeric, and tulsi were used for their antibacterial, antifungal, and antiviral properties in traditional medicine.

- **Modern Medicine:** Research confirms that these herbs have antimicrobial properties and are now used in modern pharmaceuticals and alternative medicine.

130. Use of Cow Products in Medicine (Panchagavya)

- **Ancient India:** Panchagavya, a blend of five cow products, was used for health, agriculture, and spiritual purification.
- **Modern Biomedicine:** Some studies have shown medicinal effects of cow-derived products, reflecting ancient Indian practices, though modern research continues to explore this field.

131. Meteor Impact Theories

- **Ancient India:** The ancient Indian text *Rigveda* references "fire from the sky," possibly describing meteor impacts or cosmic events.
- **Modern Geology:** Today, scientists understand that meteors and asteroid impacts have shaped Earth's geological history, aligning with ancient accounts of such cosmic occurrences.

132. Detailed Surgical Instruments

- **Ancient India:** *Sushruta Samhita* described various surgical tools, including scalpels, forceps, and needles, for performing intricate surgeries.
- **Modern Surgery:** Modern surgical instruments are similar in function and purpose to those described by Sushruta, showing continuity in medical tools and techniques.

133. Animal and Plant Husbandry

- **Ancient India**: Vedic texts describe selective breeding of animals and plants for desirable traits, a precursor to modern genetics and agriculture.

- **Modern Animal Breeding**: Genetic engineering and selective breeding in modern agriculture for better yields and livestock health echo ancient Indian practices.

134. Varna as a Social Organism

- **Ancient India**: The Varna system described society as an interconnected organism, with each class having specific roles for the well-being of the whole.

- **Modern Sociology**: The idea of functionalism in sociology, where different parts of society function for collective welfare, resembles this ancient idea.

135. Ancient Weighing and Measurement Systems

- **Ancient India**: Indian civilization had highly accurate systems for weights and measures, especially seen in the Indus Valley Civilization.

- **Modern Metrology**: Today's measurement systems, including weight, length, and volume, reflect this early standardization of units in ancient India.

136. Concept of Global Trade

- **Ancient India**: Ancient Indians were pioneers in global trade, with evidence of maritime routes linking India to the Middle East, Africa, and Southeast Asia.

- **Modern Global Trade**: International trade and commerce today reflect the networks of exchange that ancient Indian traders helped establish.

137. Conservation of Biodiversity

- **Ancient India:** Vedic and Buddhist teachings emphasized the preservation of all forms of life, supporting biodiversity long before modern environmental concerns.
- **Modern Ecology:** Biodiversity conservation is now critical for maintaining ecosystems, echoing ancient Indian reverence for life.

138. Dietary Fasting and Detoxification

- **Ancient India:** Fasting as part of spiritual and physical cleansing was practiced widely, with guidelines for balanced detoxification of the body.
- **Modern Nutrition and Detox:** Today, fasting and detox diets are popular health practices for cleansing and rejuvenating the body, similar to the ancient approach.

139. Ayurvedic Sleep Cycles

- **Ancient India:** Ayurveda emphasized the importance of regular sleep cycles (the *Dinacharya* routine), aligning with natural rhythms for optimal health.
- **Modern Sleep Science:** Modern research into sleep hygiene and circadian rhythms mirrors these ancient practices for improving sleep quality and overall health.

140. Quantum Fluctuations in Vedanta

- **Ancient India:** Vedanta philosophy discusses how the material world emerges from fluctuations in consciousness, a concept analogous to quantum fluctuations.

- **Modern Quantum Physics**: In modern quantum theory, particles emerge from fluctuations in quantum fields, resonating with the Vedantic understanding of creation.

141. Ayurvedic Diagnosis of Pulse (Nadi Pariksha)

- **Ancient India**: Nadi Pariksha was the ancient practice of diagnosing health conditions by examining the pulse, including detecting imbalances in the body's energies.
- **Modern Diagnostic Techniques**: Today's pulse-based diagnostic methods, such as pulse oximetry and cardiac analysis, parallel this ancient Ayurvedic practice.

142. The Concept of Fractals (Mandalas)

- **Ancient India**: The intricate geometric designs of *mandalas* can be seen as early representations of fractals, displaying repeating patterns at different scales.
- **Modern Mathematics**: The concept of fractals, developed in the 20th century, reflects this ancient Indian understanding of repeating patterns in nature and design.

143. Traditional Iron Smelting Techniques

- **Ancient India**: Indian blacksmiths were known for advanced iron smelting techniques, especially the production of *wootz steel*.
- **Modern Metallurgy**: The techniques used in producing wootz steel are still studied in materials science for their high-quality and resilient properties.

144. Chakras and Bioenergetic Fields

- **Ancient India**: The concept of *chakras* (energy centers) in the body is foundational in yogic and Ayurvedic teachings.
- **Modern Bioenergetics**: Research into energy fields around the human body, as well as practices like acupuncture, have parallels with the ancient chakra system.

145. Dental Surgery (Danta Chikitsa)

- **Ancient India**: Ancient texts like *Sushruta Samhita* detailed dental surgeries, including extractions and treatments for oral diseases.
- **Modern Dentistry**: Modern dental surgery, including the extraction of teeth and treatments for oral hygiene, reflects these ancient medical practices.

146. Cardiac Surgery Principles

- **Ancient India**: Ancient Ayurvedic texts mention treatments for heart conditions, focusing on herbal medicines, diet, and lifestyle adjustments.
- **Modern Cardiac Surgery**: While modern techniques are more advanced, the holistic approach to heart health in Ayurveda laid foundational principles for understanding cardiovascular care.

147. Planned Urban Drainage Systems

- **Ancient India**: The cities of the Indus Valley Civilization, like Mohenjo-Daro, had well-planned drainage systems for managing wastewater and stormwater.

- **Modern Urban Planning**: Modern sewage and drainage systems reflect the principles of efficient waste management and urban planning first seen in ancient India.

148. Theoretical Computer Science (Panini's Grammar)

- **Ancient India**: *Panini's Ashtadhyayi*, an ancient grammar text, laid out rules for linguistic structures in a manner that is algorithmic in nature.
- **Modern Computer Science**: Panini's grammar rules have been compared to algorithms in computer science, particularly in programming languages and natural language processing.

149. Herbal Cosmetics

- **Ancient India**: Ayurveda provided recipes for cosmetics made from herbs, flowers, and oils for skin and hair care.
- **Modern Cosmetics Industry**: Herbal and organic beauty products in today's market often trace their roots back to these ancient Indian formulations.

150. Ethical Codes for Doctors (Charaka Samhita)

- **Ancient India**: The *Charaka Samhita* outlined ethical guidelines for physicians, emphasizing patient care, confidentiality, and compassion.
- **Modern Medical Ethics**: The ethical standards in modern medicine, including the Hippocratic Oath, reflect many principles outlined in ancient Indian medical texts.

151. Iron Casting and Pillar Construction

- **Ancient India**: The Iron Pillar of Delhi showcases advanced casting techniques and resistance to corrosion, indicating mastery over metallurgy.
- **Modern Engineering**: Modern alloy development and anti-corrosion technologies parallel these ancient metallurgical skills.

152. Healing with Sound Therapy

- **Ancient India**: Chanting mantras and using sound vibrations for healing and meditation were integral to Indian spiritual practices.
- **Modern Medicine**: Sound therapy and binaural beats are used for stress relief, meditation, and mental health treatment.

153. Climate Adaptation in Architecture

- **Ancient India**: Stepwells and temple designs adapted to climatic conditions, such as Rajasthan's heat and humidity.
- **Modern Architecture**: Climate-resilient and sustainable building designs follow similar principles of passive cooling and water conservation.

154. Concept of the Golden Mean

- **Ancient India**: Temple construction adhered to proportional geometry resembling the golden mean for aesthetic and spiritual alignment.
- **Modern Mathematics**: The golden ratio is used in architecture, art, and design for its universally appealing proportions.

155. Antiseptic Properties of Ash

- **Ancient India**: Wood ash was used as a disinfectant and cleaning agent in rituals and daily life.
- **Modern Chemistry**: The use of alkaline solutions derived from ash serves as a natural antiseptic and cleaner.

156. Understanding Lunar Phases

- **Ancient India**: Astronomers tracked lunar cycles and used them to time religious festivals and agricultural activities.
- **Modern Astronomy**: Detailed lunar calendars are essential for space exploration, tidal studies, and global timekeeping.

157. Plant-Based Dyes

- **Ancient India**: Indigo and turmeric were used as natural dyes for textiles.
- **Modern Chemistry**: Natural dyes are being revived as eco-friendly alternatives to synthetic ones.

158. Cosmic Vibrations in Creation

- **Ancient India**: The concept of *Nada Brahma* (the universe as sound) connects creation to cosmic vibrations.
- **Modern Physics**: String theory and the study of vibrations at the quantum level mirror these ancient ideas.

159. Geometry in Temple Floor Plans

- **Ancient India**: Temples were designed based on precise geometric patterns to harmonize energy flow.

- **Modern Urban Planning:** Mathematical layouts for efficiency and harmony in city planning reflect these principles.

160. Use of Camphor in Rituals

- **Ancient India:** Camphor was burned in rituals for its antiseptic and air-purifying properties.
- **Modern Medicine:** Camphor is used in creams and inhalants for its antibacterial and soothing effects.

161. Weather Forecasting Techniques

- **Ancient India:** Observing animal behavior and cloud formations helped forecast weather.
- **Modern Meteorology:** Weather prediction uses advanced technology, but early methods often align with traditional observations.

162. Balance in Diet (Tridosha Theory)

- **Ancient India:** Ayurveda prescribed diets based on balancing the three doshas: Vata, Pitta, and Kapha.
- **Modern Nutrition:** Personalized nutrition based on body types and metabolism reflects this ancient dietary wisdom.

163. Steel Reinforcement Techniques

- **Ancient India:** Wootz steel production involved advanced forging techniques for creating durable weapons.
- **Modern Metallurgy:** High-carbon and alloyed steel production owes much to ancient techniques like those used in Wootz.

164. Acupuncture-Like Pressure Points

- **Ancient India:** *Marma Chikitsa* in Ayurveda identified pressure points for healing and energy flow.
- **Modern Medicine:** Acupuncture and acupressure therapies align closely with these concepts.

165. Concept of Rebirth in Buddhism

- **Ancient India:** Buddhism's belief in the cycle of rebirth tied to karma reflects a deep philosophical understanding of continuity.
- **Modern Psychology:** The study of behavioral patterns and generational trauma connects to these cyclical ideas.

166. Sacred Geometry in Mandalas

- **Ancient India:** Mandalas used intricate geometric designs for meditation and spiritual focus.
- **Modern Art Therapy:** Mandalas are now used for mindfulness, relaxation, and self-expression in therapy.

167. Use of Sand Filters for Water Purification

- **Ancient India:** Charcoal and sand were used to purify water in ancient systems.
- **Modern Water Treatment:** Sand filtration remains a cornerstone in modern water purification techniques.

168. Seed Preservation Techniques

- **Ancient India:** Seeds were coated with neem or turmeric for preservation and pest resistance.

- **Modern Agriculture**: Similar natural coatings are now being researched to avoid chemical treatments.

169. Mathematics of Infinite Series

- **Ancient India**: Kerala mathematicians like Madhava calculated infinite series for Pi.
- **Modern Calculus**: The foundations of infinite series underpin modern mathematics and engineering.

170. Tanning and Leather Processing

- **Ancient India**: Herbal techniques were used for tanning leather and preserving hides.
- **Modern Chemistry**: Eco-friendly leather tanning methods reflect ancient practices.

171. Military Engineering

- **Ancient India**: Forts like those in Rajasthan utilized water systems and defensive designs.
- **Modern Engineering**: Military bunkers and defensive architecture draw from similar principles.

172. Mindfulness Meditation

- **Ancient India**: Buddhist and yogic practices emphasized mindfulness for mental clarity.
- **Modern Psychology**: Mindfulness meditation is now a widely accepted technique for stress management and mental health.

173. Sacrificial Pits for Energy Generation

- **Ancient India:** Fire sacrifices (*Yajnas*) were believed to release energy and purify surroundings.

- **Modern Physics:** Controlled combustion systems reflect similar principles of energy release.

174. Cultural Preservation through Oral Traditions

- **Ancient India:** The Vedas were preserved orally for generations with remarkable precision.
- **Modern Linguistics:** Oral traditions are studied for their role in preserving languages and cultures.

175. Medicinal Properties of Frankincense

- **Ancient India:** Frankincense was used in rituals and medicine for its calming and healing properties.
- **Modern Aromatherapy:** Frankincense essential oil is widely used for stress relief and wellness.

176. Magnetized Stones for Healing

- **Ancient India:** Lodestones were used for healing and balancing energy.
- **Modern Alternative Medicine:** Magnetic therapy is used for pain relief and promoting circulation.

177. Bamboo Construction

- **Ancient India:** Bamboo was used for scaffolding, bridges, and homes due to its strength and flexibility.
- **Modern Sustainable Design:** Bamboo is now a key material in green construction projects.

178. Sun-Dried Bricks

- **Ancient India:** The Indus Valley Civilization used sun-dried bricks for durable construction.

- **Modern Green Construction:** Environmentally friendly building materials like earthen bricks mirror this technique.

179. Holistic Treatment of Fever

- **Ancient India:** Fever was treated with cooling herbs, rest, and hydration in Ayurveda.
- **Modern Medicine:** Treating fever with fluids, rest, and anti-inflammatories parallels these methods.

180. Bone Setting in Ayurveda

- **Ancient India:** Techniques for setting broken bones were described in detail in *Sushruta Samhita*.
- **Modern Orthopedics:** Bone-setting techniques evolved but retain core principles of alignment and stabilization.

181. Concept of Spacetime in Cosmology

- **Ancient India:** Indian cosmology described time and space as interconnected and cyclical.
- **Modern Physics:** Einstein's theory of spacetime parallels this ancient understanding.

182. Salt Extraction from Seawater

- **Ancient India:** Techniques for salt extraction were documented in early Indian texts.
- **Modern Chemistry:** Industrial salt extraction follows similar evaporation processes.

183. Bamboo Musical Instruments

- **Ancient India:** Bamboo flutes and other instruments were crafted for specific tonal qualities.

- **Modern Music**: Bamboo remains a key material for crafting high-quality wind instruments.

184. Traditional Hair Oils

- **Ancient India**: Herbal oils were used for hair health and scalp nourishment.
- **Modern Cosmetics**: Herbal hair oils are now part of mainstream hair care routines globally.

185. Concept of Emotional Well-Being

- **Ancient India**: Emotional health was considered integral to physical health in Ayurveda.
- **Modern Psychology**: The holistic approach to mental and emotional health reflects this philosophy.

186. Bee-Keeping for Honey

- **Ancient India**: Beekeeping was practiced for honey, wax, and medicinal uses.
- **Modern Apiculture**: Beekeeping remains a critical agricultural and medicinal practice.

187. Temple Tanks for Rainwater Storage

- **Ancient India**: Temple tanks collected rainwater for religious and community use.
- **Modern Rainwater Harvesting**: Water tanks and reservoirs are part of urban sustainability efforts.

188. Use of Sandalwood for Skin Health

- **Ancient India**: Sandalwood paste was used to treat skin conditions and improve complexion.
- **Modern Skincare**: Sandalwood is now a key ingredient in natural skincare products.

189. Solar Heat for Cooking

- **Ancient India**: Sunlight was used for drying and cooking food in solar traps.
- **Modern Solar Cookers**: Solar cooking technologies echo these ancient techniques.

190. Ayurvedic Oil Pulling

- **Ancient India**: Oil pulling was used for oral health and detoxification.
- **Modern Dentistry**: Oil pulling is gaining popularity as a natural method for improving oral hygiene.

191. Use of Honey as a Preservative

- **Ancient India**: Honey was used to preserve food and medicines due to its antimicrobial properties.
- **Modern Food Science**: Honey is still valued as a natural preservative in food products.

192. Traditional Knowledge of Earthquakes

- **Ancient India**: The *Brihat Samhita* described earthquake precursors like unusual animal behavior.
- **Modern Seismology**: These observations align with research into natural earthquake predictors.

193. Spiritual Practices for Longevity

- **Ancient India**: Practices like meditation, fasting, and yoga aimed at extending lifespan.
- **Modern Wellness**: Longevity-focused lifestyles now incorporate similar techniques.

194. Salt Lamps for Purifying Air

- **Ancient India**: Salt was used in lamps and purifying rituals to cleanse energy.
- **Modern Therapy**: Himalayan salt lamps are used for air purification and aesthetic purposes.

195. Understanding Seasonal Ailments

- **Ancient India**: Ayurveda linked health conditions to seasonal changes, suggesting preventive measures.
- **Modern Epidemiology**: Seasonal trends in diseases are now studied to predict outbreaks and plan healthcare responses.

196. Solar Worship and Health Benefits

- **Ancient India**: *Surya Namaskar* and other solar worship practices emphasized sunlight for health.
- **Modern Medicine**: Sunlight exposure is vital for vitamin D synthesis and overall health.

197. Indigo as a Natural Dye

- **Ancient India**: Indigo plants were cultivated for dyeing fabrics.
- **Modern Textiles**: Indigo remains a popular and eco-friendly dye in the fashion industry.

198. Use of Cloves for Oral Health

- **Ancient India**: Cloves were chewed to treat toothache and freshen breath.
- **Modern Dentistry**: Clove oil is used for its antiseptic and pain-relieving properties.

199. Copper Vessels for Water Storage

- **Ancient India:** Storing water in copper vessels was believed to purify and enhance its health benefits.
- **Modern Science:** Studies confirm the antimicrobial properties of copper for water purification.

200. Fumigation for Pest Control

- **Ancient India:** Burning neem and other herbs was used to repel insects and purify spaces.
- **Modern Pest Control:** Natural fumigants are being developed as safer alternatives to chemical pesticides.

Chapter 1:
Introduction

Bridging Worlds

Setting the Stage for the Exploration of Vedic Insights and Scientific Discoveries

Humanity's insatiable curiosity, an intrinsic drive to unravel the mysteries of existence, transcends time and cultures. This chapter sets the stage for a profound exploration, a journey that seeks to bridge the seemingly disparate realms of Vedic insights and scientific discoveries. As we embark on this intellectual odyssey, the convergence of ancient wisdom and modern knowledge unfolds, offering a unique perspective woven with threads of ancient scriptures and the empirical rigor of contemporary science.

The dichotomy between tradition and progress often creates a perceived schism, with science and spirituality seemingly at odds. However, a closer examination reveals a rich history of interconnectedness, where ancient civilizations, particularly the Vedic culture, harbored a holistic worldview that seamlessly integrated the spiritual and the empirical. Bridging these worlds becomes an intellectual and philosophical endeavor, inviting us to transcend preconceived notions and embrace the symbiosis of wisdom from diverse epochs.

The Human Quest for Understanding

The human quest for understanding has manifested in various forms throughout history. From the Vedic seers contemplating the cosmic order to modern scientists unraveling the mysteries of quantum mechanics, the pursuit of knowledge has been a constant, unifying thread. This chapter delves into the motivations underlying this universal quest, examining how both Vedic insights and scientific discoveries emerge from humanity's perennial desire to comprehend the intricacies of the cosmos.

Early Vedic Wisdom

The Vedic corpus, a collection of ancient Indian scriptures, stands as a testament to the profound philosophical and spiritual insights of the early Vedic seers. Rigveda, the oldest of the Vedas, contains hymns that reflect a deep reverence for nature, a cosmic interconnectedness, and a contemplation of the fundamental questions of existence. The exploration of the early Vedic mindset becomes a crucial foundation for understanding the roots of Vedic wisdom.

The roots of early Vedic wisdom delve into the cradle of ancient Indian civilization, offering profound philosophical and spiritual insights. This period, spanning from around 1500 BCE to 500 BCE, saw the composition of the Rigveda, the oldest and foundational text of the Vedas. The Vedic seers, known as Rishis, played a pivotal role in shaping the intellectual and spiritual landscape of ancient India.

Rigveda: Hymns to the Cosmic Order

At the heart of early Vedic wisdom lies the Rigveda, a collection of hymns composed in a poetic and metrical form. These hymns are dedicated to various deities, natural forces, and cosmic principles. The Rigveda is divided into ten books, or Mandalas, each reflecting a different facet of Vedic thought.

The hymns in the Rigveda are not mere expressions of devotion but intricate reflections on the nature of reality, existence, and the interconnectedness of all things. The Rishis engaged in profound contemplation, seeking to understand the mysteries of the universe and humanity's place within it. The symbolism and metaphors employed in the hymns go beyond the literal, inviting readers to explore deeper layers of meaning.

Nature Worship and Cosmic Harmony

Early Vedic thought is characterized by a deep reverence for nature and an acknowledgment of the interconnectedness of all living beings. The hymns of the Rigveda are replete with praises for natural elements such as Agni (fire), Vayu (wind), Varuna (cosmic order), and Aditi (the infinite). These elements are personified and venerated as manifestations of the divine.

The concept of Rita, often translated as cosmic order or truth, is a central theme in early Vedic thought. It represents the inherent harmony and balance in the universe, and the Rishis saw their role as aligning with this cosmic order through rituals and righteous living. The interconnectedness of all elements, both divine and earthly, reflects a holistic worldview that emphasizes the unity of the microcosm and the macrocosm.

Sacrificial Rituals and Spiritual Insights

One of the prominent features of early Vedic society was the performance of elaborate sacrificial rituals, known as Yajnas. These rituals, detailed in the Brahmanas and later in the Sutras, were intricate ceremonies involving the chanting of specific hymns, the offering of oblations into the sacred fire, and the participation of priests and patrons. While these rituals had external symbolic meanings, they were also imbued with deep spiritual significance.

The Yajnas were not mere external acts but symbolized inner transformations and a harmonious relationship between the individual and the cosmos. The fire, Agni, served as a conduit between the earthly and divine realms, symbolizing the transformative power of spiritual practices. The early Vedic seers recognized that the external rituals were a means to an inner end – the purification of the mind and the realization of higher truths.

Quest for Ultimate Reality: Brahman and Atman

Embedded within the hymns of the Rigveda is the philosophical foundation of early Vedic wisdom, introducing concepts that would later evolve into the core tenets of Vedanta. The exploration of the ultimate reality, often referred to as Brahman, transcends the limitations of anthropomorphic deities. Brahman is described as the unchanging, infinite, and eternal reality that underlies and sustains the entire cosmos.

Simultaneously, the Rigveda introduces the concept of Atman, the individual self or soul. The Rishis contemplated the relationship between Atman and Brahman, laying the groundwork for later Upanishadic thought. The realization of the oneness of Atman and Brahman became a central theme in the spiritual quest of the Vedic seers.

Evolution of Scientific Thought

Parallelly, the evolution of scientific thought has witnessed a relentless pursuit of knowledge, marked by revolutions and paradigm shifts. From the scientific renaissance of the 16th century to the quantum revolution of the 20th century, science has expanded the boundaries of human understanding, challenging conventional beliefs and opening new vistas of inquiry.

The journey of scientific thought is a riveting saga, characterized by transformative revolutions, paradigm shifts, and the relentless pursuit of knowledge. This exploration spans centuries, witnessing the birth of new ideas, the overthrow of established dogmas, and the emergence of a scientific worldview that has fundamentally reshaped our understanding of the universe.

The Scientific Renaissance (15th-17th Century)

The Scientific Renaissance marks a pivotal era where the seeds of modern scientific thought were sown, challenging the medieval scholasticism that dominated intellectual discourse. The 15th century saw the revival of classical knowledge, driven by pioneers like Leonardo da Vinci and Nicholas Copernicus. Copernicus's heliocentric model, placing the sun at the center of the solar system, challenged the geocentric view prevailing since antiquity.

The 17th century witnessed the full bloom of the Scientific Renaissance with towering figures like Galileo Galilei and Johannes Kepler. Galileo's telescopic observations provided empirical evidence for Copernican heliocentrism, while Kepler's laws of planetary motion laid the groundwork for a new understanding of celestial mechanics. Isaac Newton, with his laws of motion and universal gravitation, synthesized these ideas, providing a mathematical framework that explained both earthly and celestial phenomena.

The Age of Enlightenment (17th-18th Century)

The Enlightenment era ushered in a wave of intellectual and cultural transformation, emphasizing reason, skepticism, and the scientific method. Thinkers like René Descartes, John Locke, and Voltaire advocated for empirical inquiry and the rejection of dogma. The scientific method, characterized by systematic observation, experimentation, and the formulation of hypotheses, became the cornerstone of scientific inquiry.

In the 18th century, Carl Linnaeus's taxonomy system revolutionized the classification of living organisms, laying the foundation for modern biology. The Enlightenment spirit also influenced the development of chemistry, with Antoine Lavoisier pioneering the concept of the conservation of mass and the identification of chemical elements.

The Birth of Modern Biology (19th Century)

The 19th century witnessed the rise of modern biology, fueled by breakthroughs in various fields. Charles Darwin's theory of evolution, presented in "On the Origin of Species" (1859), revolutionized our understanding of the diversity of life. Darwin proposed the mechanism of natural selection, wherein species evolve over time through the gradual accumulation of advantageous traits.

Gregor Mendel's work on inheritance and the laws of genetics laid the groundwork for the field of genetics, though its significance was recognized later in the 20th century. Louis Pasteur's germ theory of disease, Joseph Lister's antiseptic surgical techniques, and the discovery of cell theory collectively contributed to the establishment of biology as a rigorous scientific discipline.

Physics in the 20th Century: Relativity and Quantum Mechanics

The 20th century witnessed unprecedented revolutions in physics, challenging classical Newtonian mechanics and reshaping our understanding of space, time, and matter. Albert Einstein's theory of relativity, formulated in the early 1900s, introduced a new paradigm for understanding gravity and the nature of the cosmos. Special relativity, published in

1905, challenged classical notions of simultaneity and time, while general relativity, published in 1915, provided a new understanding of gravity as the curvature of spacetime.

Simultaneously, quantum mechanics emerged as a groundbreaking theory to explain the behavior of subatomic particles. Pioneered by scientists like Max Planck, Niels Bohr, Werner Heisenberg, and Erwin Schrödinger, quantum mechanics introduced probabilistic and wave-particle duality concepts that defied classical intuition. The famous debates between Einstein and Bohr highlighted the philosophical implications of quantum mechanics, with Einstein famously stating, "God does not play dice with the universe."

The Molecular Biology Revolution (Mid-20th Century)

The mid-20th century witnessed the convergence of biology and physics, leading to the elucidation of the molecular mechanisms underlying life. The discovery of the structure of DNA by James Watson and Francis Crick in 1953 marked a watershed moment in biology, laying the foundation for the field of molecular biology. This breakthrough, combined with advancements in X-ray crystallography and the understanding of the genetic code, paved the way for exploring the molecular basis of inheritance and the mechanisms of cellular processes.

Space Exploration and Cosmology

The latter half of the 20th century saw remarkable strides in space exploration and cosmology. The launch of Sputnik 1 in 1957 marked the beginning of the space age, with subsequent achievements including human moon landings, robotic exploration of planets, and the launch of space telescopes like Hubble. These endeavors provided unprecedented insights into the cosmos, expanding our understanding of the universe's vastness, evolution, and fundamental processes.

The Information Age and Interdisciplinary Sciences

The late 20th century and the 21st century ushered in the Information Age, characterized by rapid technological advancements and the integration of disciplines. The advent of computers and the internet transformed scientific research, enabling data analysis, simulations, and global collaboration on an unprecedented scale.

Interdisciplinary sciences, such as bioinformatics, computational physics, and systems biology, became integral for addressing complex questions that transcended traditional disciplinary boundaries. The emergence of fields like nanotechnology, synthetic biology, and artificial intelligence further exemplified the interdisciplinary nature of modern scientific inquiry.

The Historical Context of Vedic Wisdom: Echoes of Ancient Realms

In this detailed exploration, we immerse ourselves in the historical context of Vedic wisdom, tracing its origins to ancient civilizations. The Rigveda, with its poetic hymns and profound philosophical insights, becomes a focal point for understanding the depth of Vedic thought. Through vivid descriptions and historical analysis, we transport readers to the cultural richness of ancient India, exploring the symbiotic relationship between Vedic insights and the vibrant societal and spiritual fabric of the time.

The historical context of Vedic wisdom spans a vast and intricate base, unfolding over millennia in the Indian subcontinent. To understand the genesis and evolution of Vedic thought, it is essential to delve into the cultural, social, and political landscapes that shaped ancient India. This exploration unfolds across distinct periods, each contributing to the rich canvas of Vedic wisdom.

Indus Valley Civilization (3300–1300 BCE):

The roots of Vedic civilization are often traced back to the ancient Indus Valley Civilization. Flourishing along the banks of the Indus River, this advanced urban culture is known for its sophisticated city planning, intricate drainage systems, and a script yet to be fully deciphered. While the direct connection between the Indus Valley Civilization and Vedic culture remains a subject of scholarly debate, some archaeological findings suggest cultural continuity.

Early Vedic Period (1500–1000 BCE):

The Early Vedic period marks the emergence of the Indo-Aryans in the northwestern regions of the Indian subcontinent. This period is closely associated with the composition of the Rigveda, the oldest of the four Vedas. The Rigveda comprises hymns dedicated to various deities and reflects the religious and philosophical outlook of the early Vedic people. Society was organized into tribal communities, and rituals, including sacrificial ceremonies, played a central role.

Late Vedic Period (1000–600 BCE):

During the Late Vedic period, societal changes unfolded, leading to the transition from tribal to more complex, agrarian societies. This era witnessed the composition of the other three Vedas (Samaveda, Yajurveda, and Atharvaveda) and the emergence of Brahmanas, texts providing explanations and guidance for Vedic rituals. The concept of Dharma, the moral and social duties, began to take prominence, shaping the ethical framework of Vedic society.

Early Upanishadic Period (800–200 BCE):

The latter part of the Vedic period saw the emergence of the Upanishads, philosophical texts that explored profound questions about the nature of reality, the self (Atman), and the ultimate reality (Brahman). This period witnessed the crystallization of key philosophical concepts, laying the groundwork for what would later be known as Vedanta. The Upanishads emphasized inner contemplation and meditation as means to attain spiritual realization.

Mahajanapadas and the Rise of Kingdoms (600–300 BCE):

As the Vedic era transitioned to the period of Mahajanapadas (great kingdoms), political structures evolved, and territorial states began to take shape. The rise of kingdoms and republics marked the onset of the "Sramanic" movements, including Jainism and Buddhism, which challenged certain aspects of Vedic rituals and societal norms.

Maurya and Gupta Empires (322 BCE–550 CE):

The Maurya Empire, under the rule of Chandragupta Maurya and later expanded by Ashoka, unified much of the Indian subcontinent. Ashoka's embrace of Buddhism had a profound impact on the spread of Buddhist teachings. The Gupta Empire, often considered a "Golden Age" of Indian civilization, witnessed advancements in science, mathematics, art, and literature. During this time, the compilation of Dharmashastra (legal and ethical texts) occurred, reflecting the evolving socio-political landscape.

Post-Gupta Period (550–1200 CE):

Following the decline of the Gupta Empire, India entered a period of regional kingdoms and cultural efflorescence. The Bhakti movement gained prominence, emphasizing devotion to a personal deity, transcending caste and ritualistic barriers.

This period also saw the compilation of the Puranas, which encapsulated mythological narratives, cosmology, and moral teachings.

Symbolism and Allegory in the Vedic Period

Central to Vedic wisdom is the use of symbolism and allegory to convey profound truths. The Rigveda's hymns, laden with metaphors and symbolic language, invite interpretations that transcend the literal. This nuanced approach to conveying knowledge adds layers of complexity to the exploration, prompting readers to unravel the hidden meanings embedded in the ancient verses.

The Vedic period, particularly in the hymns of the Rigveda, is adorned with rich symbolism and allegory, providing a window into the profound insights of the ancient seers. The use of symbolic language and allegorical expressions in the Vedic texts transcends mere poetic ornamentation; it serves as a vehicle to convey deeper cosmic truths, reaching beyond the literal and mundane. To grasp the significance of symbolism and allegory in the Vedic period, we embark on a journey through the hymns of the Rigveda and the cultural context that shaped this symbolic language.

Early Vedic Period (1500–1000 BCE):

The earliest phase of Vedic literature, the Rigvedic period, was marked by the composition of hymns that reflected the worldview and spiritual insights of the early Vedic seers. These hymns, often attributed to sages like Agastya, Vishwamitra, and Vashistha, were primarily transmitted orally before being later compiled in written form. The Rigveda comprises ten books, or Mandalas, with each Mandala containing hymns dedicated to specific deities, cosmic forces, and natural elements.

Cosmic Forces and Natural Elements:

In the Rigveda, natural elements such as Agni (fire), Varuna (cosmic order), Indra (thunder and rain), and Surya (the sun) are personified and venerated. The symbolic language employed in addressing these deities extends beyond mere praise; it becomes a means of expressing the interconnectedness between the microcosm of human existence and the macrocosm of the universe.

Agni, the Sacred Fire:

Agni, the most frequently invoked deity in the Rigveda, symbolizes not only the physical fire used in rituals but also the divine spark within every living being. The fire ritual, known as Yajna, is both a symbolic and practical act, representing the transformative power of knowledge and consciousness.

Varuna, the Cosmic Order:

Varuna, often associated with cosmic order (Rita) and moral law (Dharma), embodies the universal principles that govern the natural and metaphysical realms. The hymns addressing Varuna delve into the profound interconnectedness of all existence and the moral responsibilities inherent in cosmic harmony.

Metaphors and Allegorical Descriptions:

The Rigveda is replete with metaphors and allegorical descriptions that invite deeper contemplation. The seers employed vivid and evocative language to convey truths that transcended the limitations of ordinary discourse. For instance:

Indra's Slaying of Vritra:

The mythological narrative of Indra slaying the serpent-demon Vritra is not merely a tale of a heroic deity overcoming a foe. It symbolizes the triumph of order (Rita) over chaos and the release of life-giving waters, representing the essential cycles of nature and the cosmic balance.

Ushas, the Dawn:

The hymns dedicated to Ushas, the dawn goddess, use poetic imagery to describe the cosmic awakening. The rising of Ushas is symbolic of the eternal renewal of life, the transition from darkness to light, and the spiritual awakening within the individual.

Philosophical Themes:

As the Vedic period progressed into the later Vedic and Upanishadic periods, the symbolism in the Rigveda laid the groundwork for deeper philosophical exploration. The Upanishads, which emerged around the 8th century BCE, delved into the nature of reality, consciousness, and the ultimate truth (Brahman).

Prajapati and Sacrificial Symbolism:

The concept of Prajapati, often associated with the creator deity, is explored in the context of sacrificial symbolism. The cosmic sacrifice (Yajna) is allegorically linked to the creation and sustenance of the universe. The sacrificial rituals performed by humans mirror the cosmic processes, emphasizing the interconnectedness of the microcosm and macrocosm.

Cultural and Ritualistic Context:

Understanding the symbolism and allegory in the Vedic period requires an appreciation of the cultural and ritualistic context in which these hymns were composed and recited. The Vedic rituals, including the Yajnas, were not mere external acts but symbolic expressions of inner transformations and cosmic harmony.

Transmission and Continuity:

The symbolic language of the Rigveda was transmitted through the oral tradition, with each generation of Rishis preserving and embellishing upon the hymns. The Gurukula system, where students lived with their teachers, facilitated not only the memorization of verses but also the transmission of the esoteric meanings and allegorical interpretations.

Evolution into Vedanta:

The symbolic and allegorical dimensions of Vedic wisdom evolved over centuries, finding profound expression in the Upanishads and, eventually, in the philosophical system known as Vedanta. Vedanta, meaning the end or culmination of the Vedas, delves into the non-dualistic nature of reality (Advaita Vedanta), emphasizing the unity of the individual soul (Atman) with the ultimate reality (Brahman).

Yogic Sciences and Inner Exploration in Vedic Thought

The Vedic era witnessed the development of Yogic sciences, providing a systematic framework for inner exploration and self-realization. The Upanishads, part of the Vedic literature, delve into the nature of consciousness, the self, and the ultimate reality. This chapter unravels the intricate goldmine of Yogic philosophies, exploring how the ancient sages navigated the inner realms of the mind in their quest for transcendental wisdom.

The Vedic period witnessed the emergence of profound philosophical and spiritual insights, and among its most transformative contributions was the development of Yogic sciences. Rooted in the Upanishads, the Yogic traditions provided a systematic and holistic framework for inner exploration, self-realization, and the attainment of higher states of consciousness. To understand the depth of Yogic sciences in Vedic thought, we embark on a journey through the Upanishads and the foundational principles that guide inner exploration.

Early Vedic Seeds: Origins in the Rigveda:

The seeds of Yogic wisdom can be traced back to the Rigveda, the oldest of the Vedas. The hymns of the Rigveda, while primarily focused on external rituals and cosmic order, contained hints of inner contemplation and spiritual quest. The practice of meditation and asceticism found early expressions, setting the stage for the elaboration of Yogic sciences in later Vedic literature.

Upanishadic Unveilings (800–200 BCE):

The Upanishads, often referred to as Vedanta (the end or culmination of the Vedas), form the philosophical bedrock of Yogic sciences. These texts, composed between the 8th and 2nd centuries BCE, delve into the nature of reality, the self (Atman), and the ultimate reality (Brahman). The Upanishads lay the foundation for various paths of Yoga, each offering a unique approach to inner exploration.

Paths of Yogic Sciences:

The Upanishads outline multiple paths of Yogic sciences, each tailored to the temperament and inclination of the seeker. These paths, often referred to as Yogas, include:

1. **Jnana Yoga (Path of Knowledge):**
   - Emphasizes the discernment between the eternal and the ephemeral.

- Encourages the intellectual inquiry into the nature of reality.
- Key Upanishadic Text: Chandogya Upanishad, which explores the identity of the individual soul (Atman) with the ultimate reality (Brahman).

2. **Bhakti Yoga (Path of Devotion):**

    - Advocates the cultivation of love and devotion toward a personal deity.
    - Views surrender and devotion as means to transcend the ego.
    - Key Upanishadic Text: Bhagavad Gita, which discusses devotion and surrender as pathways to self-realization.

3. **Karma Yoga (Path of Action):**

    - Focuses on selfless action, performed without attachment to outcomes.
    - Sees every action as an offering to the divine.
    - Key Upanishadic Text: Bhagavad Gita, where Lord Krishna imparts the wisdom of performing one's duties without attachment.

4. **Raja Yoga (Path of Meditation):**

    - Involves the practice of meditation, concentration, and control of the mind.
    - Systematizes the techniques of meditation for inner exploration.
    - Key Upanishadic Text: Yoga Upanishads, which provide insights into meditative practices.

Yogic Practices in Upanishads:

The Upanishads detail specific Yogic practices aimed at realizing the transcendent truth. Some of the prominent practices include:

1. **Dhyana (Meditation):**
   - Explores different meditation techniques to still the mind and realize inner peace.
   - The Mandukya Upanishad delves into the significance of OM (AUM) as a meditative symbol representing the ultimate reality.

2. **Pranayama (Breath Control):**
   - Recognizes the intimate connection between breath and consciousness.
   - Techniques like Pranayama are hinted at in various Upanishads, emphasizing the regulation of breath for inner stillness.

3. **Mantra Yoga (Chanting of Sacred Sounds):**
   - Acknowledges the transformative power of sound vibrations.
   - The Mandukya Upanishad explores the significance of the primal sound AUM as a mantra for meditation.

4. **Neti-Neti (Not This, Not This):**
   - Encourages a negation process to realize the essence beyond the material and mental realms.
   - The Brihadaranyaka Upanishad employs the Neti-Neti approach to guide seekers toward the unchanging reality.

Concept of Atman and Brahman:

Central to Yogic sciences in the Upanishads is the exploration of the relationship between the individual self (Atman) and the ultimate reality (Brahman). The Chandogya Upanishad, for instance, employs profound metaphors and allegories to elucidate the unity of Atman with Brahman, emphasizing that the essence of the individual soul is identical to the cosmic reality.

Inner Journey and Self-Realization:

The Yogic sciences outlined in the Upanishads envision an inner journey that transcends the limitations of the material world. Through disciplined practices and profound contemplation, the seeker aims to realize the true nature of the self and, in doing so, attains liberation (Moksha) from the cycle of birth and death (Samsara).

Legacy and Influence:

The Yogic sciences presented in the Upanishads laid the groundwork for the diverse yogic traditions that evolved over the centuries. The practices and insights delineated in these ancient texts continue to inspire seekers on the path of inner exploration and self-realization. The profound wisdom encapsulated in the Upanishads serves as a timeless guide for those embarking on the transformative journey of Yogic sciences.

Bridging Worlds: The Confluence of Vedic Insights and Scientific Endeavors

The convergence of Vedic insights and scientific endeavors becomes the crux of our exploration. As we transition from the ancient realms to the contemporary scientific landscape, the inquiry into the parallels, intersections, and potential collaborations between these two domains takes center stage.

The confluence of Vedic insights and scientific endeavors is a complex and ongoing process that has unfolded over centuries. While the Vedic period itself laid the philosophical groundwork, the explicit intersection with modern scientific endeavors began to take shape during the Renaissance and gained momentum through subsequent centuries. Here's a broad timeline highlighting key periods:

1. Vedic Period (1500–500 BCE):

The ancient Indian scriptures, especially the Vedas and Upanishads, laid the foundations for philosophical and cosmological insights. These texts contain profound observations about the nature of reality, consciousness, and the interconnectedness of all existence.

2. Renaissance (14th–17th Century):

The Renaissance in Europe marked a revival of classical knowledge and a shift toward empirical inquiry. During this period, thinkers like Copernicus, Galileo, and Kepler challenged the geocentric model, initiating a paradigm shift in scientific thought.

3. 17th–18th Century:

The Scientific Revolution unfolded, characterized by the works of luminaries such as Newton, who formulated laws of motion and universal gravitation. This period saw a growing divergence between religious and scientific explanations of the natural world.

4. 19th Century:

Advances in various scientific disciplines, including biology, geology, and physics, continued to challenge traditional religious interpretations. Darwin's theory of evolution posed profound questions about the origin of life.

5. Early 20th Century:

The advent of quantum mechanics and Einstein's theory of relativity revolutionized physics. These theories introduced concepts that challenged classical notions of determinism, causality, and the nature of reality.

6. Mid-20th Century Onward:

The latter half of the 20th century and the 21st century witnessed the convergence of ancient wisdom and modern science. This period saw an increased interest in Eastern philosophies, including Vedic insights, among scientists and scholars.

7. Mind-Body Connection and Quantum Physics:

In the latter part of the 20th century, scientific inquiries into the mind-body connection gained prominence. Quantum physics, with its emphasis on interconnectedness and the role of consciousness, drew parallels with Vedic concepts.

8. Neuroscience and Consciousness Studies (21st Century):

Advancements in neuroscience have led to a deeper understanding of the brain's functioning and its relationship with consciousness. This aligns with Vedic insights into the nature of the mind and consciousness.

9. Holistic Health and Yoga Studies:

The 21st century has seen a surge in interest in holistic health and well-being, with practices like yoga gaining widespread recognition. Scientific studies have explored the physiological and psychological benefits of yoga, aligning with Vedic principles of mind-body harmony.

10. Interdisciplinary Research and Dialogues:

Ongoing interdisciplinary research and dialogues between scientists, philosophers, and spiritual leaders continue to explore the confluence of Vedic insights and scientific endeavors. Conferences, publications, and collaborative projects aim to bridge the gap between these two realms of knowledge.

Quantum Physics and Vedanta: Exploring the Correlation

In the realm of modern physics, the echoes of Vedic insights become apparent, particularly in the enigmatic world of quantum physics. The interconnectedness and non-dualistic perspectives found in Vedanta, a philosophical school derived from the Upanishads, find resonance in the fundamental principles of quantum entanglement and non-locality. This chapter dissects the parallels, inviting readers to contemplate the implications of this convergence for our understanding of reality.

The correlation between Quantum Physics and Vedanta, the ancient Indian philosophical tradition, has been a subject of fascination and exploration in the realms of science and spirituality. While Quantum Physics deals with the nature of the very small – particles at the quantum level, Vedanta explores the nature of reality, consciousness, and the self. Here, we delve into key aspects of Quantum Physics and Vedanta, highlighting their intriguing correlations.

1. Non-Locality and Interconnectedness:

Quantum Physics Perspective:

Quantum entanglement reveals a phenomenon where particles become interconnected regardless of the distance between them. Changes in one particle instantaneously affect its entangled partner, suggesting non-local connections.

Vedantic Correlation:

Vedanta teaches the interconnectedness of all existence, emphasizing an underlying unity beyond the apparent diversity. The concept of "Brahman" in Vedanta reflects an interconnected, undivided reality.

2. Observer Effect and Consciousness:

Quantum Physics Perspective:

The observer effect in Quantum Physics suggests that the act of observation influences the behavior of particles. Conscious observation plays a role in determining the properties of particles.

Vedantic Correlation:

Vedanta posits that consciousness is fundamental to reality. The idea that the observer and the observed are intertwined resonates with Vedantic teachings on the role of consciousness in shaping perception.

3. Uncertainty Principle and Cosmic Indeterminacy:

Quantum Physics Perspective:

Heisenberg's Uncertainty Principle asserts that certain pairs of properties, like position and momentum, cannot be precisely known simultaneously. It introduces an inherent indeterminacy at the quantum level.

Vedantic Correlation:

Vedanta acknowledges the impermanence and changing nature of the material world. The concept of "Maya" suggests that the phenomenal world is transient and subject to change.

4. Wave-Particle Duality and Unity of Existence:

Quantum Physics Perspective:

Particles exhibit both wave-like and particle-like behavior, depending on how they are observed. This duality challenges classical notions of a strictly deterministic reality.

Vedantic Correlation:

Vedanta teaches that the ultimate reality (Brahman) is beyond dualities and encompasses all opposites. The wave-particle duality resonates with the idea of a unified, non-dual reality.

5. Superposition and Infinite Potentials:

Quantum Physics Perspective:

Superposition allows particles to exist in multiple states simultaneously until observed, collapsing the probabilities into a definite state.

Vedantic Correlation:

Vedanta speaks of the infinite potentials within the ultimate reality. The idea of superposition aligns with the notion of an infinite, unmanifest potential before the manifestation of the universe.

6. Quantum Entropy and Cosmic Order:

Quantum Physics Perspective:

Quantum entropy reflects the degree of disorder or randomness in a system. The concept parallels the arrow of time and the progression toward greater disorder.

Vedantic Correlation:

Vedanta introduces the cosmic order (Rita) and the cyclical nature of creation and dissolution. The concept aligns with the idea of an underlying order within the apparent chaos.

7. Holistic Perspective and Wholeness:

Quantum Physics Perspective:

Quantum holism emphasizes the interconnectedness of all parts, with the whole system influencing the behavior of its individual components.

Vedantic Correlation:

Vedanta teaches that the ultimate reality is a holistic, indivisible whole. The holistic perspective in Quantum Physics resonates with Vedantic ideas of an interconnected, unified reality.

Examples of Correlation:

- **Double-Slit Experiment:** The famous double-slit experiment, where particles exhibit both wave and particle properties, aligns with the Vedantic concept of the unity of existence, transcending dualities.

- **Schrödinger's Cat:** The thought experiment highlighting superposition and the indeterminate state of particles reflects the Vedantic idea of an unmanifest potential before the manifestation of the universe.

- **Quantum Entanglement:** The non-local connections between entangled particles find a parallel in Vedanta's emphasis on the interconnectedness of all existence.

- **Observer Effect:** The role of consciousness in influencing quantum phenomena aligns with Vedantic teachings on the fundamental role of consciousness in shaping reality.

In exploring the correlation between Quantum Physics and Vedanta, it's essential to acknowledge the nuanced nature of both disciplines. While parallels exist, each offers a unique perspective on the nature of reality, inviting a profound dialogue between science and spirituality.

Neuroscience and Vedic Perspectives on Consciousness: A Symbiotic Correlation

The exploration extends into the realm of neuroscience, where the study of consciousness aligns with Vedic perspectives on the nature of awareness. As contemporary research sheds light on the neural correlates of consciousness, the ancient insights into the layers of the mind and the expansiveness of consciousness offer a holistic framework for dialogue and exploration.

The intersection of neuroscience and Vedic perspectives on consciousness presents a captivating journey into the nature of the mind and the profound insights these two disciplines offer. While neuroscience investigates the biological basis of consciousness, Vedic philosophy delves into the spiritual and metaphysical dimensions of the self. In this exploration, we uncover correlations between neuroscience findings and Vedic insights, highlighting their symbiotic relationship.

1. Neural Correlates of Consciousness:

Neuroscience Perspective:

Neuroscience research seeks to identify neural correlates associated with conscious experiences. Brain regions such as the prefrontal cortex and thalamus are implicated in various aspects of consciousness.

Vedic Correlation:

Vedic perspectives assert that consciousness transcends the physical brain. The concept of "Atman" (individual soul) implies a consciousness that extends beyond the material realm.

2. Brain Plasticity and Vedic Transformative Practices:

Neuroscience Perspective:

Neuroplasticity, the brain's ability to reorganize itself, is a key focus. It acknowledges the brain's adaptability in response to experiences and learning.

Vedic Correlation:

Vedic practices such as meditation and yoga aim at transforming consciousness. They are believed to induce changes in neural circuits, aligning with the concept of neuroplasticity.

3. Altered States of Consciousness:

Neuroscience Perspective:

Studies on altered states, induced by psychedelics or meditation, explore shifts in neural activity accompanying changes in consciousness.

Vedic Correlation:

Vedic traditions describe altered states achieved through meditation, known as "Samadhi" or transcendental consciousness. The parallels suggest commonality in experiential states.

4. Quantum Mind Theories and Vedic Cosmology:

Neuroscience Perspective:

Quantum mind theories propose quantum processes in microtubules within neurons. These theories explore quantum phenomena in consciousness.

Vedic Correlation:

Vedic cosmology describes the subtle realms of existence beyond the physical. The concept aligns with the idea that consciousness operates at levels beyond classical physics.

5. Default Mode Network and Vedic Notions of Ego:

Neuroscience Perspective:

The Default Mode Network (DMN) is associated with self-referential thoughts and the ego. Disruptions in the DMN are linked to altered states of consciousness.

Vedic Correlation:

Vedic teachings emphasize overcoming the ego (Ahamkara) for self-realization. The correlation suggests that alterations in the DMN may relate to shifts in egoic identification.

6. Consciousness as Fundamental:

Neuroscience Perspective:

Some neuroscientists propose that consciousness is a fundamental aspect of the universe, challenging the traditional materialist view.

Vedic Correlation:

Vedic perspectives posit consciousness as fundamental, existing beyond the material world. The notion aligns with the idea of an eternal, unchanging consciousness (Brahman).

Examples of Correlation:

- **Mindfulness Meditation and Brain Changes:** Studies show that mindfulness meditation induces changes in brain regions associated with attention and self-awareness. This aligns with Vedic practices emphasizing awareness and self-realization.

- **Yogic Breath Control and Autonomic Nervous System:** Yogic practices such as Pranayama influence the autonomic nervous system, showcasing the connection between breath control and neural regulation.

- **Neurofeedback and Vedic Self-Realization:** Neurofeedback techniques, where individuals learn to control brain activity, echo Vedic notions of self-realization through conscious awareness and mastery over the mind.

- **Ayurveda and Neural Harmony:** Ayurveda, a Vedic system of medicine, emphasizes holistic well-being. The harmony sought in Ayurveda aligns with neuroscience's understanding of the interconnectedness of physical and mental health.

- **Quantum Mind Theories and Vedic Cosmogony:** The exploration of quantum mind theories resonates with Vedic cosmogony, where consciousness operates in subtle realms beyond conventional understanding.

The correlation between neuroscience and Vedic perspectives on consciousness invites a holistic understanding of the mind–brain relationship. While neuroscience provides valuable insights into the neural mechanisms of consciousness, Vedic wisdom enriches the discourse by delving into the metaphysical and spiritual dimensions of the self. Together, they contribute to a more comprehensive exploration of the profound mystery that is human consciousness.

The Ethical Imperative: Wisdom for the Modern World

Beyond the intellectual exploration lies an ethical imperative. Vedic wisdom, steeped in moral and ethical considerations, provides a guiding light for seeing through the complexities of the modern world. This chapter delves into the ethical dimensions of Vedic insights, emphasizing their relevance in fostering compassion, ecological stewardship, and harmonious coexistence with the interconnected web of life.

In the hustle and bustle of the modern world, where complexities abound, Vedic wisdom serves as a guiding light, offering profound insights that resonate with contemporary challenges. Scientific experiments and studies increasingly affirm the relevance of Vedic principles in enhancing well-being, and resilience, and fostering a harmonious existence. Let's explore how Vedic wisdom provides a guiding light for through the complexities of the modern world, with examples grounded in scientific research:

1. Mindfulness and Stress Reduction:

Vedic Wisdom:

Vedic traditions, particularly through practices like meditation and mindfulness, emphasize the importance of cultivating inner peace and mental clarity.

Scientific Correlation:

Scientific studies, such as those conducted by Jon Kabat-Zinn, have demonstrated that mindfulness meditation reduces stress, lowers cortisol levels, and enhances overall well-being.

2. Ayurveda and Holistic Health:

Vedic Wisdom:

Ayurveda, an ancient Vedic system of medicine, advocates a holistic approach to health, considering the interconnectedness of the body, mind, and spirit.

Scientific Correlation:

Research has shown that Ayurvedic practices, including herbal remedies, dietary adjustments, and lifestyle changes, can positively impact various health conditions, promoting overall well-being.

3. Yoga for Physical and Mental Health:

Vedic Wisdom:

Yoga, a Vedic practice, integrates physical postures, breath control, and meditation for holistic health and balance.

Scientific Correlation:

Numerous scientific studies have affirmed the physical and mental health benefits of yoga, including improved flexibility, reduced anxiety, and enhanced cognitive function.

4. Mind-Body Connection:

Vedic Wisdom:

Vedic philosophy underscores the intrinsic connection between the mind and body, recognizing that mental well-being significantly influences physical health.

Scientific Correlation:

Scientific research in psychoneuroimmunology demonstrates the profound impact of mental states on the immune system, showcasing the intricate mind-body relationship.

5. Quantum Physics and Consciousness:

Vedic Wisdom:

Vedic thought posits that consciousness is fundamental and extends beyond the material realm, aligning with the concept of Brahman.

Scientific Correlation:

Quantum physics explores the role of consciousness in shaping reality, with theories such as the observer effect highlighting the inseparable link between the observer and the observed.

6. Environmental Stewardship:

Vedic Wisdom:

Vedic teachings emphasize reverence for nature and ecological balance, considering the environment as an extension of the self.

Scientific Correlation:

Modern environmental science supports the idea that sustainable practices, aligned with Vedic principles, are crucial for preserving the planet's health and biodiversity.

7. Emotional Intelligence and Interpersonal Harmony:

Vedic Wisdom:

Vedic texts highlight the importance of cultivating emotional intelligence and harmonious relationships for personal and societal well-being.

Scientific Correlation:

Studies in psychology affirm that emotional intelligence contributes to mental health, resilience, and positive social interactions, reinforcing Vedic teachings on emotional well-being.

8. Non-Attachment and Mental Resilience:

Vedic Wisdom:

Vedic philosophy encourages non-attachment, teaching that detachment from outcomes fosters mental resilience and inner peace.

Scientific Correlation:

Research in positive psychology suggests that cultivating a non-attached mindset contributes to greater emotional resilience and adaptive coping strategies in the face of challenges.

As scientific research continues to unravel the intricate connections between mind, body, and the broader cosmos, the wisdom embedded in Vedic traditions gains recognition for its holistic and timeless relevance in promoting well-being, resilience, and harmonious existence.

Ecological Consciousness in Vedic Traditions

The ecological consciousness embedded in Vedic traditions becomes a poignant focal point. The reverence for nature, the sacredness attributed to the elements, and the interconnectedness of all living beings present a holistic ecological paradigm. In a world grappling with environmental challenges, this chapter explores how Vedic insights can inform contemporary approaches to sustainability and environmental ethics.

Vedic traditions hold a profound ecological consciousness, recognizing the interconnectedness between humanity and the natural world. This ecological awareness is deeply embedded in the scriptures, rituals, and lifestyle practices, emphasizing the importance of living in harmony with nature. Here are key aspects illustrating the significance of ecological consciousness in Vedic traditions, along with examples:

1. Reverence for Nature:

Vedic Perspective:

Vedic texts, including the Vedas and Upanishads, express reverence for the natural elements, considering them sacred manifestations of the divine. Nature is viewed not merely as a resource but as a living, conscious entity deserving respect.

Example:

The Atharva Veda includes hymns dedicated to various aspects of nature, celebrating the Earth as a nurturing mother and the rivers as life-giving goddesses.

2. Rituals and Eco-Friendly Practices:

Vedic Perspective:

Vedic rituals often involve offerings to nature, acknowledging the interconnectedness between humans and the environment. Practices such as Yajna (fire ceremonies) symbolize the symbiotic relationship between humanity and the elements.

Example:

Yajnas involve the use of natural substances like ghee, grains, and herbs, promoting sustainable and eco-friendly practices. The ritual is seen as a way to express gratitude and maintain environmental balance.

3. Ahimsa (Non-Violence) and Environmental Ethics:

Vedic Perspective:

The principle of Ahimsa extends beyond human interactions to encompass all living beings, fostering an ethical stance towards the environment. Avoiding harm to animals, plants, and ecosystems aligns with Vedic values.

Example:

The concept of Jivamrita in Vedic ecology involves offering water mixed with Tulsi leaves to plants, symbolizing a commitment to non-violence and nurturing the well-being of all life forms.

4. Cyclical Understanding of Time and Nature:

Vedic Perspective:

Vedic cosmology views time as cyclical, with periods of creation, sustenance, and dissolution. This cyclic understanding encourages a sense of responsibility towards preserving the balance of nature.

Example:

The concept of Yugas (epochs) in Vedic philosophy emphasizes the cyclical nature of cosmic time, fostering an awareness of the need for sustainable practices to ensure the longevity of the Earth.

5. Living in Harmony with Seasons:

Vedic Perspective:

Vedic lifestyle, including dietary practices, is attuned to the changing seasons. This harmony with nature is reflected in the celebration of festivals and rituals aligned with natural cycles.

Example:

Festivals like Makar Sankranti mark the transition of the sun into the northern hemisphere, signifying the onset of longer days. Traditional foods associated with these festivals are often seasonally available and locally sourced.

6. Conservation of Biodiversity:

Vedic Perspective:

Vedic wisdom recognizes the diversity of flora and fauna as integral to the cosmic order. Preserving biodiversity is seen as a duty to maintain the intricate balance of the ecosystem.

Example:

The Atharva Veda acknowledges the interconnectedness of all living beings and underscores the importance of protecting plant and animal species for the well-being of the Earth.

7. Sustainable Agriculture Practices:

Vedic Perspective:

Vedic agriculture practices emphasize the importance of sustainable cultivation methods, crop rotation, and organic farming to ensure the fertility of the soil and the health of ecosystems.

Example:

The concept of 'Krsi Parashara' in Vedic agriculture guides farmers on sustainable land management, promoting ecological harmony and minimizing the ecological footprint of agricultural activities.

Ecological consciousness in Vedic traditions goes beyond a mere acknowledgment of the environment; it is deeply interwoven with a spiritual understanding of the sacredness of nature. By embodying values of reverence, ethical conduct, and sustainable practices, Vedic wisdom serves as an enduring guide for fostering a harmonious relationship between humanity and the natural world.

The Historical Context of Vedic Wisdom and the Evolution of Modern Scientific Thought

The Vedic period laid the groundwork for the development of Vedic wisdom, encompassing religious, philosophical, and scientific ideas. It is interesting to note that Vedic wisdom and modern scientific thought emerged in different cultural and historical contexts, there are intersecting points, particularly in their holistic perspectives and contributions to mathematics and cosmology. Both traditions reflect humanity's enduring curiosity and quest for understanding the mysteries of the universe.

Vedic Wisdom:

Cosmology and Philosophy: The Vedas contain hymns and rituals that reflect a cosmological understanding, describing the universe's interconnectedness and the cyclical nature of creation, preservation, and destruction. The philosophical aspects of the Vedas are embodied in texts like the Upanishads, which delve into the nature of reality, self, and ultimate truth (Brahman).

Ayurveda: Vedic knowledge also contributed to the field of medicine through Ayurveda. Ayurveda emphasizes a holistic approach to health, focusing on balance and harmony within the body, mind, and spirit.

Mathematics and Astronomy: The Vedic period saw advancements in mathematics with the development of the decimal system and concepts of zero. Additionally, Vedic texts contain references to celestial bodies, indicating a rudimentary understanding of astronomy.

Evolution of Modern Scientific Thought:

Greek and Hellenistic Influence: The evolution of modern scientific thought in the Western world was heavily influenced by Greek philosophers like Aristotle and Plato. Their emphasis on observation, reasoning, and the search for natural explanations laid the groundwork for the scientific method.

Medieval Islamic Golden Age: During the medieval period, Islamic scholars preserved and expanded upon Greek knowledge. They made significant contributions to various fields, including astronomy, medicine, mathematics, and optics.

Renaissance and Scientific Revolution: The Renaissance marked a revival of interest in classical learning, fostering a spirit of inquiry and exploration. This period paved the way for the Scientific Revolution in the 16th and 17th centuries, characterized by figures like Copernicus, Galileo, and Newton, who challenged traditional views and established the foundations of modern science.

Empirical Observation and Experimentation: Modern scientific thought is characterized by its emphasis on empirical observation, experimentation, and the formulation of testable hypotheses. This approach distinguishes it from earlier philosophical and speculative traditions.

Intersecting Points:

Holistic Perspectives: Both Vedic wisdom and modern scientific thought share an appreciation for holistic perspectives. Ayurveda, for example, considers the interconnectedness of various aspects of life, similar to the interdisciplinary approach in modern science.

Cyclical Nature of Time: Vedic cosmology depicts time as cyclical, a concept that finds resonance in modern scientific theories like the cyclical nature of the universe proposed in certain cosmological models.

Mathematical Advancements: The Vedic decimal system and mathematical concepts, such as zero, contributed to the development of mathematical thought. Modern science heavily relies on advanced mathematical principles for modeling and understanding the natural world.

Chapter 2:
The Nature of Reality

Concepts like Brahman, Maya, and the interconnectedness of all existence

Vedic Perspectives

1. Brahman:

In Vedic philosophy, Brahman is the ultimate reality, the unchanging, eternal, and infinite source of all that exists. It is described as formless, beyond attributes, and the essence of the universe. The concept of Brahman is prominently featured in the Upanishads, which are considered the culmination of Vedic thought.

Sacred Text Reference:

Chandogya Upanishad (6.2.1): "That which is invisible, ungraspable, without family, without caste, without eyes or ears, without hands or feet, eternal, all-pervading, omnipresent, exceedingly subtle – that is the Imperishable."

2. Maya:

Maya refers to the illusion or deceptive power that veils the true nature of reality. It is the cosmic illusion that makes the finite world appear as separate from Brahman. The concept of Maya is found in various Upanishads and is central to understanding the nature of existence.

Sacred Text Reference:

Chandogya Upanishad (6.8.4): "Now that serene being is verily the same as this person. And that which is beyond mind and speech, and which the mind cannot comprehend – That alone is true. That is the essence of the world. That is the Self. That thou art, O Svetaketu."

3. Interconnectedness of All Existence:

Vedic philosophy emphasizes the interconnectedness of all existence, asserting that everything in the universe is interconnected and interdependent. This interconnectedness is often described through the concept of "Vasudhaiva Kutumbakam," meaning "the world is one family."

Sacred Text Reference:

Rig Veda (1.164.46): "Ekam sat vipra bahudha vadanti" – "Truth is one, the wise call it by many names."

These concepts collectively form the basis of Vedic perspectives on the nature of reality, highlighting the transcendental nature of Brahman, the illusory nature of the world (Maya), and the interconnected oneness of all existence. The Upanishads, particularly the Chandogya Upanishad and the Rig Veda, provide profound insights into these philosophical ideas, shaping the spiritual and metaphysical aspects of Vedic thought.

Insights from Ancient Texts on the Illusory Nature of the Material World

Verses from the Vedas convey the idea that the material world is a projection, an illusion and that true understanding comes from realizing the underlying unity of existence beyond the apparent diversity. The concept of Maya is a recurring theme in Vedic philosophy, encouraging seekers to transcend the illusions of the material world to realize the ultimate reality, Brahman.

Upanishads, in particular, contain hymns and verses that delve into the illusory nature of the material world, emphasizing the concept of Maya. Here are some quotes and evidence from the Vedas that highlight this perspective:

1. Chandogya Upanishad:

The Chandogya Upanishad (6.8.7) speaks about the illusory nature of the material world, describing it as a mirage:

"Just as, my dear, by knowing one lump of clay, all that is made of clay is known, the difference being only in name, arising from speech, but the truth being that all is clay. And as, my dear, by knowing one gold nugget, all that is made of gold is known, the difference being only in name, arising from speech, but the truth being that all is gold. So, my dear, is that instruction."

2. Brihadaranyaka Upanishad:

The Brihadaranyaka Upanishad (2.4.14) explores the idea that the material world is a result of a covering or projection:

"As a spider sends forth and draws in its thread, as plants grow on the earth, as hair grows on the head and body of a living person, so from the Imperishable arises this universe."

3. Rig Veda:

The Rig Veda (10.90.2) hints at the interconnectedness and transient nature of the material world:

"The wise who have searched their hearts with wisdom and learned it know that which is kin to that which is not kin; for kin and not kin all proceed from One, from that which is and from that which is not."

4. Mundaka Upanishad:

The Mundaka Upanishad (1.1.9) describes the illusory nature of the world as a magic show:

"As water on a lotus leaf, as a mustard seed on the point of a needle, he is without contact with water, without contact with the earth, without contact with fire, without contact with air, he is without contact with the ether, without contact with the senses, without contact with the Manas (mind), without contact with intellect, without contact with egoism, without contact with the great one, without contact with the unmanifest; he is without contact with all this; and he is without contact, without stain."

---

*Quantum Mechanics and the Enigmatic
Nature of Subatomic Particles*

Scientific Understanding

Quantum mechanics, the branch of physics that deals with the behavior of particles on the smallest scales, has revolutionized our understanding of the universe. At the heart of quantum mechanics lies the study of subatomic particles, the building blocks of matter. These particles exhibit behaviors that challenge our classical intuitions and give rise to a host of enigmatic phenomena.

Foundations of Quantum Mechanics:

At the turn of the 20th century, physicists were grappling with phenomena that classical physics couldn't explain. The discovery of phenomena like the photoelectric effect and blackbody radiation led to the development of quantum theory. In 1900, Max Planck proposed that energy is quantized, coming in discrete packets called quanta. This idea laid the groundwork for quantum mechanics.

Wave-Particle Duality:

One of the most perplexing aspects of quantum mechanics is the wave-particle duality of subatomic particles. In classical physics, particles like electrons were thought to behave like tiny billiard balls. However, in the quantum realm, particles exhibit both wave-like and particle-like characteristics.

Example: *Double-Slit Experiment:*

The famous double-slit experiment demonstrates wave-particle duality. When particles such as electrons or photons are fired through two slits onto a screen, they create an interference pattern, characteristic of waves. However, when observed, the particles behave like discrete particles, forming a pattern consistent with their particle nature. This duality challenges our classical intuition and suggests that particles don't have definite positions until observed.

Quantum Superposition:

Quantum superposition is another perplexing concept in quantum mechanics. It asserts that particles can exist in multiple states simultaneously until they are observed or measured. This is in stark contrast to classical objects, which exist in well-defined states.

Example: *Schrödinger's Cat:*

In Schrödinger's thought experiment, a cat is placed in a box with a radioactive atom that may or may not decay, triggering a poison and potentially killing the cat. According to quantum mechanics, before observation, the atom is in a superposition of decayed and undecayed states, implying the cat is simultaneously alive and dead. It's only when someone opens the box and observes the cat that the superposition collapses into one definite state.

Quantum Entanglement:

Quantum entanglement is a phenomenon where two or more particles become interconnected and share a state, regardless of the distance between them. Changes to one particle instantaneously affect the other, defying classical notions of locality.

Example: *EPR Paradox:*

The Einstein-Podolsky-Rosen (EPR) paradox involves entangled particles. According to quantum mechanics, measuring one entangled particle's state instantaneously determines the state of the other, no matter how far apart they are. Einstein famously referred to this as "spooky action at a distance," challenging classical ideas about information transfer.

Uncertainty Principle:

Formulated by Werner Heisenberg, the uncertainty principle states that there is an inherent limit to the precision with which certain pairs of properties, such as position and momentum, can be known simultaneously. The more precisely we know one property, the less precisely we can know the other.

Example: *Uncertainty in Electron Position and Momentum:*

In the case of an electron, the more accurately we determine its position, the less accurately we can know its momentum, and vice versa. This principle introduces a fundamental indeterminacy into the microscopic world, emphasizing the limits of classical concepts of measurement and determinism.

Quantum Tunneling:

Quantum tunneling allows particles to pass through energy barriers that, according to classical physics, should be insurmountable. It's a phenomenon where particles can appear on the other side of a barrier without having sufficient energy to cross it.

Example: *Tunneling Microscope:*

The scanning tunneling microscope (STM) is a practical application of quantum tunneling. By exploiting the tunneling of electrons between a sharp metal tip and a sample, researchers can create detailed images of surfaces at the atomic level. This technology has revolutionized nanoscience and nanotechnology.

Quantum Computing:

Quantum mechanics has given rise to the field of quantum computing, promising a paradigm shift in computation. Quantum computers use quantum bits or qubits, which can exist in superpositions of 0 and 1 simultaneously. This allows them to perform complex calculations exponentially faster than classical computers for certain tasks.

Example: *Quantum Superposition in Quantum Computing:*

In a classical computer, bits can be either 0 or 1. In a quantum computer, qubits can exist in superpositions of 0 and 1, allowing for parallel processing of information. This enables quantum computers to tackle problems like factorization and optimization much more efficiently than classical computers.

Challenges and Interpretations:

Quantum mechanics challenges our classical intuitions, leading to various interpretations of its fundamental concepts. The most famous of these is the Copenhagen interpretation, which emphasizes the role of observation in collapsing quantum states. Other interpretations include the many-worlds interpretation, suggesting that every quantum possibility plays out in a separate parallel universe.

Applications and Future Directions:

Quantum mechanics has found applications in various fields, including technology, medicine, and materials science. Quantum computers are a burgeoning area of research, with the potential to revolutionize fields like cryptography and optimization. Quantum communication promises secure communication channels using the principles of entanglement.

Quantum mechanics has fundamentally altered our understanding of the nature of reality at the microscopic level. The enigmatic behaviors of subatomic particles challenge classical notions of determinism, locality, and objective reality. Wave-particle duality, quantum superposition, entanglement, and the uncertainty principle reveal the richness and complexity of the quantum world.

While the theory has been immensely successful in explaining experimental observations, it continues to spark philosophical debates about the nature of existence and the role of observation in shaping reality. As technology advances, the practical applications of quantum mechanics are becoming increasingly apparent, ushering in a new era of scientific exploration and technological innovation. The enigma of the quantum world persists, inviting scientists and philosophers to delve deeper into the mysteries that lie at the heart of the smallest scales of the universe.

Establishing Parallels Between Quantum Mechanics and Vedic Maya

Drawing parallels between the concepts of quantum mechanics and the Vedic concept of Maya involves exploring the fundamental nature of reality, the role of observation, and the illusory aspects of the material world. While the two systems of thought arise from different cultural and historical contexts, there are intriguing similarities in their attempts to explain the mysteries of existence.

1. Illusory Nature of Reality:

Quantum Mechanics:

Quantum mechanics challenges the classical notion of an objective reality. The wave-particle duality and superposition suggest that the state of a particle is not determined until observed, emphasizing the illusory nature of properties like position and momentum.

Vedic Maya:

Maya in Vedic philosophy is the cosmic illusion that veils the true nature of reality. It suggests that the material world is not as it appears and that there is a deeper, unchanging reality (Brahman) beyond the transient and deceptive nature of the phenomenal world.

Parallel:

Both quantum mechanics and Vedic philosophy posit that the material world may not be as solid and objective as it seems. Observations in quantum mechanics and the concept of Maya imply that reality is influenced by perception and may not have a fixed, independent existence.

2. Role of Consciousness and Observation:

Quantum Mechanics:

The role of observation is central to quantum mechanics. The act of measurement collapses the wave function, determining the outcome of a quantum system. The observer is an integral part of the process, influencing the observed reality.

Vedic Maya:

Maya, in Vedic thought, is often associated with the play of consciousness. The Upanishads emphasize the importance of self-realization and transcending the illusory aspects of the material world through higher consciousness.

Parallel:

Both quantum mechanics and Vedic philosophy highlight the significance of consciousness and observation in shaping our understanding of reality. The observer's role in quantum mechanics resonates with the idea that our perception and consciousness play a crucial role in navigating the illusory aspects of the world, as suggested by the concept of Maya.

3. Non-local Connections and Interconnectedness:

Quantum Mechanics:

Quantum entanglement reveals non-local connections between particles, where the state of one particle is instantly correlated with the state of another, regardless of the distance between them.

Vedic Maya:

Vedic philosophy emphasizes the interconnectedness of all existence. The concept of Vasudhaiva Kutumbakam, "the world is one family," reflects the idea that all things are interconnected in a cosmic unity.

Parallel:

Both quantum mechanics and Vedic philosophy suggest a profound interconnectedness in the fabric of reality. Quantum entanglement challenges classical notions of locality, and the Vedic concept of interconnectedness implies a unity that transcends the apparent diversity of the material world.

4. Limitations of Language and Concepts:

Quantum Mechanics:

Quantum mechanics often encounters challenges when attempting to describe phenomena at the quantum level using classical language and concepts. The nature of particles and their behaviors defy easy representation in classical terms.

Vedic Maya:

Maya is considered beyond the grasp of ordinary language and conceptualization. The Upanishads often speak of Brahman as "neti neti – not this, not this," indicating the ineffability of the ultimate reality.

Parallel:

Both quantum mechanics and Vedic philosophy acknowledge the limitations of language and conventional concepts in capturing the essence of their respective domains. The elusive nature of quantum phenomena and the ineffable nature of Maya point to the difficulty of expressing these profound realities using ordinary language.

In summary, while quantum mechanics and Vedic philosophy arise from distinct cultural and intellectual traditions, there are intriguing parallels in their exploration of the illusory nature of reality, the role of observation and consciousness, the interconnectedness of existence, and the challenges posed by language and concepts in describing fundamental truths. These parallels offer a fascinating bridge between scientific inquiry and ancient metaphysical wisdom, inviting contemplation on the nature of reality from different perspectives.

Theories on the Nature of Matter, Energy, and the Fabric of Reality

The nature of matter, energy, and the fabric of reality has been a subject of intense exploration and speculation across different scientific and philosophical traditions. Various theories have been proposed to explain the fundamental building blocks of the universe and the nature of the space-time fabric that underlies reality. Here are some key theories:

1. Classical Mechanics: Newton's Laws and Determinism

The journey begins with classical mechanics, a framework formulated by Sir Isaac Newton in the 17th century. Newton's laws of motion and the law of universal gravitation provided a deterministic view of the universe. According to classical mechanics, particles have well-defined trajectories, and physical properties can be precisely determined. The clockwork universe envisioned by Newtonian physics suggested a world governed by predictable laws, where the motion of celestial bodies and the behavior of objects could be accurately calculated.

Despite its success in describing macroscopic phenomena, classical mechanics faced challenges when confronted with the behavior of particles at the atomic and subatomic scales. The deterministic nature of classical physics proved inadequate in explaining certain phenomena, such as the photoelectric effect and the behavior of electrons in atoms.

2. Quantum Mechanics: The Dance of Particles and Waves

The early 20th century witnessed a scientific revolution with the advent of quantum mechanics. Pioneered by physicists like Max Planck, Albert Einstein, Niels Bohr, Werner Heisenberg, and Erwin Schrödinger, quantum mechanics introduced a paradigm shift in our understanding of the microscopic world.

At the heart of quantum mechanics lies the wave-particle duality, challenging classical notions of particles as distinct, solid entities. Particles at the quantum level, such as electrons and photons, exhibit both wave-like and particle-like characteristics. The famous double-slit experiment, where particles create an interference pattern reminiscent of waves when not observed and form distinct particles when observed, highlights the inherent duality of quantum entities.

Uncertainty becomes a central theme in quantum mechanics through Heisenberg's Uncertainty Principle. This principle asserts that there is an intrinsic limit to the precision with which certain pairs of properties, such as position and momentum, can be simultaneously known. The more precisely one property is known, the less precisely the other can be determined, introducing a fundamental indeterminacy into the microscopic world.

Quantum mechanics introduces the concept of superposition, suggesting that particles can exist in multiple states simultaneously until observed or measured. This concept challenges classical intuitions, emphasizing that a particle's properties are not determined until an observation is made.

Entanglement is another enigmatic phenomenon in quantum mechanics. When particles become entangled, the state of one particle is instantaneously correlated with the state of another, even if they are light-years apart. This non-local connection defies classical notions of locality and suggests a profound interconnectedness in the fabric of reality.

While quantum mechanics has proven highly successful in explaining experimental observations, it also gives rise to conceptual challenges and philosophical implications. The role of observation and the influence of consciousness on quantum states raise questions about the nature of reality and the relationship between the observer and the observed.

3. General Relativity: The Curvature of Spacetime

While quantum mechanics explores the microscopic realm, Albert Einstein's general theory of relativity revolutionized our understanding of the large-scale structure of the universe. Published in 1915, general relativity describes gravity as the curvature of space-time caused by the presence of mass and energy. Massive objects, such as planets and stars, create "dimples" in the fabric of space-time, influencing the paths of other objects that move through this curved space.

General relativity provides a comprehensive framework for understanding gravity and cosmology, predicting phenomena like time dilation near massive objects and the bending of light around massive bodies, known as gravitational lensing. It has been experimentally confirmed in various settings, from the precession of Mercury's orbit to the detection of gravitational waves by LIGO and Virgo observatories.

Despite its success, general relativity and quantum mechanics present a fundamental challenge when attempts are made to unify them in a single, coherent framework. This challenge has led to the exploration of theories that seek to reconcile these two pillars of modern physics.

4. Standard Model of Particle Physics: The Dance of Subatomic Particles

The Standard Model of particle physics, developed in the mid-20th century, provides a comprehensive framework for understanding the fundamental particles and forces in the universe. This quantum field theory describes three of the four fundamental forces: electromagnetism, the weak nuclear force, and the strong nuclear force.

The Standard Model introduces elementary particles such as quarks, leptons (including electrons and neutrinos), and force carriers like photons and W/Z bosons. The successful predictions of the Higgs boson's existence, confirmed by experiments at the Large Hadron Collider (LHC), represented a significant triumph for the Standard Model.

However, the Standard Model is not without limitations. It does not incorporate gravity and cannot explain certain phenomena, such as dark matter and dark energy, which together constitute the majority of the universe's mass-energy content. The search for a more complete and unified theory continues.

5. String Theory: Vibrations in the Cosmic Symphony

String theory represents a radical departure from traditional particle physics. It suggests that the fundamental building blocks of the universe are not point-like particles but tiny, vibrating strings. These strings can vibrate at different frequencies, giving rise to the various particles observed in nature. The theory proposes extra dimensions beyond the familiar three spatial dimensions and one time dimension.

String theory has the potential to unify quantum mechanics and general relativity, providing a framework that encompasses all forces and particles in a single coherent theory. However, as of now, string theory remains a candidate for a unified theory of fundamental physics, with many challenges and open questions to address.

6. Loop Quantum Gravity: Quantizing the Fabric of Space-Time

Loop quantum gravity is another approach to reconciling quantum mechanics and general relativity. Unlike string theory, which focuses on the nature of particles, loop quantum gravity aims to quantize the fabric of space-time itself. In this framework, space-time is viewed as a network of interconnected loops, with discrete, quantized properties.

Loop quantum gravity addresses the challenges associated with the singularity problem in general relativity, where space-time curvature becomes infinitely large. The theory suggests that at extremely small scales, space-time exhibits a granular structure, avoiding the singularities encountered in classical general relativity.

While loop quantum gravity is still a work in progress, it offers a novel perspective on the nature of space-time and the possibility of a quantum theory of gravity.

7. Grand Unified Theories (GUTs): Unifying Forces at High Energies

Grand Unified Theories (GUTs) seek to unify the electromagnetic, weak, and strong nuclear forces into a single theoretical framework. GUTs propose that at high energies, these forces were once indistinguishable, providing a more comprehensive understanding of particle interactions.

While GUTs have not been experimentally confirmed, they represent an important step toward the ultimate goal of a "Theory of Everything" that unifies all forces and particles in a single, elegant framework.

8. Quantum Field Theory:

Quantum field theory, a foundational framework in particle physics, treats particles as excitations of underlying fields. It describes the interactions between particles in terms of the exchange of force-carrying particles.

9. Information Theory and Holography: Universe Is Nothing but a Holograph

Some theories propose that the fabric of reality is fundamentally informational. The holographic principle suggests that the information describing a three-dimensional volume can be encoded on its two-dimensional boundary. This idea has connections to black hole physics and the nature of space-time.

These theories represent ongoing efforts to unravel the mysteries of the universe, and some are more speculative than others. The quest for a unified theory that explains the fundamental nature of matter, energy, and the fabric of reality continues to be a central focus of scientific inquiry and philosophical exploration.

10. Multiverse Hypothesis: Universes within Universes

The multiverse hypothesis suggests that our universe is one of many universes that exist in a vast cosmic ensemble. Different regions of the multiverse may have different physical constants and laws of physics, leading to diverse universes. The multiverse hypothesis is a speculative and intriguing concept that suggests our universe is just one of many universes that exist in a vast and diverse cosmic ensemble. This hypothesis proposes that there are multiple, perhaps an infinite number of universes, each with its own set of physical laws, constants, and properties. The idea of a multiverse challenges traditional views of a single, unique cosmos and has gained attention in cosmology, theoretical physics, and philosophical discussions.

- **Origins of the Multiverse Hypothesis:**

The concept of a multiverse arose as a way to address certain puzzles and inconsistencies in our understanding of the universe. One of the key motivations comes from the field of cosmology and the study of the early universe. The observed uniformity and isotropy of the cosmic microwave background radiation, coupled with the large-scale structure of the cosmos, have led scientists to consider scenarios beyond what a single universe could explain.

- **Types of Multiverse Hypotheses:**

There are several distinct proposals within the multiverse framework, each addressing different aspects of cosmological questions. Some of the prominent types include:

   a. *Cosmological Multiverse:* This type suggests that our universe is just one of many "bubbles" in a larger inflating space. Each bubble represents a separate universe with its own distinct physical properties.

   b. *Quantum Multiverse:* Based on the principles of quantum mechanics, this hypothesis posits that every possible outcome of a quantum event is realized in a separate universe. It suggests that all the potential branches of reality, resulting from quantum probabilities, exist simultaneously in different universes.

   c. *Landscape Multiverse:* In the context of string theory, the landscape multiverse proposes that the multitude of possible vacuum states or configurations in string theory's extra dimensions gives rise to different universes with varying physical constants and properties.

d. **Parallel Universes:** This idea suggests that there are universes that exist in parallel with ours, occupying the same space but remaining undetectable due to the differences in vibrational frequencies or other physical properties.

e. *Holographic Multiverse*: Drawing inspiration from the holographic principle, this hypothesis suggests that the information describing a three-dimensional volume can be encoded on its two-dimensional boundary. Each universe in the multiverse could be a holographic projection of information encoded on a lower-dimensional boundary.

- **Experimental and Observational Implications:**

One of the challenges of the multiverse hypothesis lies in its testability. Many versions of the multiverse may forever remain beyond the reach of direct observation or experimental verification. However, some proposals could, in principle, leave observable imprints or signatures on our own universe.

a. *Cosmic Microwave Background (CMB):* The cosmic microwave background radiation, considered the afterglow of the Big Bang, may contain evidence of interactions with other universes in the multiverse. Anomalies or patterns in the CMB might be indicative of such interactions.

b. *Quantum Effects:* If quantum mechanics plays a role in generating the multiverse, there could be subtle quantum signatures or correlations between our universe and others that might be detected through advanced experiments.

c. ***Gravitational Effects:*** The gravitational influence of neighboring universes might cause observable effects in our own. Anomalies in the motion of galaxies or the distribution of matter could be potential indicators.

- **Criticisms and Challenges:**

The multiverse hypothesis is not without its critics and challenges. Some scientists argue that invoking a multiverse might be seen as a "cop-out," as it allows for a wide range of possibilities without the need for a deeper understanding of the fundamental laws governing our universe.

Critics also point out that, without clear experimental evidence, the multiverse remains a speculative concept rather than a proven scientific theory. The lack of direct observability raises questions about the scientific validity of the multiverse hypothesis.

- *Philosophical Implications:*

The multiverse hypothesis has profound philosophical implications. It challenges our intuitions about uniqueness, determinism, and the nature of reality. The idea that every conceivable possibility is realized in some universe raises questions about the nature of choice, free will, and the meaning of our existence.

The concept also intersects with discussions about the anthropic principle, which suggests that the observed properties of our universe are compatible with the existence of intelligent life. In a multiverse scenario, the anthropic principle could be invoked to explain why our universe has the conditions necessary for the emergence of life.

- *The Search for a Unified Theory:*

The quest for a unified theory that explains the fundamental laws of physics, including the potential existence of a multiverse, continues to be a driving force in theoretical physics. Some researchers hope that a successful theory of everything, merging quantum mechanics and general relativity, will naturally incorporate or predict the existence of a multiverse.

- **Popular Culture and Public Interest:**

The multiverse hypothesis has captured the imagination of the public and has become a popular theme in science fiction and popular culture. The idea of parallel worlds and alternate realities has been explored in literature, movies, and television, contributing to its widespread recognition beyond scientific circles.

In conclusion, the multiverse hypothesis represents a fascinating and speculative avenue of exploration at the intersection of cosmology, quantum mechanics, and theoretical physics. While it remains a topic of ongoing research and debate, the multiverse concept has sparked new ways of thinking about the nature of reality and our place within the vast cosmic landscape. As scientific inquiry continues and our understanding of the universe deepens, the multiverse hypothesis stands as a testament to the richness and complexity of the questions that drive our exploration of the cosmos.

Drawing Parallels Between Multiverse Hypothesis and Existence of Lokas as Mentioned in Vedas

The parallels between the multiverse hypothesis in modern physics and the concept of Lokas in Vedic literature offer a fascinating exploration of diverse cosmic structures, interconnected realms, and the limits of human understanding. While the multiverse hypothesis is rooted in the scientific inquiry of the cosmos, the Vedic Lokas derive from ancient Indian scriptures, particularly the Puranas and the Upanishads. Let's delve deeper into these parallels with more details and quotes from Vedic scriptures:

1. Multiple Realms and Dimensions:

Multiverse Hypothesis: The multiverse posits the existence of numerous universes, potentially with distinct physical laws and properties, existing simultaneously in different dimensions beyond our direct perception.

Vedic Scriptures: The Vedic literature, including the Puranas, describes Lokas as distinct realms or dimensions. The Rigveda, one of the oldest Vedic texts, mentions different planes of existence. For instance, in the Purusha Sukta (Rigveda 10.90), the cosmic being Purusha is described as having seven layers, each associated with a specific realm.

"The Purusha has seven fuel-sticks, twenty-one are his kindling-places; when the gods performed the sacrifice with Purusha as the offering, these were the moulding sticks."

2. Diversity of Realities:

Multiverse Hypothesis: Each universe in the multiverse may exhibit diverse physical constants, laws of nature, and types of matter, leading to a multitude of possible realities.

Vedic Scriptures: The Vedic concept of Lokas emphasizes the diversity of cosmic realms. The Bhagavad Gita (15.6) speaks of an inverted cosmic tree with roots in the heavens and branches reaching downwards, symbolizing the interconnectedness of different realms.

"The branches of this tree extend downwards and upwards, nourished by the three gunas, with the mortal world as its buds; and its roots extend upwards into the higher worlds, causing the tree itself to continue to grow."

3. Non-Local Connections and Interconnectedness:

Multiverse Hypothesis: Some multiverse theories propose interconnectedness between universes, suggesting that the influence of one universe may extend to another.

Vedic Scriptures: The interconnectedness of Lokas is a recurrent theme in Vedic philosophy. The Brihadaranyaka Upanishad (2.4.5) highlights the idea of Lokas being linked through cosmic axes, emphasizing the unity of the cosmos.

"As the web issues out of the spider, as tiny sparks come out of the fire, even so from this Self appear all creation, and the whole universe issues from the Self."

4. Higher Realms and Conscious Beings:

Multiverse Hypothesis: Higher dimensions in the multiverse may be inhabited by conscious beings or entities operating under different physical laws.

Vedic Scriptures: The Vedic Lokas include higher realms inhabited by celestial beings and deities. The Chandogya Upanishad (8.1.6) speaks of the celestial realms, stating that the sun, moon, and other luminaries are heavenly beings residing in these realms.

"Now that light which shines above this heaven, higher than all, higher than everything, in the highest world, beyond which there are no other worlds, that is the same light which is within man."

5. Concept of Ascension and Descent:

Multiverse Hypothesis: In certain multiverse scenarios, beings or entities may ascend or descend between different universes or dimensions.

Vedic Scriptures: Vedic literature often describes ascension and descent between Lokas as a part of the cosmic order. The Bhagavad Gita (8.16) speaks of the cyclical nature of creation, dissolution, and the potential for beings to ascend to higher realms.

"From the highest planet in the material world down to the lowest, all are places of misery wherein repeated birth and death take place. But one who attains to My abode, O son of Kunti, never takes birth again."

6. Mystical and Beyond Ordinary Perception:

Multiverse Hypothesis: The multiverse involves realms and structures beyond the limits of direct observation, requiring theoretical constructs that challenge ordinary perception.

Vedic Scriptures: The Lokas in Vedic philosophy is often described in mystical and symbolic terms, transcending ordinary human experience. The Mundaka Upanishad (1.1.3) describes the pursuit of knowledge that goes beyond the material realm.

"One should know that by which he knows all this. Seek to know that. All that is seen and unseen will then be known to you."

7. Philosophical Implications:

Multiverse Hypothesis: The multiverse raises philosophical questions about the nature of reality, existence, and the role of consciousness in perceiving diverse realms.

Vedic Scriptures: The Lokas in Vedic philosophy have deep philosophical significance, reflecting on the interconnectedness of all existence and the pursuit of spiritual understanding beyond the material plane. The Bhagavad Gita (2.16) emphasizes the impermanence of the material world.

"There is no existence for the unreal, and the real never ceases to be; the seers of truth have concluded the same, as perceiving the real and the unreal."

In conclusion, the parallels between the multiverse hypothesis and the Vedic concept of Lokas offer a mind-boggling perspective on cosmic exploration, interconnected realms, and the perennial quest for understanding the mysteries of existence. While one arises from the cutting-edge inquiries of modern physics and the other from ancient philosophical traditions, their thematic resonances invite contemplation on the nature of reality from diverse perspectives.

Chapter 3:
Consciousness and Self-awareness

The Atman and the Journey of Self-realization

Vedic Insights

In the vast treasure of Vedic wisdom, the concept of Atman stands as a luminous thread, weaving through the philosophical and spiritual landscape of ancient India. The journey of self-realization, as expounded in Vedic scriptures, is a profound odyssey that invites individuals to embark on a quest to unveil the true nature of the self. This discourse explores the essence of the Atman, tracing the path of self-realization through hymns and shlokas from the Vedas and Upanishads.

The Essence of Atman:

The term "Atman" refers to the eternal and unchanging essence within an individual, representing the true self beyond the physical, mental, and emotional layers. It is the divine spark, the innermost core that connects every living being to the cosmic order. The journey of self-realization, according to Vedic philosophy, involves realizing the profound truth that the individual Atman is inseparable from the universal Brahman, the ultimate reality.

Atman in the Vedas:

The Vedas, the oldest scriptures of Hinduism, provide glimpses of the Atman through hymns that celebrate the cosmic order and the interconnectedness of all existence. Let us delve into some of these hymns to understand the Vedic perspective on the Atman.

1. Rigveda (10.90.2):

> *"Two birds, inseparable companions,*
> *Perch on the same tree.*
> *One eats the fruits of pleasure,*
> *The other looks on without eating."*

This shloka from the Rigveda metaphorically captures the duality inherent in human existence. The Atman, like the witnessing bird, observes the experiences of pleasure and pain without being entangled in them. This sets the stage for the journey toward self-realization, where the individual transcends identification with transient experiences.

2. Atharva Veda (12.1.1):

> *"The Self (Atman) is the honey of all beings,*
> *And all beings are the honey of the Self.*
> *The world is a honeycomb,*
> *And the individual souls are its cells."*

This hymn from the Atharva Veda beautifully illustrates the interconnectedness of all beings through the metaphor of a honeycomb. The Atman is the essence that permeates every soul, emphasizing the unity and interdependence of the individual with the entire cosmos.

The Journey of Self-Realization:

The path of self-realization, according to Vedic teachings, involves a transformative journey from ignorance to wisdom, from identification with the ephemeral to the realization of the eternal. This journey unfolds in stages, each marked by a deeper understanding of the nature of the self.

1. Realizing the Impermanence of the Physical Self:

Teaching from the Upanishads:

Chandogya Upanishad (6.1.2) declares, *"That which is finite is the Self made up of food; the same is immortal, for food is the eater of food."*

Interpretation:

This teaching underscores the impermanence of the physical body, which is sustained by food. The realization that the physical self is transient paves the way for seeking the immortal essence within.

2. Recognizing the Mind as the Seat of Ego:

Teaching from the Upanishads:

Brihadaranyaka Upanishad (4.4.5) states, *"It is the mind that thinks, and that is what the ego is. By seeing who the thinker is, the ego is transcended."*

Interpretation:

This teaching directs attention to the mind as the seat of the ego. Through self-inquiry and introspection, individuals can discern the nature of the ego and realize the thinker behind the thoughts.

3. Unveiling the Witnessing Consciousness:

Teaching from the Upanishads:

Mandukya Upanishad (7) elucidates, *"The Self is not this, not that. It is incomprehensible, for it cannot be comprehended; undecaying, for it never decays; unattached, for it does not attach itself; unfettered – no one frees it."*

Interpretation:

The Upanishad negates all attributes to describe the true nature of the Self. This points to the transcendental aspect of the Atman, which is beyond conceptualization and is free from all attachments.

Meditative Practices for Self-Realization:

The Vedic tradition prescribes various meditative practices to aid individuals on their journey of self-realization. These practices are designed to quiet the mind, turn inward, and unveil the Atman. Here are key meditative principles and corresponding teachings:

1. Dhyana (Meditation):

Teaching from the Bhagavad Gita (6.6):

"For him who has conquered the mind, the mind is the best of friends; but for one who has failed to do so, his mind will remain the greatest enemy."

Interpretation:

The Bhagavad Gita emphasizes the significance of conquering the mind through meditation. A disciplined mind becomes a steadfast ally on the path to self-realization.

2. Pranayama (Breath Control):

Teaching from the Prashna Upanishad (4.4):

"The one who knows the prana as Brahman, by which the mind remains established in the heart, knows the ultimate goal of life and becomes immortal."

Interpretation:

Pranayama, the control of breath, is seen as a means to connect with the vital life force (prana) that sustains both the body and the mind. By understanding prana as Brahman, one attains immortality.

The Culmination: Realizing Oneness with Brahman:

As the journey progresses, the culmination of self-realization lies in the profound understanding that the individual Atman is none other than the universal Brahman. This realization is encapsulated in the famous phrase "*Tat Tvam Asi*" (*That Thou Art*) from the Chandogya Upanishad.

Chandogya Upanishad (6.8.7):

"Aham Brahmasmi" (I am Brahman)

This proclamation signifies the ultimate realization where the individual recognizes their identity with the supreme reality. The journey of self-realization transforms into an awareness of oneness, where distinctions dissolve, and the Atman merges with Brahman.

The Vedic odyssey of self-realization, with the Atman as its guiding light, beckons individuals to embark on an inner journey of profound discovery. Through the wisdom embedded in hymns and shlokas from the Vedas and Upanishads, the Vedic tradition imparts timeless teachings that remain relevant to seekers of truth across epochs. The journey unfolds through stages of realizing the impermanence of the physical self, recognizing the mind as the seat of ego, unveiling the witnessing consciousness, and ultimately culminating in the profound realization of oneness with Brahman. As individuals traverse this sacred path, the Atman becomes not just a concept but a living, experiential reality – a radiant spark that illuminates the sheer awe of existence.

The Role of Consciousness in Vedic Philosophy: Piloting the Cosmos Within

In Vedic philosophy, the concept of consciousness occupies a central and transcendent position. Rooted in ancient wisdom, Vedic thought delves into the nature of consciousness, its relationship with the self, and its expansive connection to the cosmic order. This discourse explores the multifaceted role of consciousness in Vedic philosophy, unraveling its significance, nuances, and profound implications.

Consciousness emerges as the radiant thread that binds the self to the cosmos. It is the essence of reality, the silent witness to the play of existence, and the key to unlocking the mysteries of the self. From the cosmic perspective to the individual journey of self-realization, consciousness weaves through the philosophical landscape, inviting seekers to explore the depths of their being. In the words of the Upanishads, *"Lead me from the unreal to the real. Lead me from darkness to light. Lead me from mortality to immortality."* In this quest for enlightenment, consciousness serves as the guiding light, illuminating the path to transcendence and oneness with the eternal reality.

1. Consciousness as the Essence of Reality:

In Vedic philosophy, consciousness is not merely an attribute of the mind; it is the foundational essence of reality itself. The understanding is rooted in the notion that consciousness (Chit) is inherent in the ultimate reality (Brahman). The Chandogya Upanishad (6.2.1) declares, "Satyam, Jnanam, Anantam Brahman" (Brahman is Truth, Knowledge, and Infinite). Here, consciousness is inseparable from the ultimate truth, emphasizing its primordial and eternal nature.

2. Levels of Consciousness:

Vedic philosophy recognizes different levels of consciousness, each corresponding to a layer of the self. These levels are often delineated as waking consciousness (Jagrat), dream consciousness (Swapna), deep sleep consciousness (Sushupti), and the transcendental consciousness beyond these states (Turiya). The Mandukya Upanishad and its Karika provide a profound exploration of these states, guiding seekers to understand the subtleties of consciousness.

3. Inner Exploration through Yogic Sciences:

The Vedic tradition places great emphasis on inner exploration through Yogic sciences. Practices such as Dhyana (meditation), Pranayama (breath control), and Dharana (concentration) aim to quiet the mind and unveil deeper layers of consciousness. The Yoga Sutras of Patanjali, an influential text in Vedic philosophy, provides a systematic guide to harnessing and expanding consciousness through these practices.

4. Cosmic Consciousness:

Vedic thought envisions a cosmic consciousness that permeates the entire universe. The Rigveda (1.164.20) encapsulates this cosmic perspective with the famous hymn known as the Nasadiya Sukta, stating, *"Whence this creation has arisen – perhaps it formed itself, or perhaps it did not – the one who looks down on it, in the highest heaven, only He knows – or perhaps, He does not know."*

5. Role of Consciousness in Creation:

The Vedas describe a dynamic interplay between consciousness and the cosmic creative process. The Rigveda (10.129) contemplates the mystery of creation, pondering the origin of existence. It suggests a cosmic consciousness that precedes the material world, with the hymn stating, "Then even nothingness was not, nor existence; there was no air then, nor the heavens beyond it."

6. Unity of Individual and Universal Consciousness:

Vedic philosophy asserts the unity of individual consciousness (Jivatman) and universal consciousness (Paramatman or Brahman). The Upanishads, particularly the Mandukya Upanishad, elaborate on the profound realization that the individual self and the cosmic self are ultimately one. The Mahavakyas (great sayings) encapsulate this truth, with statements like "Aham Brahmasmi" (I am Brahman) and "Tat Tvam Asi" (That Thou Art).

7. Consciousness and Karma:

Vedic philosophy intertwines consciousness with the concept of Karma, the law of cause and effect. The Bhagavad Gita elucidates the role of consciousness in the cycle of action and its consequences. Lord Krishna imparts wisdom about detached action, emphasizing the importance of performing duties without attachment to the fruits of those actions, thus elevating one's consciousness.

8. Vedanta and Advaita:

Vedanta, a major school of Vedic philosophy, delves into the nature of consciousness with particular focus on non-dualism (Advaita). The foundational text of Advaita Vedanta, the Brahma Sutras, explores the identity of the individual self with the ultimate reality. Adi Shankaracharya, a prominent philosopher of Advaita Vedanta, emphasizes the realization that the individual's Atman is none other than Brahman, underscoring the oneness of consciousness.

9. Consciousness and Sankhya Philosophy:

Sankhya, one of the classical schools of Vedic philosophy, provides a systematic analysis of the elements of creation and the nature of consciousness. Sankhya philosophy, as outlined in the Sankhya Karika, identifies consciousness (Purusha) as distinct from matter (Prakriti). It delves into the intricate dance between the unchanging consciousness and the ever-changing material world, elucidating the role of self-awareness in realizing the transcendent nature of the self.

10. Consciousness in Rituals and Sacrifices:

The Vedic tradition places a significant emphasis on rituals and sacrifices (Yajnas) as a means to connect with the divine and harmonize individual consciousness with cosmic forces. The Yajur Veda details various rituals, highlighting the sacredness of conscious offerings and the symbolism behind each action. These rituals are seen as a way to purify the mind and attune individual consciousness to higher spiritual frequencies.

11. Devotion and Bhakti Yoga:

Vedic philosophy encompasses the path of Bhakti Yoga, the yoga of devotion, as a powerful means to elevate consciousness. Devotees engage in acts of love and surrender to the divine, recognizing that devotion leads to a profound merging of individual consciousness with the universal consciousness. Bhakti literature, including the Bhagavad Gita and the works of saint-poets like Tulsidas and Meera, beautifully expresses the transformative power of divine love in expanding consciousness.

12. Consciousness in Art and Aesthetics:

Vedic philosophy recognizes the arts as a medium to transcend the mundane and elevate consciousness. The Natya Shastra, attributed to Sage Bharata, outlines the principles of classical Indian performing arts. According to this text, the purpose of art is to evoke specific emotional states (Rasas) in the audience, leading to an aesthetic experience that transcends ordinary perception. Through music, dance, and drama, individuals can access higher states of consciousness and experience a profound connection with the divine.

13. Consciousness and Sound (Nada Brahman):

The Vedic tradition regards sound as a fundamental aspect of the cosmos, resonating with the concept of Nada Brahman – the sound of the ultimate reality. The Upanishads often speak of the divine syllable 'Om' as a manifestation of this cosmic sound. Chanting and meditating on sacred sounds are considered potent practices for attuning individual consciousness to the cosmic vibration, facilitating a deeper connection with the divine.

14. Consciousness and Ethics:

Vedic philosophy underscores the importance of ethical living as a means to purify consciousness. The Dharma Shastras provide guidelines for righteous conduct, emphasizing values such as truthfulness, compassion, and non-violence. Living in accordance with dharma is seen as essential for elevating consciousness and progressing on the spiritual path.

The multifaceted role of consciousness in Vedic philosophy extends beyond metaphysical contemplation to practical applications in daily life. Whether through yogic practices, rituals, devotion, art, or ethical living, the Vedic tradition presents a holistic approach to expanding consciousness and realizing the interconnectedness of the individual with the cosmic whole. Consciousness, in its myriad expressions, remains the unifying force that beckons seekers on a transformative journey from self-awareness to self-realization, ultimately leading to the profound realization of the oneness of all existence. In the words of the ancient seers, "*Ayam Atma Brahma*" – *This Self is Brahman.*

These shlokas below reflect the profound wisdom embedded in Vedic scriptures regarding the nature of consciousness, the self, and the ultimate reality.

Rigveda (1.164.20):

"Two birds, inseparable companions,
Perch on the same tree.
One eats the fruits of pleasure,
The other looks on without eating."

Atharva Veda (12.1.1):

"The Self (Atman) is the honey of all beings,
And all beings are the honey of the Self.
The world is a honeycomb,
And the individual souls are its cells."

Chandogya Upanishad (6.2.1):

"Satyam, Jnanam, Anantam Brahman"
(Brahman is Truth, Knowledge, and Infinite)

Mandukya Upanishad (7):

"The Self is not this, not that. It is incomprehensible,
for it cannot be comprehended; undecaying, for it never decays; unattached, for it does not attach itself;
unfettered – no one frees it."

Bhagavad Gita (2.20):

"The soul (Atman) is never born and never dies, nor does

it ever become, having been, it will never not be. Unborn, eternal, perpetual, and ancient, it is not killed when the body is killed."

Bhagavad Gita (2.47):

"You have a right to perform your prescribed duties, but you are not entitled to the fruits of your actions. Never consider yourself to be the cause of the results of your activities, nor be attached to inaction."

Chandogya Upanishad (6.8.7):

"Aham Brahmasmi"
(I am Brahman)

Taittiriya Upanishad (2.1.1):

"From Brahman, verily, are these beings born; having been born, by Brahman they live; into Brahman they depart, when they die."

Isha Upanishad (1):

"Isha Vasyam Idam Sarvam"
(All this is enveloped by the Divine)

Rigveda (10.129):

"Then even nothingness was not, nor existence; there was no air then, nor the heavens beyond it."

Bhagavad Gita (4.24):

"Brahman is the oblation; Brahman is the clarified butter; by Brahman is the oblation poured into the fire consumed; Brahman is that which is to be attained by him who makes the oblation."

Brihadaranyaka Upanishad (4.4.5):

"It is the mind that thinks, and that is what the ego is. By seeing who the thinker is, the ego is transcended."

Katha Upanishad (2.2.15):

"When all desires that dwell in the heart cease, then the mortal becomes immortal, and here attains Brahman."

Mundaka Upanishad (2.2.8):

"The wise, having realized the Self as ever-existent, as seated in the hearts of all beings, become immortal."

Rigveda (10.90.2):

"The one who knows Brahman becomes Brahman."

Bhagavad Gita (15.7):

"The living entities in this conditioned world are My eternal fragmental parts. Due to conditioned life, they are struggling very hard with the six senses."

Taittiriya Upanishad (2.7.1):

"From joy all beings have come, by joy they are sustained, and to joy they all return. This is the Brahman, the Supreme."

Maitri Upanishad (6.22):

"He who knows the joy of Brahman, from that joy, verily, does he become Brahman."

Bhagavad Gita (9.22):

"To those who are constantly devoted to serving Me with love, I give the understanding by which they can come to Me."

Chandogya Upanishad (7.23.1):

"All this has a devata, a presiding deity.
Verily, that devata is the consciousness in me."

Scientific Exploration

Neuroscientific Perspectives on Consciousness and the Mind

In the intricate landscape of neuroscience, the pursuit of understanding consciousness and the mind stands as a formidable challenge and an intellectual frontier. The human brain, a complex web of interconnected neurons, is the orchestrator of subjective experiences, thoughts, and emotions. This exploration delves deeper into neuroscientific perspectives on consciousness, shedding light on the intricate mechanisms that underlie our conscious awareness.

1. The Neural Symphony of Consciousness:

At the heart of neuroscience's quest lies the endeavor to decipher the neural symphony responsible for consciousness. Researchers aim to pinpoint specific brain regions and networks crucial for generating conscious experiences. The cortex, with its intricate folds and diverse functions, and the thalamus, acting as a relay for sensory information, emerge as focal points in this neuroscientific odyssey.

2. Thalamus: The Gateway to Consciousness:

The thalamus, often dubbed the brain's gateway to consciousness, plays a pivotal role in processing and relaying sensory information to the cortex. Neuroscientific investigations indicate that the thalamus acts as a filter, selectively allowing certain stimuli to reach conscious awareness. Its intricate dance with various sensory and motor regions shapes our perceptual experiences.

3. Global Workspace Theory: A Symphony of Integration:

Bernard Baars' Global Workspace Theory proposes that consciousness arises from the brain's ability to integrate and broadcast information globally. In this neural symphony, specific brain regions act as a "global workspace," broadcasting selected information to various regions, creating a unified and coherent conscious experience. The theory illuminates the dynamic interplay between localized and global neural processes.

4. Default Mode Network (DMN): The Resting Mind's Stage:

The Default Mode Network (DMN) takes center stage in neuroscientific discussions about consciousness during moments of rest. Traditionally associated with daydreaming and self-referential thoughts, the DMN's role in shaping our sense of self and contributing to conscious experiences is an area of ongoing investigation. Its activation during periods of rest highlights the brain's continuous engagement with self-reflection.

5. Neural Correlates of Consciousness (NCC): Decrypting the Neural Code:

Neuroscientists strive to identify Neural Correlates of Consciousness (NCC) – specific neural activities or patterns that correlate with conscious experiences. Through meticulous studies of brain activity during various cognitive tasks, researchers aim to unveil the neuronal processes responsible for different facets of consciousness, such as perception, attention, and self-awareness.

6. Quantum Consciousness Hypothesis: Exploring the Unconventional:

In the quest for a comprehensive understanding of consciousness, some neuroscientists entertain unconventional ideas, including the Quantum Consciousness Hypothesis. This speculative theory suggests that quantum processes within neuronal structures contribute to conscious experiences. Though met with skepticism, it underscores the field's openness to diverse perspectives and the ongoing exploration of consciousness beyond classical frameworks.

7. Brain-Computer Interfaces (BCIs): Directing the Orchestra:

Advancements in Brain-Computer Interfaces (BCIs) offer a unique lens into the neural processes underlying conscious intentions. These interfaces facilitate direct communication between the brain and external devices, providing researchers with insights into how neural activity translates into external actions. BCIs not only unveil the intricacies of conscious decision-making but also hold promise for applications in neuroprosthetics and cognitive augmentation.

8. Altered States of Consciousness: Thraveling Uncharted Waters:

The study of altered states of consciousness, induced through meditation, psychedelic substances, or neurostimulation, provides a window into the brain's flexibility. Neuroscientific investigations into these states offer glimpses into the neural mechanisms contributing to shifts in perception, self-awareness, and the boundaries of consciousness. These explorations illuminate the brain's capacity to undergo transformative experiences beyond ordinary states of awareness.

9. Neural Plasticity and Learning: Shaping the Brain's Landscape:

Neural plasticity, the brain's ability to reorganize itself in response to experience, emerges as a fundamental force in shaping the brain's landscape. Neuroscientific research delves into the changes in synaptic connections and neural networks that occur during learning and memory processes. Understanding neural plasticity provides insights into the neurobiology of cognition and the conscious processing of information.

10. Consciousness and Unconscious Processes: A Dynamic Duo:

Neuroscience acknowledges that much of cognitive processing occurs unconsciously. The interplay between conscious and unconscious processes constitutes a dynamic area of investigation. Studies reveal how unconscious mechanisms influence decision-making, emotions, and even complex cognitive functions, emphasizing the intricate dance between conscious awareness and automatic, unconscious processes.

The exploration of consciousness and the mind from a neuroscientific perspective stands as an ongoing symphony, a dynamic interplay of research, discovery, and theoretical exploration. As neuroscience advances, the quest to unravel the neural intricacies of consciousness remains an exciting endeavor. The interdisciplinary nature of this inquiry underscores the complexity of understanding the conscious mind, weaving insights from philosophy, psychology, and physics into the evolving narrative. In the grand orchestration of the brain's network, each neuroscientific discovery resonates as a note, contributing to the harmonious composition that defines the enigma of consciousness. The journey continues, promising deeper insights into what it means to be conscious beings in the vast and interconnected universe of the mind.

The Mystery of Self-awareness and its Scientific Examination

The scientific examination of self-awareness has journeyed through a labyrinth of experiments, each shedding light on different facets of this intricate phenomenon. From the mirror test's revelations about self-recognition to the profound implications of split-brain studies, the startling results challenge our preconceptions and prompt us to reconsider the nature of consciousness.

As technology and methodologies evolve, the scientific community is poised to delve even deeper into the mystery of self-awareness. The enigma persists, inviting researchers to design ever-more ingenious experiments and unravel the secrets encoded within the neural fabric of our conscious selves. The journey continues, promising new vistas in our understanding of what it means to be aware of oneself in the vast landscape of the mind.

1. The Mirror Test:

One of the pioneering experiments in the exploration of self-awareness is the mirror test. Developed by psychologist Gordon Gallup Jr. in 1970, this experiment assesses an individual's ability to recognize themselves in a mirror. When marked with a colored spot on their face, animals or humans with self-awareness will attempt to remove the mark after seeing themselves in the mirror. Surprisingly, great apes, dolphins, and elephants have demonstrated this capacity, suggesting a level of self-awareness once considered exclusive to humans.

2. Rubber Hand Illusion:

In the realm of body ownership and self-awareness, the Rubber Hand Illusion stands out. In this experiment, participants experience a disconnect between their visual and tactile perceptions. By watching a rubber hand being stroked while their own unseen hand is simultaneously stroked, participants often report a sense of ownership over the rubber hand. This illusion reveals the brain's ability to integrate visual and tactile information, highlighting the malleability of our perception of self.

3. Out-of-Body Experience (OBE) Studies:

Studies on out-of-body experiences provide a unique window into the exploration of self-awareness. In one remarkable experiment, researchers induced an illusion of self-perception outside the physical body using virtual reality and multisensory stimulation. Participants reported a vivid sense of being located outside their bodies, shedding light on the plasticity of self-awareness and the brain's role in constructing our sense of bodily existence.

4. Split-Brain Studies:

Experiments involving individuals with a split-brain – a condition where the corpus callosum, the bundle of nerves connecting the brain hemispheres, is severed – have yielded startling insights. Research by Michael Gazzaniga and Roger W. Sperry involved presenting stimuli to one hemisphere without the other being aware. The experiments showcased the brain's capacity to create narratives and explanations for actions performed without conscious awareness, revealing the intricate dance between consciousness and the divided brain.

5. Cognitive Neuroscience of Metacognition:

Recent advancements in cognitive neuroscience have delved into the neural correlates of metacognition – the ability to reflect on one's own thoughts. Functional magnetic resonance imaging (fMRI) studies have identified brain regions associated with metacognitive processes. Surprisingly, the prefrontal cortex, anterior cingulate cortex, and insula play pivotal roles, offering insights into the neural underpinnings of self-awareness and introspection.

6. Consciousness in Anesthesia:

The study of consciousness under anesthesia has also provided unexpected findings. In experiments exploring the neural correlates of consciousness, researchers have uncovered that certain brain regions remain active even when individuals are in a deep anesthetic state. These findings challenge traditional views of complete unconsciousness during anesthesia and prompt a reevaluation of our understanding of altered states of consciousness.

7. Neuroimaging and Resting-State Networks:

Advancements in neuroimaging, particularly resting-state functional magnetic resonance imaging (rs-fMRI), have enabled researchers to investigate the default mode network (DMN). The DMN is active during rest and self-referential thinking. Studies reveal that disruptions in the DMN are associated with alterations in self-awareness, emphasizing the crucial role of specific brain networks in sustaining our sense of self.

8. Quantum Consciousness Hypothesis:

In the quest for understanding self-awareness, some researchers have ventured into the realm of quantum consciousness. While highly speculative, the Quantum

Consciousness Hypothesis proposes that quantum processes at the neuronal level contribute to consciousness. Experiments exploring quantum entanglement in biological systems and the potential role of quantum effects in cognitive processes challenge conventional views of the mind.

Parallels Between Vedic Insights and Scientific Exploration on Consciousness and Self-Awareness

The exploration of consciousness and self-awareness stands as a fascinating intersection between ancient Vedic insights and modern scientific inquiry. While originating from distinct cultural and historical contexts, both traditions share compelling parallels in their attempts to unravel the mysteries of the mind. This exploration aims to highlight the resonances between Vedic wisdom and scientific endeavors in understanding consciousness and self-awareness.

The parallels between Vedic insights and scientific exploration on consciousness and self-awareness are remarkable. Both traditions, separated by time and cultural contexts, converge in their recognition of the profound nature of the mind and the interconnected fabric of consciousness. While Vedic wisdom draws from millennia of contemplative inquiry, modern science brings empirical rigor to the exploration of the same profound questions. The synthesis of these perspectives holds the promise of a more holistic understanding of consciousness, bridging ancient wisdom and contemporary scientific inquiry in a shared quest for unraveling the mysteries of the mind.

1. Contemplative Practices:

Vedic Insights: Vedic traditions, particularly those encapsulated in the Upanishads, emphasize contemplative practices such as meditation and introspection. The ancient seers engaged in profound self-inquiry to explore the nature of consciousness.

Scientific Exploration: Contemporary scientific research acknowledges the transformative impact of contemplative practices on consciousness. Studies on mindfulness meditation and other contemplative techniques demonstrate measurable changes in brain activity, highlighting the potential for conscious awareness to be cultivated through deliberate mental exercises.

2. Concept of the Self:

Vedic Insights: The Upanishadic concept of "Atman," often translated as the inner self or soul, delves into the essence of individual consciousness. The self, according to Vedic wisdom, transcends the physical body and is interconnected with the universal consciousness, known as "Brahman."

Scientific Exploration: Neuroscientific studies and cognitive psychology explore the nature of self-awareness by investigating how the brain constructs a sense of self. The concept of the self, as an integrated and dynamic entity, aligns with the evolving understanding of the neural basis of consciousness.

3. Universal Consciousness:

Vedic Insights: Vedic traditions posit the existence of a universal consciousness, where individual consciousness is seen as a manifestation of cosmic intelligence. The interconnectedness of all living beings is emphasized, suggesting a shared foundation of consciousness.

Scientific Exploration: The field of quantum physics, with its exploration of entanglement and non-locality, presents parallels with the Vedic idea of a universal consciousness. Some scientists propose that the interconnectedness observed at the quantum level might hint at a deeper, universal consciousness underlying reality.

4. Layers of Consciousness:

Vedic Insights: Vedic philosophy delineates different layers of consciousness, ranging from the waking state ("Jagrat") to the dream state ("Swapna") and the deep sleep state ("Sushupti"). Beyond these, the Upanishads describe a transcendent state of consciousness called "Turiya."

Scientific Exploration: The study of altered states of consciousness, including dreaming, deep sleep, and various meditative states, aligns with the Vedic categorization. Neuroscientific investigations explore the neural correlates of these states, providing insights into the shifting dynamics of consciousness.

5. Non-Duality:

Vedic Insights: Advaita Vedanta, a school of Vedic philosophy, expounds non-duality, asserting that the individual self ("Atman") and the universal consciousness ("Brahman") are ultimately one. The illusion of separation is seen as a result of ignorance.

Scientific Exploration: The idea of non-duality finds echoes in the scientific understanding of the interconnected nature of reality. The exploration of entanglement in quantum physics challenges the classical notions of separate, isolated entities, suggesting a fundamental unity underlying the diversity of the cosmos.

6. Inner Exploration:

Vedic Insights: The Upanishads and other Vedic texts advocate turning inward for self-discovery. Practices like introspection, self-inquiry, and meditation are pathways to uncovering the depths of consciousness.

Scientific Exploration: Neuroscience and psychology acknowledge the importance of introspection and self-inquiry for understanding consciousness. Brain imaging studies reveal the neural mechanisms associated with self-reflection, affirming the relevance of inner exploration in scientific inquiry.

Chapter 4:
Cosmology and the Universe

Vedic Cosmology and Cycles of Creation and Destruction (Yugas)

Vedic cosmology articulates a cyclical view of time, manifesting in the concept of Yugas, which are epochs representing different phases in the cosmic cycle of creation, preservation, and destruction. These Yugas, each with its distinct characteristics, collectively form a larger time cycle known as a Mahayuga. The four Yugas are Satya Yuga, Treta Yuga, Dvapara Yuga, and Kali Yuga. This cosmic perspective provides a profound understanding of the eternal and cyclical nature of existence.

1. Satya Yuga (The Golden Age):

- Duration: 1.728 million years
- Characteristics:
- Virtue and righteousness (Dharma) prevail.
- Truthfulness is inherent, and people possess deep spiritual wisdom.
- Virtue is so abundant that there is no need for external rituals.

2. Treta Yuga (The Silver Age):

- Duration: 1.296 million years
- Characteristics:
- A gradual decline in virtue and righteousness.
- Introduction of rituals and sacrifices to uphold Dharma.

- People start to lose touch with their inherent spirituality.

3. Dvapara Yuga (The Bronze Age):

- Duration: 864,000 years
- Characteristics:
- A further decline in virtue and adherence to Dharma.
- The introduction of organized religion and devotion.
- The advent of Lord Krishna takes place during this Yuga.

4. Kali Yuga (The Iron Age):

- Duration: 432,000 years
- Characteristics:
- A significant decline in virtue and righteousness.
- Materialism, greed, and ignorance become prominent.
- Spiritual wisdom is scarce, and people are easily swayed by base desires.

5. Mahayuga (Great Epoch):

- Total Duration: 4.32 million years
- Composition: Consists of four Yugas – Satya, Treta, Dvapara, and Kali Yugas.

6. Manvantara:

- Total Duration: 308.571 million years
- Composition: Encompasses 71 Mahayugas.
- Characteristics: Each Manvantara is presided over by a specific Manu, who imparts knowledge and guidance.

7. Kalpa:

- Total Duration: 4.32 billion years
- Composition: Consists of 1,000 Mahayugas.
- Characteristics: Marks one full day (Day of Brahma) in the cosmic cycle.

8. Pralaya (Cosmic Dissolution):

- The end of a Kalpa signifies the cosmic dissolution.
- All physical forms are withdrawn, and the universe returns to a state of potentiality.
- A period of rest and rejuvenation before the next cycle of creation begins.
- This cyclic model of time in Vedic cosmology emphasizes the impermanence of material existence and the eternal nature of the soul. The Yugas provide a framework for understanding the fluctuations in human and cosmic evolution, offering spiritual insights into the purpose of life and the pursuit of higher consciousness.

Hymns Written About Each Yuga:

Vedic cosmology, encapsulated in hymns and shlokas, illuminates the cyclical nature of creation and destruction. These Yugas, representing distinct phases, symbolize the eternal rhythm of cosmic existence. The wisdom embedded in these verses beckons individuals to navigate the currents of time with spiritual discernment, recognizing the transient nature of material pursuits and emphasizing the timeless pursuit of spiritual knowledge and righteousness.

1. Satya Yuga (The Golden Age):

Hymn:

> "Sahasra-yuga-paryantam ahar yad brahmaṇo viduḥ,
> yuga-sahasra-antām ahaṁ teṣu āvṛtātmānaṁ kṛtam."

Translation:

"They understand that the duration of the four yugas, multiplied by one thousand, constitutes one day of Brahma, and that his night has the same duration."

In Satya Yuga, righteousness prevails, and truth reigns supreme. It is the age of virtue, where dharma (righteousness) is unblemished.

2. Treta Yuga (The Silver Age):

Hymn:

> "Tretāyāṁ dvāpare varṣe nṛiṇāṁ saṅkhye ca pārthiva,
> tretāyām eka-varṣeṇāpy anyat-kāmaṁ labhate nṛpa."

Translation:

"In Tretā-yuga, O king, a man who offers a horse sacrifice lives for eleven thousand years, and in one year he enjoys sense gratification as desired."

Treta Yuga witnesses a decline in virtue, and rituals and sacrifices become prominent.

3. Dvapara Yuga (The Bronze Age):

Hymn:

> "Dvāpare samanuprāpte tṛtīye yuga-paryaye,
> kṛṣṇe tu bhagavān svayaṁ jātaḥ karuṇāya ātmanā."

Translation:

"In the Dvāpara-yuga, which is the third of the yugas, the Lord, Śrī Kṛṣṇa, appeared as the son of Vasudeva, being compassionate to fallen souls."

Dvapara Yuga witnesses the advent of Lord Krishna, representing a period of devotion and divine intervention.

4. Kali Yuga (The Iron Age):

Hymn:

> "Dāmpatye 'bhirucir hetur māyaiva vyāvahārike,
> strītve puṁstve ca hi ratir vipratve sūtram eva hi."

Translation:

"In Kali-yuga, the duration of life is shortened. People are not happy; they do not have sufficient food, and they are very rarely happy in family life. Most people are ignorant, and therefore their only interest is in the present body."

Kali Yuga is characterized by a decline in righteousness, with a prevalence of ignorance and materialism.

5. Cosmic Dissolution (Pralaya):

Hymn:

> "Saṅkṣepe sarva-kāryeṣu saṅgrahaḥ kṛta ucyate,
> pralaye sarva-karmāṇi saṅgrahaḥ kṛtas tataḥ."

Translation:

"When all the activities and endeavors of the living entities become an amalgamated whole in the final dissolution, that is, at the time of the annihilation of the material creation, the living entities remain in that condition."

Pralaya marks the cosmic dissolution, where the universe undergoes a state of rest before the next cycle of creation begins.

The Cosmic Dance of Shiva and the Eternal Nature of the Universe

The cosmic dance of Shiva, known as the "Tandava," is a profound and symbolic representation in Hindu mythology that encapsulates the eternal nature of the universe, the cycle of creation, preservation, and destruction, and the cosmic forces that govern existence.

Shiva's Tandava: The Dance of Creation and Destruction

1. Nataraja: The Lord of Dance

Shiva, in his cosmic dance form known as Nataraja, is envisioned as the Lord of Dance. The dance is both an expression of the divine and a symbolic representation of the cosmic cycles. Nataraja is often depicted with multiple arms and in a dynamic pose, surrounded by a circle of fire.

2. Ananda Tandava: The Dance of Bliss

Shiva's dance is often referred to as the "Ananda Tandava," which translates to the Dance of Bliss. This emphasizes the joy inherent in the cosmic play of creation and destruction. It signifies the divine ecstasy that permeates the universe.

3. Symbolism in the Dance:

Destruction and Creation: Shiva's Tandava represents the eternal rhythm of creation and destruction. The universe undergoes constant cycles of birth, existence, and dissolution.

Five Acts (Pancha Krityas): Shiva's dance is often associated with five activities – creation (Srishti), protection (Sthiti), destruction (Samhara), hiding or veiling (Tirobhava), and grace or liberation (Anugraha). These activities signify the cosmic processes at play.

Duality and Unity: The dance symbolizes the interplay of opposites – creation and destruction, birth and death, joy and sorrow. Shiva, through his dance, harmonizes these dualities into a unified whole.

4. The Cosmic Symbolism:

Damaru (Drum): Shiva holds a small drum, symbolizing the primordial sound of creation, the heartbeat of the universe.

Fire Circle (Prabha Mandala): The circle of fire represents the cosmic cycle and the continuous flow of energy in the universe.

Ganges (Ganga): The Ganges flowing from Shiva's hair symbolizes the purifying and life-giving force, transcending earthly limitations.

Eternal Nature of the Universe:

The Tandava portrays the cyclical nature of time, where the universe goes through infinite cycles of creation and dissolution. It emphasizes the impermanence of the material world and the eternal, unchanging nature of the divine.

Philosophical Significance:

Timelessness: Shiva's dance is timeless, reflecting the eternal nature of the cosmic processes.

Renewal and Regeneration: The dance signifies the continual process of renewal and regeneration, where the old gives way to the new.

Transcendence: Shiva, through the Tandava, transcends the limitations of the material world, symbolizing the ultimate reality beyond the visible universe.

Shiva's Tandava encapsulates the cosmic harmony and the interconnectedness of all existence. It serves as a source of spiritual inspiration, encouraging individuals to recognize the transient nature of the material world, embrace the cyclical rhythms of life, and seek the eternal truth beyond the dance of creation and destruction. In essence, Shiva's cosmic dance invites contemplation on the profound mysteries of existence and the timeless nature of the universe.

Scientific Theories

The Big Bang theory is the prevailing cosmological model that describes the origin and evolution of the universe. It proposes that the universe began as an extremely hot and dense state approximately 13.8 billion years ago and has been expanding ever since. Here is an overview of the key concepts and evidence supporting the Big Bang theory:

1. Cosmic Microwave Background (CMB):

- Observation: The discovery of the Cosmic Microwave Background radiation in 1965 by Arno Penzias and Robert Wilson provided strong evidence for the Big Bang. This faint radiation is uniform across the sky and is considered the residual heat from the early stages of the universe.

- Explanation: The CMB is consistent with the prediction that the universe was once in a hot, dense state. As the universe expanded, the radiation cooled and shifted towards longer wavelengths, eventually becoming the microwave background we observe today.

2. Redshift of Galaxies:

- Observation: Edwin Hubble's observations in the 1920s revealed that galaxies are moving away from each other. This was evidenced by the redshift of their light, indicating that the universe is undergoing expansion.

- Explanation: The redshift of light is a consequence of the stretching of space itself. The more distant a galaxy, the greater its redshift, indicating a faster recession. This expansion is a fundamental prediction of the Big Bang model.

3. Abundance of Light Elements:

- Observation: The observed abundances of light elements, such as hydrogen, helium, and small traces of lithium, match the predictions of nucleosynthesis during the early moments of the universe.

- Explanation: In the first few minutes after the Big Bang, the conditions were hot and dense enough for nuclear fusion to occur, forming light elements. The observed ratios of these elements in the universe align with the predictions based on the Big Bang model.

4. Large-Scale Structure:

- Observation: The distribution of galaxies and cosmic structures across the universe exhibits a large-scale, filamentary pattern.

- Explanation: The gravitational influence of dark matter and dark energy, combined with the initial density fluctuations from quantum fluctuations during the early universe, led to the formation of large-scale structures observed today.

5. Hubble's Law:

- Observation: The relationship between the velocity of a galaxy and its distance, known as Hubble's Law, further supports the concept of an expanding universe.

- Explanation: The linear relationship between velocity and distance implies a uniform expansion of the universe. This observational evidence is consistent with the predictions of the Big Bang theory.

6. Dark Energy Acceleration:

- Observation: In the late 20th century, observations of distant supernovae revealed an unexpected acceleration in the expansion of the universe.

- Explanation: The accelerated expansion is attributed to dark energy, a mysterious form of energy that permeates space and counteracts the gravitational attraction between matter. This discovery added a crucial element to the understanding of cosmic evolution.

7. Galactic Evolution and Age:

- Observation: The study of galaxies and their evolution, along with the ages of the oldest stars, provides consistent evidence for a universe that is approximately 13.8 billion years old.

- Explanation: The age of the universe is inferred from the expansion rate and the observed properties of celestial objects. This age aligns with the time elapsed since the initial singularity in the Big Bang model.

8. Inflationary Universe:

- Observation: In the 1980s, the concept of cosmic inflation was introduced to address certain questions about the uniformity of the universe on large scales.

- Explanation: Cosmic inflation proposes that the universe underwent an exponential expansion in the first moments after the Big Bang. This rapid expansion helps explain the observed uniformity of the cosmic microwave background and the large-scale structure of the universe.

9. Formation of Cosmic Microwave Background Anisotropies:

- Observation: Observations of the cosmic microwave background reveal small fluctuations or anisotropies in temperature.

- Explanation: Quantum fluctuations in the early universe, magnified during cosmic inflation, left imprints on the cosmic microwave background. These fluctuations eventually led to the formation of galaxies and other cosmic structures through gravitational instability.

10. Galaxy Formation and Evolution:

- Observation: Detailed observations of galaxies and their properties provide insights into their formation and evolution.

- Explanation: The hierarchical growth of cosmic structures, driven by gravitational interactions and the interplay between dark matter and baryonic matter, aligns with the predictions of the Big Bang model. Computer simulations based on the principles of the Big Bang theory can reproduce the observed distribution and properties of galaxies.

11. Dark Matter:

- Observation: Observations of galaxy rotation curves, gravitational lensing, and large-scale structure indicate the presence of non-luminous, or dark, matter.

- Explanation: The Big Bang model incorporates the existence of dark matter, a form of matter that does not emit, absorb, or reflect light. Dark matter plays a crucial role in the formation and evolution of cosmic structures, influencing the observed motions and distributions of galaxies.

12. Quantum Fluctuations and Structure Formation:

- Observation: The cosmic microwave background and the large-scale distribution of galaxies show patterns consistent with quantum fluctuations in the early universe.

- Explanation: Quantum fluctuations in the fabric of space during the early moments of the universe, combined with the influence of dark matter and dark energy, shaped the large-scale structure observed today. These fluctuations provide the seeds for the formation of galaxies and galaxy clusters.

13. Formation of Elements in Stars:

- Observation: The abundance of elements in the universe, beyond the light elements formed during the initial moments of the Big Bang, is largely shaped by nuclear processes within stars.

- Explanation: Stars, through their life cycles, synthesize heavier elements through nuclear fusion. Supernova explosions then disperse these elements into space, enriching the interstellar medium. The observed abundance of elements aligns with the predictions based on stellar nucleosynthesis.

14. Future Evolution and Fate of the Universe:

- Observation: Observations of distant galaxies and the rate of cosmic expansion provide insights into the future of the universe.

- Explanation: Depending on the balance between dark energy, dark matter, and ordinary matter, the fate of the universe may involve continued expansion, eventual slowing, or even a cosmic contraction. Current observations suggest a universe that will continue to expand at an accelerating rate due to the dominance of dark energy.

The Big Bang theory, with its extensions like inflation and incorporation of dark matter and dark energy, provides a comprehensive narrative for the origin and evolution of the universe. From the initial moments of rapid expansion to the formation of galaxies, elements, and cosmic structures, the theory seamlessly integrates observations across various scales. The successful predictions and alignment with observational evidence make the Big Bang theory a foundational framework in cosmology, guiding our understanding of the universe's past, present, and potential future. Ongoing observations and research continue to refine and enhance our knowledge, deepening our grasp of the cosmic order painted by the Big Bang.

Current Cosmological Models and Scientific Understanding of the Cosmos

our understanding of the cosmos has advanced significantly, and cosmological models continue to evolve. While the Big Bang theory remains the prevailing framework for explaining the observable universe's origin and expansion, several key developments and areas of exploration have emerged. Please note that there might be further advancements or refinements beyond my last update.

1. Lambda Cold Dark Matter (ΛCDM) Model:

- Overview: The ΛCDM model is an extension of the Big Bang theory and is the current standard cosmological model. It includes the presence of dark energy (Λ) and cold dark matter (CDM) as essential components influencing the evolution of the universe.

- Dark Energy: Dark energy is hypothesized to be responsible for the observed accelerated expansion of the universe. Its nature remains one of the most significant mysteries in cosmology.

2. Cosmic Microwave Background (CMB) Experiments:

- Advancements: Ongoing experiments, such as those conducted by the Planck satellite, have provided increasingly precise measurements of the CMB's temperature fluctuations. These measurements offer insights into the early universe's conditions and the distribution of matter.

3. Large-Scale Structure Surveys:

- Surveys: Projects like the Sloan Digital Sky Survey (SDSS) and the Dark Energy Survey (DES) have mapped the large-scale structure of the universe, revealing the distribution of galaxies and cosmic voids. These surveys contribute to our understanding of the cosmic web and the role of dark matter.

4. Inflationary Cosmology:

- Inflation Models: Inflationary cosmology, originally proposed to address certain issues with the standard

Big Bang model, continues to be explored. Various inflationary models provide mechanisms for the rapid expansion of the universe in its early moments.

5. Quantum Cosmology and Multiverse Hypotheses:

- Quantum Effects: The intersection of quantum mechanics and cosmology explores the quantum nature of the early universe. The application of quantum principles to cosmological models aims to understand the origin of the universe itself.

- Multiverse Hypotheses: Some speculative theories propose the existence of a multiverse, where our observable universe is just one of many universes with different physical properties.

6. Dark Matter Detection Experiments:

- Direct Detection: Efforts to directly detect dark matter particles are ongoing. Underground experiments, such as those involving sensitive detectors, aim to identify the elusive particles that constitute dark matter.

7. Advanced Gravitational Wave Observations:

- LIGO and Virgo Collaborations: The Laser Interferometer Gravitational-Wave Observatory (LIGO) and Virgo collaborations have detected gravitational waves from merging black holes and neutron stars. These observations provide a new tool for exploring extreme astrophysical phenomena and testing general relativity.

8. Cosmic Acceleration Studies:

- Supernova Surveys: Ongoing surveys of distant supernovae, such as the Dark Energy Survey

Supernova Program, contribute to our understanding of cosmic acceleration and the role of dark energy.

9. Advancements in High-Energy Astrophysics:

- Gamma-Ray Bursts: High-energy astrophysics, including the study of gamma-ray bursts and high-energy cosmic rays, provides insights into extreme cosmic events and the energetic processes in the universe.

10. Future Space Telescopes and Observatories:

- James Webb Space Telescope (JWST): Scheduled for launch, JWST is expected to be a powerful tool for studying the early universe, the formation of galaxies, and the atmospheres of exoplanets.

- Next-Generation Surveys: Upcoming surveys and observatories, like the Vera C. Rubin Observatory and the Nancy Grace Roman Space Telescope, aim to address fundamental questions about dark matter, dark energy, and the large-scale structure of the universe.

The field of cosmology is dynamic and continuously evolving, with ongoing observations, experiments, and theoretical developments. As technology advances, new discoveries are made, challenging our understanding of the cosmos and leading to refinements or revisions of existing models. The quest to unravel the mysteries of dark matter, dark energy, and the ultimate origins of the universe remains at the forefront of cosmological research, shaping our evolving comprehension of the vast cosmic landscape.

Do Vedic Theories of Creation Overlap with Modern Theories of Creation?

Vedic theories of creation, rooted in ancient Indian philosophical and religious texts such as the Vedas and Puranas, provide a unique and intricate perspective on the origin and nature of the universe. While the language and conceptual framework of Vedic cosmology differ from modern scientific theories, some intriguing parallels and symbolic resonances can be identified. It's essential to approach this comparison with an understanding that Vedic narratives are often allegorical and symbolic, conveying spiritual and philosophical truths rather than scientific descriptions.

Key Points of Overlap

Cycles of Creation and Destruction:

Vedic Perspective: The concept of "Yugas" in Vedic cosmology describes cycles of creation, preservation, and destruction. These cosmic cycles, known as Mahayugas, consist of four ages: Satya Yuga, Treta Yuga, Dvapara Yuga, and Kali Yuga, repeating in a continuous cycle.

Modern Parallel: Modern cosmology, particularly the concept of the Big Bang followed by cosmic expansion and eventual contraction or heat death, also involves a cyclical view of the universe. The idea of a cosmic cycle is explored in certain cosmological models.

Symbolism of Cosmic Elements:

Vedic Perspective: Vedic hymns often use symbolic language to describe the creation of the universe, attributing it to the divine play (Lila) of the Supreme Being. Elements like fire, water, air, and space are symbolically represented in the process of creation.

Modern Parallel: Modern cosmology describes the evolution of the universe in terms of fundamental forces and elements. The formation of cosmic structures involves the interplay of gravity, electromagnetic forces, and the fundamental particles that make up matter.

Cosmic Sound (Om) and Vibration:

Vedic Perspective: The cosmic sound "Om" holds significant importance in Vedic philosophy. It is considered the primordial sound, representing the essence of the ultimate reality and the vibrational energy that initiated creation.

Modern Parallel: In modern physics, the concept of cosmic vibrations is explored through the study of cosmic microwave background radiation. This faint radiation, a remnant of the early universe, carries information about the initial conditions and fluctuations that led to the formation of cosmic structures.

Consciousness and Universal Connectivity:

Vedic Perspective: Vedic philosophy emphasizes the interconnectedness of all living beings and the universe. Consciousness is considered fundamental, and the divine is seen as immanent in all aspects of creation.

Modern Parallel: Certain aspects of quantum physics explore the interconnected nature of particles, suggesting non-local correlations. The study of entanglement and quantum coherence hints at a level of interconnectedness that challenges classical notions of separateness.

Points of Departure

Literal vs. Symbolic Interpretations:

Vedic Perspective: Vedic cosmology often employs symbolic and allegorical language to convey metaphysical truths. The emphasis is on spiritual and philosophical insights rather than precise scientific descriptions.

Modern Perspective: Modern cosmology relies on empirical observations, mathematical models, and scientific principles to describe the physical universe. The language used in scientific theories aims for precise and testable statements.

Timelines and Specifics:

Vedic Perspective: Vedic cosmology presents cyclical timeframes and cosmic epochs without specifying exact timelines. The emphasis is on the eternal nature of creation and dissolution.

Modern Perspective: Modern cosmology provides detailed timelines based on observable phenomena, from the cosmic microwave background radiation to the formation of galaxies. The emphasis is on understanding the chronological evolution of the universe.

Purpose of Creation:

- ***Vedic Perspective:*** Vedic cosmology often intertwines the cosmic creation with spiritual and ethical teachings, emphasizing the cyclical nature of existence and the pursuit of higher consciousness.
- ***Modern Perspective:*** Scientific theories, by design, focus on empirical observations and explanations for the physical processes governing the universe. Questions of purpose and meaning fall outside the scope of scientific inquiry.

While there are intriguing parallels between Vedic cosmology and modern scientific theories, it's crucial to recognize the distinct purposes and contexts of these narratives. Vedic cosmology offers a profound peep of symbolic, allegorical, and philosophical insights into the nature of reality, consciousness, and existence. Modern cosmology, grounded in empirical evidence and mathematical models, provides a detailed understanding of the observable universe. Both perspectives contribute to humanity's exploration of the profound questions surrounding our existence and the cosmos.

Chapter 5:
Time and Space

Vedic Concepts

Time as a Cyclical Phenomenon (Kalachakra)

The concept of time as a cyclical phenomenon is deeply embedded in various ancient philosophies and religious traditions, including the Vedic and Hindu traditions. In Hindu cosmology, this cyclical nature of time is often referred to as "Kalachakra," where "Kala" means time, and "Chakra" means cycle or wheel. The idea of Kalachakra reflects a cyclic view of time, with the universe undergoing repeated cycles of creation, preservation, and dissolution.

Key Aspects of Kalachakra:

Yugas (Ages):

The cyclical nature of time is manifested through the concept of Yugas, which are epochs or ages. According to Hindu cosmology, there are four Yugas: Satya Yuga, Treta Yuga, Dvapara Yuga, and Kali Yuga. Each Yuga represents a specific phase in the cosmic cycle, characterized by different moral, social, and spiritual conditions.

Creation, Preservation, and Dissolution:

The universe undergoes a continuous process of creation (Srishti), preservation (Sthiti), and dissolution (Samhara). This cosmic cycle is governed by the divine principles of Brahma (the creator), Vishnu (the preserver), and Shiva (the destroyer).

Symbolic Representation:

The Kalachakra is often symbolically represented as a wheel with distinct spokes, each spoke representing a specific Yuga. This symbol encapsulates the perpetual movement and cyclical nature of time, emphasizing the transient and ever-changing aspects of the material world.

Duration of Yugas:

The duration of each Yuga varies, forming a descending order of time spans. Satya Yuga is the longest and most virtuous, followed by Treta Yuga, Dvapara Yuga, and Kali Yuga, which is the shortest and characterized by a decline in righteousness.

Interpretations and Symbolism:

Spiritual Evolution:

The cyclical nature of time in Kalachakra is not only a cosmic phenomenon but also holds symbolic significance for spiritual evolution. It suggests that individuals and societies undergo cycles of growth, decline, and renewal on both a cosmic and personal level.

Moral and Ethical Lessons:

Each Yuga is associated with specific moral and ethical characteristics, reflecting the cyclical nature of societal virtues and vices. This provides a framework for understanding the challenges and opportunities presented in different phases of time.

Detachment and Liberation:

The cyclical view of time encourages individuals to cultivate detachment (Vairagya) from the transient aspects of the material world. By recognizing the impermanence of worldly phenomena, one can strive for spiritual liberation (Moksha) from the cycle of birth and rebirth (Samsara).

Cosmic Harmony:

The cyclical concept of time also underscores the idea of cosmic harmony, where the universe follows a natural rhythm governed by divine principles. This harmony involves a dynamic interplay of creation, preservation, and dissolution to maintain cosmic balance.

Kalachakra in Vedic Hymns

1. Bhagavad Gita:

In the Bhagavad Gita, a sacred dialogue between Lord Krishna and Arjuna, there are verses that allude to the cyclic nature of time and creation:

Chapter 8, Verse 17:

"By human calculation, a thousand ages taken together form the duration of Brahma's one day. And such also is the duration of his night."

This verse hints at the cyclical nature of time, where the day and night of Brahma, the creator deity, represent immense time spans.

2. Mahabharata:

The Mahabharata, a monumental epic that includes the Bhagavad Gita, also contains references to the cosmic cycles:

Book 3, Vana Parva, Section CCCXXXVII:

"When the universal dissolution comes, all the seas together boil up and burn with a great flame. The mountains also burn, as also the earth and the sky, and the Wind, the Firmament, Yama, and the Destroyer, and the regions that are above, below, and the cardinal and the subsidiary points of the compass. Indeed, O best of kings, all the points of the compass, cardinal and subsidiary,

> *and inter-cardinal, burn with the energy of the weapon of the high-souled Maheswara."*

This excerpt describes the cataclysmic events during the dissolution (Pralaya) phase of the cosmic cycle.

3. Puranas:

The Puranas, especially the Vishnu Purana and Bhagavata Purana, provide detailed accounts of the Yugas and the cosmic cycles:

Vishnu Purana:

The Vishnu Purana describes the four Yugas – Satya, Treta, Dvapara, and Kali – each with its distinct characteristics and durations. The cyclic pattern of creation, preservation, and dissolution is evident throughout these Yugas.

Bhagavata Purana:

In the Bhagavata Purana, the cosmic cycles are expounded, emphasizing the transient nature of material existence and the importance of spiritual pursuits. The duration of each Yuga is delineated, reinforcing the cyclical nature of time.

4. Srimad Devi Bhagavatam:

Book 3, Chapter 6:

> *"O King! Again and again the world is created; again and again it is dissolved. This wheel of creation and dissolution is rolling on. Again and again the beings are born; again and again they die. This wheel, thus continuously turning, is without any beginning. It is without any string, without any support, and is full of error and illusion."*

This passage from the Srimad Devi Bhagavatam emphasizes the perpetual nature of the cosmic wheel, symbolizing the continuous cycles of creation and dissolution.

5. Vedic Hymns and Upanishads:

While the concept of Kalachakra may not be explicitly mentioned in the Rigveda or Upanishads, the Vedic hymns and philosophical dialogues often delve into the nature of time, the eternal reality (Brahman), and the cyclical aspects of creation.

Rigveda:

> *"Thou only knowest, Thou only O Creator, how this wheel of creation, dissolution, and preservation turns, O God."*

This hymn from the Rigveda reflects on the divine understanding of the cyclical wheel of creation, dissolution, and preservation.

In essence, Kalachakra, as portrayed in these scriptures, represents the eternal rhythm of the cosmos, where time unfolds in cyclical patterns, emphasizing the impermanence of the material world and the eternal nature of the spiritual reality.

The Eternal Nature of Space and the Interplay of Time

The Eternal Nature of Space in Vedic Thought:

In Vedic thought, the concept of space transcends the conventional understanding of physical dimensions. The term "Akasha" is used to describe the cosmic space that encompasses and permeates the entire universe. It is not merely an empty void but is considered the subtlest and most fundamental aspect of creation. The Rigveda often alludes to this expansive, boundless space, portraying it as a divine reality beyond the reach of ordinary perception.

Rigveda 10.90.4:

"That which is above the sky, that which is beneath the earth, that which is between these two, sky and earth, that which the people call the world, envelops this universe. Therein a golden egg arose."

This hymn from the Rigveda metaphorically describes the all-encompassing nature of Akasha, suggesting a cosmic unity that extends beyond the visible realms.

The Interplay of Time in Vedic Cosmology:

Vedic cosmology views time not as a linear progression but as a dynamic force intimately linked with the cosmic order. The concept of "Kala" represents time as a multifaceted principle governing the cyclical processes of creation, preservation, and dissolution. Time, in this context, is a cosmic force that orchestrates the unfolding of the universe.

Chandogya Upanishad 7.26.1:

"Kala (time) is Brahman. Kala (time) is the great destroyer of the world, because it is identical with Brahman."

This Upanishadic insight underscores the profound connection between time and the ultimate reality (Brahman), portraying time not just as a chronological measure but as a transformative and powerful cosmic principle.

Time as a Cyclical Phenomenon:

The Vedic perspective introduces the cyclical nature of time through the concept of Yugas – distinct epochs that delineate different phases in the cosmic cycle. The Yugas, namely Satya Yuga, Treta Yuga, Dvapara Yuga, and Kali Yuga, represent varying levels of moral, spiritual, and societal conditions. This cyclic pattern emphasizes the perpetual motion of the cosmic wheel.

Bhagavad Gita 8.19:

"Again and again, when Brahma's day comes, all living entities come into being, and with the arrival of Brahma's night, they are helplessly annihilated."

This verse from the Bhagavad Gita elucidates the cyclical rhythm of creation and dissolution within the grand framework of cosmic time.

The Timeless Soul and Eternal Reality:

In the Vedic understanding, the eternal nature of space and time is intricately linked to the individual soul (Atman) and the ultimate reality (Brahman). The soul is considered timeless, unbreakable, and unaffected by the temporal flow. It is eternal and interconnected with the cosmic reality.

Bhagavad Gita 2.24:

"This individual soul is unbreakable and insoluble, and can be neither burned nor dried. He is everlasting, present everywhere, unchangeable, immovable, and eternally the same."

This verse highlights the eternal nature of the individual soul, suggesting a profound connection to the timeless and unchanging fabric of the cosmos.

The Vedic perspective on space and time transcends mundane notions, offering a holistic and interconnected view of the cosmos. Akasha is the boundless canvas upon which the cosmic drama unfolds, and Kala is the rhythmic force orchestrating the cosmic symphony. This understanding encourages individuals to contemplate the profound mysteries of existence, recognizing their timeless essence within the eternal dance of space and the interplay of cosmic time.

Scientific Theories

Einstein's Theory of Relativity and the Concept of Spacetime

Albert Einstein's theories of relativity, formulated in the early 20th century, represent a paradigm shift in our comprehension of space, time, and gravity. The twin theories – special relativity and general relativity – ushered in a new era of theoretical physics, fundamentally altering our understanding of the fabric of the universe. Central to this transformation is the concept of spacetime, a revolutionary idea that unifies the three spatial dimensions with the dimension of time. This exploration delves into the intricacies of Einstein's theories, their impact on our view of the cosmos, and the profound concept of spacetime.

Special Theory of Relativity: Rewriting the Laws of Physics

1. Time Dilation and Length Contraction:

Einstein's special theory of relativity, published in 1905, introduced groundbreaking concepts that challenged classical Newtonian physics. One of the key tenets is time dilation – the notion that time is not an absolute, universal constant. Instead, it is relative and dependent on the observer's motion. As an object approaches the speed of light, time for that object appears to slow down, a phenomenon confirmed by subsequent experiments with high-speed particles.

This revelation was accompanied by the concept of length contraction, where objects in motion are observed to contract in the direction of their motion. Both time dilation and length contraction were experimentally validated, emphasizing the departure from classical physics.

2. Spacetime Diagrams and Relativity of Simultaneity:

Special relativity also introduced the concept of spacetime diagrams, a visual representation where time and space are integrated into a four-dimensional continuum. Events that were once considered simultaneous for all observers are now perceived as part of a unified spacetime. The relativity of simultaneity implies that events occurring at the same time for one observer may appear sequential or simultaneous for another moving at a different velocity.

General Theory of Relativity: Gravity as Curvature of Spacetime

1. Gravity Redefined:

Einstein's general theory of relativity, unveiled in 1915, redefined our understanding of gravity. Unlike Newton's gravitational force acting at a distance, Einstein proposed that gravity arises due to the curvature of spacetime caused by the presence of mass and energy. Massive objects, such as planets and stars, create dimples or warps in the fabric of spacetime, altering the trajectory of objects moving through this curved space.

2. Equivalence Principle and Curved Spacetime:

The equivalence principle, a cornerstone of general relativity, posits that locally, the effects of gravity are indistinguishable from acceleration. This profound insight led Einstein to the idea that gravity is not a force but a manifestation of curved spacetime. Objects moving within this curved spacetime follow paths known as geodesics, which represent the straightest possible lines.

3. Gravitational Time Dilation and Black Holes:

General relativity predicted several phenomena later confirmed by experiments and observations. Gravitational time dilation, an effect where clocks in stronger gravitational fields run slower than those in weaker fields, was verified through experiments involving precise timekeeping instruments. Additionally, Einstein's equations predicted the existence of black holes – regions of spacetime where gravity is so intense that nothing, not even light, can escape. Observations of stellar orbits around invisible companions supported the existence of these enigmatic cosmic objects.

Spacetime: Unifying Space and Time

1. Spacetime as a Fabric:

The concept of spacetime emerged as a unifying framework in general relativity. In this view, spacetime is envisioned as a four-dimensional fabric, where the three dimensions of space and the fourth dimension of time are integrated. Massive objects create warps or distortions in this fabric, influencing the motion of other objects within their gravitational influence.

2. Black Holes and Wormholes:

Spacetime around black holes is profoundly distorted, creating extreme conditions where traditional laws of physics break down. The event horizon, a boundary beyond which nothing can escape a black hole's gravitational pull, exemplifies the influence of spacetime curvature. Additionally, the idea of wormholes – hypothetical tunnels through spacetime – arose from the mathematics of general relativity, presenting intriguing possibilities for cosmic shortcuts.

Impact on Cosmology and Astrophysics

1. Big Bang Theory and Cosmic Microwave Background:

General relativity played a pivotal role in the development of the Big Bang theory, describing the expansion of the universe from an initial singularity. The theory predicts the cosmic microwave background radiation – a faint glow permeating the universe, remnants from the early hot and dense state. The discovery of this radiation in 1965 provided compelling evidence in favor of the Big Bang model.

2. Black Hole Astrophysics:

General relativity has significantly influenced our understanding of astrophysical phenomena involving black holes. Observations of gravitational waves – ripples in spacetime – generated by the collision of black holes have provided direct evidence of these cosmic entities. The study of black hole accretion disks, jets, and interactions with companion stars has become a thriving field within astrophysics.

Philosophical Implications and Ongoing Research

1. Time Travel and Grandfather Paradox:

Einstein's theories have sparked numerous discussions about time travel, a concept theoretically permitted by solutions to his field equations. However, the infamous "grandfather paradox" – the idea of going back in time and potentially altering the past – poses intriguing challenges and has led to debates within the scientific and philosophical communities.

2. Quantum Gravity and Unification:

Despite its successes, general relativity encounters limitations when applied to the quantum realm. The quest for a theory of quantum gravity – a framework that unifies general relativity with quantum mechanics – remains a fundamental challenge in contemporary theoretical physics. String theory and loop quantum gravity are among the approaches aiming to reconcile these two pillars of modern physics.

Albert Einstein's theories of relativity, with their profound impact on our understanding of space, time, and gravity, represent a cornerstone of modern physics. The elegant simplicity of $E=mc^2$ and the radical reimagining of gravity as the curvature of spacetime have stood the test of time, shaping the landscape of theoretical physics and astrophysics. Spacetime, as a unified framework, continues to be a rich avenue for exploration, with ongoing research pushing the boundaries of our comprehension of the cosmos. Einstein's legacy endures not only in equations but in the way we perceive the very fabric of reality.

Modern Physics' Exploration of the Nature of Time

Modern physics has delved into the nature of time with great depth, revealing a complex and nuanced understanding that challenges classical notions. Several key theories and concepts have shaped the exploration of time in contemporary physics, reshaping our perception of this fundamental dimension. Here are some aspects of modern physics' exploration of the nature of time:

1. Relativity and Time Dilation:

Theory of Special Relativity:

Albert Einstein's special theory of relativity, formulated in 1905, revolutionized our understanding of space and time. One of its profound implications is time dilation, where time can appear to pass differently for observers in relative motion. The faster an object moves, the slower time elapses for it compared to a stationary observer.

Theory of General Relativity:

Einstein's general theory of relativity, developed in 1915, further expanded our understanding of time in the presence of gravity. Massive objects, such as planets and stars, create curvature in spacetime, affecting the flow of time. Clocks in stronger gravitational fields run slower, a phenomenon confirmed by experiments and observations.

2. Quantum Mechanics and Time:

Quantum Indeterminacy:

In the realm of quantum mechanics, the behavior of particles is subject to indeterminacy. The Heisenberg Uncertainty Principle challenges the notion of precisely measuring both the position and momentum of a particle simultaneously. This indeterminacy introduces a fundamental uncertainty into the very fabric of reality.

Quantum Entanglement and Nonlocality:

Entangled particles, no matter the distance separating them, exhibit correlated behavior instantaneously when a property of one particle is measured. This nonlocal connection challenges classical notions of time and locality, suggesting a form of interconnectedness beyond our classical understanding.

3. Arrow of Time and Thermodynamics:

Entropy and the Second Law of Thermodynamics:

The arrow of time, associated with the directionality of cause and effect, is intimately tied to the increase of entropy. The second law of thermodynamics states that in a closed system, entropy tends to increase over time. This unidirectional increase in disorder provides a directionality to time, aligning with our everyday experience.

4. Quantum Gravity and Unified Theories:

Challenges in Unifying Quantum Mechanics and General Relativity:

Efforts to unify quantum mechanics and general relativity, seeking a theory of quantum gravity, encounter challenges related to the nature of time. The discrete nature of quantum mechanics clashes with the continuous nature of spacetime in general relativity, posing fundamental questions about the nature of time at the quantum level.

String Theory and Loop Quantum Gravity:

Theoretical frameworks like string theory and loop quantum gravity are attempts to reconcile these two pillars of modern physics. These theories introduce novel concepts such as extra dimensions and discrete quantum geometry, offering potential insights into the nature of spacetime at its most fundamental level.

5. Multiverse Hypothesis:

The concept of a multiverse, arising from certain interpretations of quantum mechanics and cosmological models, introduces the idea that our universe is one of many. Time may unfold differently in other universes, challenging our traditional understanding of a singular, linear timeline.

6. Philosophical Implications:

The exploration of time in modern physics has profound philosophical implications. Questions about the nature of the present moment, the reality of the past and future, and the nature of causality continue to be subjects of intense debate and speculation.

Modern physics has transformed our conception of time, revealing a dynamic and multifaceted dimension that interacts with gravity, quantum phenomena, and the very fabric of the cosmos. The unification of quantum mechanics and general relativity remains a central challenge, and the nature of time at the quantum level continues to be a frontier of exploration. As our understanding evolves, the exploration of time in modern physics invites us to reconsider our intuitive notions and embrace the richness and complexity of this fundamental aspect of reality.

Similarities Between Vedic Kalachakra and Modern Theories of Time and Space

The Vedic concept of Kalachakra and modern theories of time and space, especially those stemming from theoretical physics, share intriguing similarities. While the language and frameworks differ, certain underlying principles suggest a convergence of thought across these seemingly disparate realms. Let's explore the commonalities between Vedic Kalachakra and modern theories:

1. Cyclical Nature of Time:

Vedic Kalachakra:

The Vedic perspective on time, as embodied in the concept of Kalachakra, emphasizes its cyclical nature. The Yugas – Satya Yuga, Treta Yuga, Dvapara Yuga, and Kali Yuga – represent distinct epochs with varying moral, spiritual, and societal characteristics. The cyclical pattern of creation, preservation, and dissolution aligns with the recurrent themes in Vedic cosmology.

Modern Theories:

In modern physics, particularly in cosmology, cyclic models of the universe propose a cyclical pattern of cosmic expansion and contraction. The idea of an oscillating universe, where periods of expansion are followed by contraction and vice versa, resonates with the cyclical nature embedded in Vedic cosmology.

2. Interconnectedness of Time and Space:

Vedic Kalachakra:

In Vedic thought, time (Kala) and space are not separate entities but interconnected aspects of a unified cosmic order. The dynamic interplay between time and space is integral to understanding the unfolding of the cosmos.

Modern Theories:

Einstein's theory of relativity introduced the concept of spacetime, where time and space are interwoven into a single fabric. The curvature of spacetime, influenced by mass and energy, dictates the motion of objects. This interconnected view aligns with the Vedic understanding of the inseparable relationship between time and space.

3. Non-Linearity of Time:

Vedic Kalachakra:

Vedic cosmology portrays time as non-linear, with cycles of creation and dissolution. The Yugas illustrate that time does not follow a linear progression but involves distinct phases and rhythms.

Modern Theories:

Einstein's theory of relativity challenged the Newtonian concept of absolute time. Time in relativity is relative and can be dilated or contracted depending on factors like gravity and velocity. The non-linearity of time, where the flow of time is influenced by the conditions of the observer, resonates with the Vedic understanding.

4. Cosmic Cycles and Renewal:

Vedic Kalachakra:

The concept of Yugas in Vedic cosmology embodies the idea of cosmic cycles, with each cycle representing a phase of spiritual and cosmic evolution. Dissolution is not the end but a prelude to a new cycle of creation.

Modern Theories:

In modern cosmology, the cyclic model proposes an eternal cosmic cycle of expansion and contraction. The universe undergoes a series of Big Bangs and Big Crunches, suggesting a continuous process of renewal and rebirth on a cosmic scale.

5. Quantum Indeterminacy and Vedic Philosophy:

Vedic Kalachakra:

Vedic philosophy often emphasizes the impermanence of the material world and the illusory nature of reality. The interplay of karma and the dynamic nature of existence align with the idea that the fabric of reality is not predetermined.

Modern Theories:

Quantum mechanics introduces the concept of indeterminacy, where the behavior of particles is inherently probabilistic. The uncertainty principle challenges the notion of a deterministic universe, reflecting a level of unpredictability that echoes certain aspects of Vedic philosophy.

6. Consciousness and Observer Effect:

Vedic Kalachakra:

Vedic thought often integrates consciousness into the fabric of existence, acknowledging the role of the observer in shaping reality. The relationship between consciousness and the unfolding of cosmic events is central to many Vedic teachings.

Modern Theories:

In quantum physics, the observer effect highlights the influence of consciousness on the behavior of quantum systems. The act of observation collapses the wave function, emphasizing the interconnectedness of consciousness and the quantum realm, aligning with certain aspects of Vedic insights.

The parallels between Vedic Kalachakra and modern theories of time and space suggest a shared resonance in fundamental concepts. Both traditions grapple with the cyclical nature of the cosmos, the interconnectedness of time and space, and the dynamic, non-linear unfolding of reality. While expressed in diverse languages and frameworks, the common thread of exploring the profound mysteries of existence runs through both Vedic philosophy and modern theoretical physics, inviting contemplation on the timeless and universal aspects of the cosmos.

Chapter 6: Healing and Wellness

Ayurveda and Vedic Approaches

Holistic Health in Ayurveda

Holistic health in Ayurveda is a comprehensive approach that seeks to achieve harmony and balance in the physical, mental, and spiritual aspects of an individual. Ayurveda, the ancient system of traditional medicine originating in India, views health not merely as the absence of disease but as a state of complete well-being. The holistic principles of Ayurveda are deeply rooted in a personalized understanding of an individual's constitution, lifestyle, and environment. Here are key components of holistic health in Ayurveda:

1. Prakriti (Constitution):

Ayurveda recognizes that each person is unique, and their constitution is determined by the three doshas – Vata, Pitta, and Kapha. Understanding one's Prakriti allows for personalized health recommendations, including dietary choices, lifestyle practices, and therapeutic measures. Holistic health involves aligning daily routines with individual constitution to maintain balance.

2. Dinacharya (Daily Routine):

Ayurveda emphasizes the importance of a daily routine, or Dinacharya, to synchronize with the natural rhythms of the day. This includes activities like waking up early, practicing oral hygiene, and engaging in self-care rituals. Aligning daily activities with the body's natural cycles promotes balance and supports overall well-being.

3. Ritucharya (Seasonal Routine):

Harmony with nature extends to seasonal routines or Ritucharya. Ayurveda recognizes the influence of seasons on the doshas and prescribes specific dietary and lifestyle recommendations for each season. Adapting to seasonal changes helps prevent imbalances and promotes holistic health.

4. Ahara (Nutrition):

Ayurvedic nutrition is an integral part of holistic health. It emphasizes the importance of mindful eating, choosing foods based on one's constitution and the seasons. Ayurveda categorizes foods based on their tastes (rasa), qualities (guna), and post-digestive effects (vipaka), providing a comprehensive understanding of the impact of food on the body and mind.

5. Panchakarma (Detoxification):

Holistic health in Ayurveda includes periodic detoxification through Panchakarma therapies. Panchakarma aims to eliminate accumulated toxins (ama) from the body, balancing the doshas and rejuvenating the system. Common Panchakarma therapies include massage, herbal therapies, and cleansing procedures.

6. Yoga and Pranayama:

Physical exercise, particularly in the form of yoga, is an essential aspect of Ayurvedic holistic health. Yoga postures (asanas) and breath control (pranayama) help balance the doshas, improve circulation, and enhance overall well-being. Yoga practices are tailored to an individual's constitution and health needs.

7. Meditation and Mindfulness:

Mental well-being is integral to Ayurvedic holistic health. Practices like meditation and mindfulness are encouraged to calm the mind, reduce stress, and enhance mental clarity. Ayurveda recognizes the mind-body connection and emphasizes the role of mental health in overall wellness.

8. Herbal Medicine:

Ayurvedic herbal formulations play a crucial role in holistic health. Herbs are chosen based on their properties and effects on the doshas. They are utilized for preventive measures, promoting balance, and addressing specific health concerns.

9. Sattvic Living:

Ayurveda encourages a sattvic lifestyle, characterized by purity, simplicity, and positivity. This includes fostering harmonious relationships, engaging in meaningful activities, and cultivating a positive mindset.

10. Spiritual Well-being:

Holistic health in Ayurveda extends beyond the physical and mental realms to include spiritual well-being. Practices like prayer, meditation, and connecting with one's inner self are considered vital for achieving holistic balance.

11. Svasthavritta (Personal and Social Conduct):

Holistic health in Ayurveda extends beyond individual practices to include personal and social conduct. Maintaining ethical and righteous behavior (Dharma) is considered crucial for overall well-being. This involves fostering positive relationships, practicing gratitude, and contributing to the welfare of society.

12. Achara Rasayana (Code of Conduct):

Ayurveda recognizes the importance of a disciplined and balanced lifestyle as a form of Rasayana or rejuvenation. Achara Rasayana includes adhering to ethical conduct, practicing moderation, and cultivating virtues such as compassion and non-violence. This code of conduct contributes to mental and emotional well-being.

13. Nidra (Sleep Hygiene):

Adequate and quality sleep is a cornerstone of holistic health in Ayurveda. Nidra (sleep) is considered one of the three pillars of health, along with proper diet and lifestyle. Establishing a consistent sleep routine and creating a conducive sleep environment are emphasized for overall balance.

14. Marma Therapy:

Marma points are vital energy points in the body, and Marma therapy is an aspect of Ayurveda that involves gentle manipulation of these points for balancing energy flow. This therapy not only supports physical health but also influences mental and emotional states, contributing to holistic well-being.

15. Sound Therapy (Nada Yoga):

Ayurveda acknowledges the therapeutic effects of sound on the body and mind. Nada Yoga, or sound therapy, involves the use of specific sounds, chants, or music to balance the doshas and promote overall harmony. This holistic approach recognizes the vibrational influence of sound on the entire being.

16. Jyotish Shastra (Vedic Astrology):

Vedic astrology is integrated into Ayurveda for a holistic understanding of an individual's health. The positioning of celestial bodies is believed to influence doshic balance and health patterns. Jyotish Shastra is consulted for insights into potential health challenges and suitable preventive measures.

17. Dinachikitsa (Daily Health Practices):

Daily health practices are integral to Ayurvedic holistic health. These include practices like tongue scraping, oil pulling, and self-massage, which are incorporated into daily routines to promote oral hygiene, detoxification, and circulation.

18. Counseling and Psychological Support:

Recognizing the mind-body connection, Ayurveda includes counseling and psychological support as part of holistic health. Addressing stress, emotional imbalances, and mental health concerns is considered essential for maintaining overall well-being.

19. Family and Community Health:

Holistic health in Ayurveda extends to the family and community. Creating a healthy and supportive environment within the family, as well as contributing positively to the community, is seen as beneficial for the well-being of individuals and society as a whole.

20. Continual Learning and Self-Reflection:

Ayurveda encourages a mindset of continual learning and self-reflection. Understanding one's own body, mind, and spirit, and adapting health practices accordingly, is considered key to maintaining holistic health. This involves staying informed about one's own needs and making conscious choices for well-being.

In essence, holistic health in Ayurveda encompasses a wide spectrum of practices and principles that address the entirety of an individual's existence. By considering physical, mental, emotional, social, and spiritual aspects, Ayurveda offers a holistic framework for achieving and maintaining optimal health throughout the journey of life.

The Mind-Body Connection in Vedic Healing Practices

The mind-body connection is a foundational concept in Vedic healing practices, reflecting the profound understanding that the state of one's mind has a direct impact on physical health and vice versa. Vedic healing, deeply rooted in ancient Indian wisdom, acknowledges the inseparable relationship between the mind and the body. Here's an exploration of the mind-body connection in Vedic healing practices:

1. Ayurveda and the Doshas:

Mind-Body Types (Doshas):

Ayurveda, the ancient system of medicine, recognizes three fundamental mind-body types known as doshas – Vata, Pitta, and Kapha. Each dosha is associated with specific physical and mental attributes. Understanding one's doshic constitution allows for personalized health recommendations that address both physical and mental well-being.

Emotional Influence on Doshas:

Ayurveda emphasizes that emotions directly impact the balance of doshas. For example, excessive stress or anxiety can aggravate Vata, while anger or intense emotions can disturb Pitta. Balancing emotions is considered essential for maintaining overall health.

2. Yoga and Pranayama:

Balancing Life Force Energy (Prana):

Yoga and pranayama (breath control) play a significant role in the mind-body connection. Through mindful movement and breath regulation, these practices aim to balance the flow of prana, the life force energy. This not only enhances physical health but also promotes mental clarity and emotional balance.

Chakras and Energy Centers:

Vedic healing acknowledges the presence of energy centers or chakras in the body. Each chakra is associated with specific physical and emotional attributes. Practices such as meditation and yoga aim to balance and harmonize these energy centers, fostering overall well-being.

3. Meditation and Mindfulness:

Cultivating Mental Clarity:

Meditation is a core practice in Vedic healing for calming the mind and cultivating mental clarity. By observing thoughts without attachment and cultivating mindfulness, individuals can achieve a state of inner balance that positively influences both mental and physical health.

Mantras and Vibrational Healing:

Chanting mantras is another aspect of Vedic healing that involves using sound vibrations for therapeutic purposes. Mantras are believed to have a calming effect on the mind, promoting emotional well-being and influencing the subtle energy system.

4. Jyotish Shastra (Vedic Astrology):

Planetary Influences on the Mind:

Vedic astrology, known as Jyotish Shastra, explores the influence of celestial bodies on an individual's life, including mental and emotional states. Understanding one's astrological chart is considered valuable for gaining insights into potential mental health challenges and suitable remedies.

5. Ayurvedic Psychology:

Tridosha Psychology:

Ayurvedic psychology delves into the tridosha system, recognizing the influence of doshas on mental attributes. Vata, for instance, is associated with creativity and adaptability but can lead to anxiety when imbalanced. Pitta governs intellect and can lead to perfectionism when in excess. Kapha is linked to emotional stability but can manifest as lethargy when imbalanced.

Sattvic Living:

Ayurvedic psychology encourages sattvic living – adopting a lifestyle characterized by purity, simplicity, and positivity. This includes fostering positive thoughts, engaging in activities that promote joy, and maintaining harmonious relationships.

6. Ayurvedic Nutrition:

Gut-Brain Connection:

Ayurvedic nutrition recognizes the gut-brain connection, emphasizing that the digestive system influences mental well-being. A healthy digestive system is considered crucial for assimilating nutrients that support both physical and mental health.

Rasayana and Mental Rejuvenation:

Rasayana, the branch of Ayurveda focused on rejuvenation, includes practices and herbs that enhance mental clarity and cognitive function. By nourishing the mind, rasayana contributes to overall well-being.

7. Sound Therapy (Nada Yoga):

Vibrational Healing:

Sound therapy, or Nada Yoga, involves using specific sounds or music for therapeutic purposes. The vibrational quality of sound is believed to influence both the mind and the body. Listening to calming sounds or chanting specific sounds can have a harmonizing effect on the nervous system.

8. Herbal Medicine:

Adaptogenic Herbs:

Ayurvedic herbal medicine includes adaptogenic herbs that help the body and mind adapt to stressors. These herbs are believed to modulate the stress response, supporting mental resilience and overall health.

The mind-body connection in Vedic healing practices reflects a holistic understanding of health, recognizing that mental and physical well-being are intricately linked. By addressing imbalances at the level of both the mind and the body, Vedic healing promotes a state of harmony and optimal health, embracing the interconnectedness of these essential aspects of human existence.

9. The Concept of Mann in Vedic Healing:

Understanding Mann:

In Vedic philosophy, particularly in the context of Ayurveda, the term "Mann" is often used to refer to the mind. It goes beyond the mere cognitive aspect and encompasses emotions, thoughts, and consciousness. Mann is considered a dynamic force that influences both mental and physical health.

Tridosha Influence on Mann:

Similar to its influence on the body, the tridosha system plays a pivotal role in shaping the nature of Mann. Vata dominance may lead to a restless mind, Pitta dominance to intense emotions, and Kapha dominance to a more stable but potentially lethargic mental state. Balancing the doshas is crucial for a harmonious Mann.

10. Ayurvedic Psychology and Mann:

Tridosha Psychology Applied to Emotions:

Ayurvedic psychology explores the connection between doshas and emotions, providing insights into how imbalances can manifest in the mind. For example, excess Vata may contribute to anxiety, while heightened Pitta can result in anger. Ayurvedic psychology offers holistic approaches to address these emotional imbalances.

Sattvic Living for a Tranquil Mann:

Sattvic living, as recommended in Ayurveda, is not just about physical health but extends to fostering a tranquil Mann. Engaging in positive activities, cultivating a serene environment, and practicing mindfulness contribute to the cultivation of Sattva – purity and harmony – in the mind.

11. Mann and Yoga Practices:

Yoga for Mental Equilibrium:

Yoga, as a mind-body practice, plays a profound role in achieving mental equilibrium. Asanas (postures) and pranayama (breath control) are designed to calm the mind, enhance concentration, and promote a sense of inner peace.

The integration of physical postures with breath awareness directly impacts Mann.

Meditation for Mann Shuddhi (Purification):

Meditation is a key component of Vedic healing practices aimed at Mann Shuddhi, the purification of the mind. Regular meditation is believed to quieten the fluctuations of the mind (chitta vrittis) and bring about a state of mental clarity and tranquility.

12. Jyotish Shastra and Mann:

Astrological Influences on the Mind:

Jyotish Shastra not only provides insights into physical health but also sheds light on potential mental predispositions based on astrological charts. It recognizes that planetary positions at the time of birth can influence aspects of Mann, guiding individuals in understanding and decoding their mental landscape.

13. Ayurvedic Nutrition and Mann:

Nutritional Influence on Cognitive Function:

Ayurvedic nutrition acknowledges that the quality of food directly impacts the mind. The consumption of Sattvic foods, which are pure, fresh, and harmonious, is believed to promote mental clarity and balance. Conversely, Tamasic foods, which are heavy and dull, may cloud the mind.

Herbs for Cognitive Support:

Certain Ayurvedic herbs are renowned for their impact on cognitive function and Mann. For instance, Brahmi is traditionally used to enhance memory and cognitive abilities. Including such herbs in one's diet is considered a holistic approach to supporting mental well-being.

14. Sound Therapy and Mann:

Mantras for Mental Harmony:

The chanting of mantras, a form of sound therapy, is deeply rooted in Vedic traditions. Mantras are believed to have a vibrational impact on the mind, influencing mental states positively. This practice is often employed for promoting mental focus, emotional balance, and spiritual connection.

15. Ayurvedic Counseling for Mann:

Psychological Support through Ayurveda:

Ayurvedic counseling recognizes the interconnectedness of the mind and body. Professionals in this field provide guidance on lifestyle, nutrition, and practices to support mental well-being. Counseling sessions may include strategies for stress management, emotional balance, and overall mental health.

The concept of Mann in Vedic healing practices underscores the holistic nature of well-being, emphasizing the inseparable connection between the mind and the body. By integrating Ayurvedic principles, yoga practices, astrological insights, and mindful living, Vedic healing offers a comprehensive approach to cultivating a balanced, tranquil, and harmonious Mann – a state essential for overall health and spiritual growth.

Integration with Modern Medicine

Scientific Research Supporting Holistic Health Practices

Scientific research has increasingly recognized the efficacy of holistic health practices in promoting overall well-being. Holistic approaches, rooted in ancient traditions and often encompassing physical, mental, and spiritual dimensions, have gained attention in the scientific community. Here are examples of scientific research supporting various holistic health practices:

1. Mindfulness Meditation:

Scientific Findings:

Numerous studies, including those conducted at institutions like Harvard and Johns Hopkins, have demonstrated the positive impact of mindfulness meditation on mental health. Research indicates reductions in stress, anxiety, and symptoms of depression. Additionally, studies using neuroimaging have shown changes in brain structures associated with improved emotional regulation and attention.

References:

- Harvard Health Publishing
- Johns Hopkins Medicine

2. Yoga and Physical Health:

Scientific Findings:

Research on yoga has demonstrated its positive effects on physical health. Studies show that regular yoga practice can improve cardiovascular health, reduce inflammation, and enhance flexibility and balance. Yoga has also been linked to improved immune function and a reduction in chronic pain conditions.

References:

- American Osteopathic Association
- International Journal of Yoga

3. Ayurvedic Medicine and Wellness:

Scientific Findings:

Studies have explored the efficacy of Ayurvedic practices in promoting wellness. Research on Ayurvedic herbs, such as Ashwagandha and Turmeric, has shown anti-inflammatory and stress-reducing effects. Ayurvedic dietary recommendations have also been associated with improved digestive health.

References:

- Journal of Ayurveda and Integrative Medicine
- Critical Reviews in Food Science and Nutrition

4. Acupuncture for Pain Management:

Scientific Findings:

Acupuncture, an integral part of Traditional Chinese Medicine, has garnered attention for its effectiveness in pain management. Scientific studies have shown that acupuncture can alleviate chronic pain conditions, such as lower back pain, osteoarthritis, and migraines. Neuroimaging studies also suggest changes in brain activity associated with pain modulation.

References:

- National Center for Complementary and Integrative Health (NCCIH)
- The Journal of Alternative and Complementary Medicine

5. Holistic Nutrition and Mental Health:

Scientific Findings:

Research has explored the link between nutrition and mental health. Nutrient-rich diets, including the Mediterranean diet and those emphasizing fruits, vegetables, and omega-3 fatty acids, have been associated with a lower risk of depression and anxiety. The gut-brain axis, connecting the microbiome to mental health, is an area of growing interest.

References:

- World Journal of Psychiatry
- Nutritional Neuroscience

6. Sound Therapy and Stress Reduction:

Scientific Findings:

Research on sound therapy, including practices like music therapy and Tibetan singing bowl therapy, indicates stress reduction benefits. Studies have shown that listening to calming music or engaging in sound-based practices can lower cortisol levels, reduce anxiety, and enhance overall well-being.

References:

- Journal of Music Therapy
- Frontiers in Psychology

Scientific research continues to validate the efficacy of holistic health practices, providing evidence for their positive impact on physical, mental, and emotional well-being. As the body of research grows, there is increasing recognition of the value of integrating holistic approaches into conventional healthcare for a more comprehensive and patient-centered approach to health and wellness.

7. Herbal Medicine for Immune Support:

Scientific Findings:

Holistic approaches often incorporate herbal medicine for immune support. Research on herbs like Echinacea, Elderberry, and Astragalus has shown potential benefits in boosting immune function. These herbs are believed to possess antiviral and immunomodulatory properties.

References:

- Phytomedicine
- Nutrients

8. Breathwork and Stress Reduction:

Scientific Findings:

Breathwork, an integral part of many holistic practices, has been studied for its impact on stress reduction. Techniques like deep breathing and diaphragmatic breathing have been shown to activate the relaxation response, reduce cortisol levels, and improve overall mental well-being.

References:

- Frontiers in Psychology
- Journal of Clinical Psychology

9. Energy Healing Modalities:

Scientific Findings:

While the scientific exploration of energy healing modalities is ongoing, some studies have shown promising results. For instance, Reiki, a form of energy healing, has been associated with reduced anxiety and pain perception. Research on biofield therapies suggests their potential impact on the body's energy fields.

References:

- Journal of Alternative and Complementary Medicine
- Journal of Pain Research

10. Forest Bathing (Shinrin-Yoku):

Scientific Findings:

Forest bathing, a practice rooted in Japanese tradition, involves immersing oneself in nature. Scientific studies have indicated various health benefits, including reduced cortisol levels, lower blood pressure, and improvements in mood. Nature exposure has been linked to enhanced mental well-being.

References:

- Environmental Health and Preventive Medicine
- International Journal of Environmental Research and Public Health

11. Holistic Approaches to Pain Management:

Scientific Findings:

Holistic approaches, such as acupuncture, yoga, and mindfulness-based stress reduction (MBSR), have been studied for their efficacy in pain management. Research indicates that these approaches can reduce pain intensity and improve the quality of life for individuals with chronic pain conditions.

References:

- Journal of Pain
- The Clinical Journal of Pain

12. Positive Psychology and Well-Being:

Scientific Findings:

Positive psychology, focusing on strengths, virtues, and factors contributing to a fulfilling life, has garnered attention. Research suggests that interventions promoting gratitude, mindfulness, and positive emotions can enhance overall well-being and contribute to mental health.

References:

- Journal of Positive Psychology
- The Journal of Positive Psychology and Wellbeing

13. Tai Chi for Balance and Cognitive Function:

Scientific Findings:

Tai Chi, an ancient Chinese martial art involving slow and deliberate movements, has been studied for its impact on balance and cognitive function. Research indicates that regular practice of Tai Chi can improve balance, reduce the risk of falls, and enhance cognitive abilities.

References:

- The Journals of Gerontology
- Frontiers in Aging Neuroscience

Scientific research continues to explore the multifaceted benefits of holistic health practices. From immune support and stress reduction to pain management and cognitive enhancement, the evidence base for these approaches is expanding. As the integration of holistic practices with conventional healthcare becomes more prevalent, the potential for comprehensive and personalized approaches to health and well-being becomes increasingly promising.

The Potential Synergy Between Traditional and Modern Approaches in Medicine and Healing

The potential synergy between traditional and modern approaches in medicine and healing represents a promising paradigm that acknowledges the strengths of both systems, aiming to provide comprehensive and patient-centered care.

This integration can lead to a holistic understanding of health, combining the ancient wisdom of traditional practices with the scientific advancements of modern medicine. Here are key aspects of the potential synergy:

1. Comprehensive Patient Care:

Traditional Approach:

Traditional medicine often emphasizes personalized care, considering not only physical symptoms but also emotional, mental, and spiritual well-being. Practices such as Ayurveda and Traditional Chinese Medicine (TCM) aim to restore balance in the body, mind, and spirit.

Modern Approach:

Modern medicine excels in diagnostic precision and acute care interventions. Advanced technologies and pharmaceuticals play a crucial role in managing acute conditions and emergencies.

Synergy:

By integrating both approaches, patients can benefit from a comprehensive healthcare model. Traditional practices may support overall well-being and preventive care, while modern medicine can address acute conditions and complex medical issues.

2. Mind-Body Connection:

Traditional Approach:

Traditional systems often recognize the intimate connection between mental and physical health. Practices like yoga, meditation, and mindfulness are integral to maintaining this balance.

Modern Approach:

Modern psychology and psychiatry emphasize the importance of mental health in overall well-being. Therapies, medications, and interventions target mental health conditions with a scientific understanding of the mind.

Synergy:

Combining traditional mind-body practices with modern mental health interventions can offer a holistic approach to mental well-being. Integrative therapies may enhance the effectiveness of treatments for conditions like anxiety and depression.

3. Preventive Medicine:

Traditional Approach:

Many traditional systems focus on preventive measures, including dietary guidelines, lifestyle recommendations, and herbal remedies to maintain health and prevent diseases.

Modern Approach:

Modern medicine is increasingly recognizing the importance of preventive care, with vaccinations, screenings, and lifestyle interventions playing a crucial role in reducing the risk of diseases.

Synergy:

The synergy lies in merging traditional preventive strategies with modern screening and diagnostic tools. This comprehensive approach can identify potential risks early and implement preventive measures based on both systems.

4. Chronic Disease Management:

Traditional Approach:

Traditional systems often use holistic approaches for managing chronic conditions, incorporating dietary modifications, herbal remedies, and lifestyle changes to address the root causes.

Modern Approach:

Modern medicine provides advanced medications and interventions for chronic diseases, offering precise management strategies and monitoring tools.

Synergy:

Integrating both approaches can result in a more effective and holistic chronic disease management plan. Traditional practices may complement modern interventions, promoting overall well-being and minimizing side effects.

5. Cultural Sensitivity and Patient Preferences:

Traditional Approach:

Traditional medicine is deeply rooted in cultural practices, reflecting the diversity of approaches worldwide. Patient preferences and cultural beliefs are integral to treatment.

Modern Approach:

Modern medicine strives for cultural competence, recognizing the significance of understanding diverse perspectives to provide patient-centered care.

Synergy:

A collaborative approach considers cultural sensitivity and patient preferences, integrating traditional practices where appropriate. This ensures a more inclusive and patient-centric healthcare experience.

6. Herbal Medicine and Modern Pharmacology:

Traditional Approach:

Herbal medicine, a cornerstone of traditional healing systems, utilizes plant-derived compounds for therapeutic purposes. Traditional herbal remedies often have a holistic approach, addressing both the symptoms and underlying imbalances.

Modern Approach:

Modern pharmacology isolates active compounds from plants to create pharmaceutical drugs. The rigorous scientific process in drug development ensures standardization, potency, and safety.

Synergy:

Integrating herbal medicine with modern pharmacology allows for a broader range of treatment options. Research on herbal remedies can inform drug development, and some traditional remedies may serve as complementary therapies, potentially reducing side effects.

7. Energy Healing and Modern Medicine:

Traditional Approach:

Energy healing practices, such as Reiki and acupuncture, focus on the body's energy systems. Traditional systems believe that imbalances in energy flow can lead to illness, and these practices aim to restore balance.

Modern Approach:

While the concept of energy flow is not part of mainstream medical understanding, some studies suggest that practices like acupuncture may influence the nervous system and release endorphins, contributing to pain relief.

Synergy:

Integrating energy healing into a patient's care plan can complement modern medical treatments, especially in managing chronic pain, reducing stress, and improving overall well-being. It can be offered as a complementary therapy with appropriate informed consent.

8. Integrative Cancer Care:

Traditional Approach:

Certain traditional practices, like Ayurveda and Traditional Chinese Medicine, have been used to support cancer patients by addressing overall well-being, managing side effects of treatments, and boosting the immune system.

Modern Approach:

Modern cancer care involves surgery, chemotherapy, and radiation therapy. Advances in targeted therapies and immunotherapy are transforming treatment options.

Synergy:

Integrative cancer care combines traditional supportive therapies with modern medical treatments. Practices like yoga, meditation, and nutritional support can enhance the quality of life for cancer patients, potentially mitigating side effects and improving mental health.

9. Genomic Medicine and Ayurvedic Principles:

Traditional Approach:

Ayurveda categorizes individuals into different constitutional types or doshas – Vata, Pitta, and Kapha – based on inherent characteristics. This personalized approach guides lifestyle, diet, and treatment recommendations.

Modern Approach:

Genomic medicine explores the influence of genetic factors on health, offering personalized insights into disease risk and treatment responses.

Synergy:

Integrating Ayurvedic constitutional principles with genomic data can enhance personalized medicine. Understanding how an individual's dosha type may interact with genetic predispositions can inform lifestyle and treatment strategies.

10. Cross-Cultural Collaborations in Research:

Traditional Approach:

Traditional healing systems often involve a wealth of knowledge passed down through generations. Collaborative research within traditional healing communities contributes to the understanding of diverse health practices.

Modern Approach:

Modern research involves rigorous scientific methodologies and technological advancements. Cross-cultural collaborations aim to bridge the gap between traditional knowledge and contemporary scientific inquiry.

Synergy:

By fostering collaborations between traditional healers and modern researchers, a wealth of knowledge can be shared and validated. This approach respects the strengths of both systems, promoting mutual learning and understanding. The potential synergy between traditional and modern approaches in medicine and healing extends across various facets of healthcare. By embracing a collaborative model, individuals can benefit from a more nuanced and personalized healthcare experience that draws on the strengths of both traditional wisdom and modern scientific advancements.

Chapter 7:
Meditation and Mind-Body Connection

Vedic Meditation Practices

Techniques like Transcendental Meditation and Mindfulness

Meditation has been a core aspect of Vedic traditions, providing profound insights into the nature of consciousness and the self. Two prominent meditation techniques within the Vedic framework are Transcendental Meditation (TM) and mindfulness. Both approaches offer distinct methodologies rooted in ancient wisdom but with variations in practice and objectives.

TM:

TM, introduced by Maharishi Mahesh Yogi in the mid-20th century, is a mantra-based meditation technique. It involves the silent repetition of a specific mantra, a word or sound with no inherent meaning. The practitioner sits comfortably with closed eyes, allowing the mind to naturally settle into a state of deep inner quietness.

Key Principles of TM:

Effortless Nature:

TM emphasizes effortlessness. Unlike concentration-based practices, where the meditator actively focuses the mind, TM encourages the mind to effortlessly transcend ordinary thought.

Mantra Usage:

The mantra used in TM is chosen individually for each practitioner based on their age and gender. The mantra serves as a vehicle for transcending the surface levels of thinking.

Restful Alertness:

TM aims to induce a state of restful alertness, where the mind experiences deep inner silence while remaining alert and aware. This unique state is believed to promote holistic well-being.

Twenty Minutes, Twice Daily:

TM is typically practiced for twenty minutes, twice daily. This regular practice is thought to lead to cumulative benefits, including reduced stress and increased clarity of mind.

Mindfulness Meditation:

Mindfulness meditation, rooted in Buddhist traditions, gained widespread popularity due to its secular adaptation. It involves cultivating present-moment awareness without judgment. Mindfulness can be applied to various activities, but formal practice often includes focused attention on the breath or body sensations.

Key Principles of Mindfulness:

Present-Moment Awareness:

Mindfulness emphasizes being fully present in the current moment. Practitioners are encouraged to observe thoughts and sensations without attachment or judgment.

Breath as Anchor:

Many mindfulness practices use the breath as an anchor. Focused attention on the breath helps ground the mind and cultivate awareness of the present.

Non-Judgmental Observation:

Mindfulness encourages non-judgmental observation of thoughts and emotions. Instead of reacting impulsively, practitioners learn to respond with awareness.

Integration into Daily Life:

Mindfulness is not confined to formal meditation sessions. The goal is to integrate mindful awareness into daily activities, fostering a continuous state of presence.

Commonalities and Distinctions:

Rooted in Vedic Tradition:

Both TM and mindfulness have roots in Vedic traditions. TM, despite being introduced in a more contemporary context, draws from ancient Vedic principles of transcending thought. Mindfulness, though originating in Buddhism, shares foundational concepts with Vedic teachings.

Approach to Thoughts:

TM encourages transcending thought, aiming for a state of pure awareness beyond the mental chatter. Mindfulness, on the other hand, involves observing thoughts without attachment, allowing them to come and go.

Mantra vs. Breath:

TM uses a mantra as a focal point, while mindfulness often centers on the breath. The mantra in TM is a tool for transcending thought, whereas breath awareness in mindfulness serves as an anchor to the present moment.

Effortlessness vs. Focus:

TM places a strong emphasis on effortlessness, allowing the mind to naturally settle into a state of transcendence.

Mindfulness involves focused attention on the breath or sensations, requiring a deliberate effort to stay present.

Benefits and Scientific Research:

Stress Reduction:

Both TM and mindfulness have shown efficacy in reducing stress. Scientific studies suggest that regular practice can lead to decreased cortisol levels and improved overall well-being.

Enhanced Cognitive Function:

Research indicates that both practices may positively impact cognitive function. TM has been associated with improved attention and memory, while mindfulness has shown benefits in areas such as working memory and cognitive flexibility.

Emotional Well-Being:

TM and mindfulness have been linked to enhanced emotional well-being. Studies suggest reductions in symptoms of anxiety and depression, as well as improvements in mood and overall emotional resilience.

Physiological Effects:

Both practices have demonstrated physiological benefits. TM, in particular, has been associated with changes in autonomic nervous system function and cardiovascular health. Mindfulness has shown positive effects on heart rate variability and immune function.

TM and mindfulness, despite their differences, share a common thread of promoting inner exploration and self-awareness. Whether one is drawn to the effortless transcending nature of TM or the focused awareness of mindfulness, both approaches offer valuable tools for sailing through the complexities of the mind and fostering holistic well-being. As scientific research continues to unravel the benefits of these practices, individuals can explore and integrate them into their lives, tapping into the timeless wisdom embedded in Vedic traditions.

The Impact of Meditation on Mental and Physical Well-being

Meditation, an ancient practice with roots in various spiritual and cultural traditions, has gained widespread recognition for its profound impact on mental and physical well-being. This essay explores the multifaceted effects of meditation, examining its influence on mental health, cognitive function, and physiological well-being.

Mental Well-Being:

Stress Reduction:

Meditation is renowned for its stress-relieving effects. Mindfulness meditation, in particular, teaches individuals to cultivate present-moment awareness, reducing the grip of stressors by promoting a non-reactive and accepting mindset. Studies suggest that regular meditation can lower cortisol levels, the hormone associated with stress.

Anxiety and Depression:

Numerous studies have demonstrated the efficacy of meditation in reducing symptoms of anxiety and depression. Mindfulness-based interventions, such as Mindfulness-Based Stress Reduction (MBSR) and Mindfulness-Based Cognitive Therapy (MBCT), have been integrated into clinical settings to complement traditional therapeutic approaches.

Enhanced Emotional Regulation:

Meditation fosters emotional regulation by encouraging individuals to observe their thoughts and feelings without attachment or judgment. This non-reactive awareness can lead to greater emotional resilience and a more balanced emotional state.

Improved Attention and Concentration:

Various forms of meditation, including focused attention and mindfulness practices, have been associated with improvements in attention and concentration. The cultivation of sustained attention allows individuals to become more present in their daily activities, leading to heightened cognitive performance.

Cognitive Function:

Memory Enhancement:

Research suggests that meditation may positively impact memory function. Both short-term and long-term memory improvements have been observed, with mindfulness practices showing promise in enhancing working memory and cognitive flexibility.

Cognitive Flexibility:

Meditation encourages cognitive flexibility, the ability to adapt and shift thinking patterns when needed. This mental agility is crucial for problem-solving, decision-making, and adapting to changing circumstances.

Brain Plasticity:

Neuroscientific studies indicate that regular meditation may contribute to changes in brain structure and function. Increased gray matter density in areas associated with memory, self-awareness, and compassion has been observed in long-term meditators.

Physiological Well-Being:

Cardiovascular Health:

Meditation has been linked to improvements in cardiovascular health. TM has shown to reduce blood pressure and decrease the risk of cardiovascular diseases. The relaxation response induced by meditation contributes to overall heart health.

Immune System Function:

The mind-body connection is evident in the impact of meditation on immune system function. Studies suggest that regular meditation can enhance immune response, promoting a more robust defense against infections and illnesses.

Pain Management:

Mindfulness meditation has proven effective in pain management. By fostering a non-judgmental awareness of pain sensations, individuals can alter their perception and response to pain, leading to improved pain tolerance and reduced reliance on analgesic medications.

Holistic Integration:

The impact of meditation on mental and physical well-being is not isolated to individual components but reflects the interconnectedness of mind, body, and spirit. Holistic integration involves incorporating meditation into one's lifestyle as a regular practice, recognizing its potential to promote overall health and harmony.

Meditation emerges as a transformative tool that transcends cultural and spiritual boundaries, offering a pathway to enhanced mental and physical well-being. As scientific research continues to unveil the intricate mechanisms through which meditation exerts its effects, individuals are empowered to harness the potential of this ancient practice for holistic health. Whether seeking stress relief, emotional balance, cognitive enhancement, or physiological well-being, meditation stands as a timeless and accessible resource for cultivating a healthier and more fulfilling life.

Scientific Research

The intersection of meditation, neuroplasticity, and mental health has become a focal point of scientific inquiry, with numerous studies exploring the transformative effects of meditation on the brain and its implications for mental well-being. This synthesis delves into key research findings that illuminate the intricate relationship between meditation practices, the brain's plasticity, and mental health outcomes.

Neuroplasticity and Meditation:

Structural Changes in the Brain:

Hippocampus: A landmark study by Dr. Sara Lazar and her team at Harvard found that mindfulness meditation is associated with an increased gray matter density in the hippocampus, a region vital for memory and learning.

Amygdala: Meditation has been linked to reduced amygdala activity, a key player in the brain's stress response. This suggests that meditation may modulate emotional reactivity and contribute to stress resilience.

Enhanced Connectivity:

Research utilizing neuroimaging techniques, such as functional Magnetic Resonance Imaging (fMRI), indicates that meditation is correlated with increased connectivity between different brain regions. This enhanced connectivity is believed to support integrative and flexible cognitive processing.

Thicker Cortical Regions:

Long-term meditation practitioners have demonstrated thicker cortical regions associated with attention, sensory processing, and interoception. This suggests that meditation may contribute to improved cognitive functions and heightened self-awareness.

Mental Health Outcomes:

Reduction in Anxiety and Depression:

Meta-analyses and systematic reviews consistently point to the positive impact of meditation on reducing symptoms of anxiety and depression. Mindfulness-Based Interventions (MBIs) have emerged as effective strategies for individuals dealing with various mental health challenges.

Stress Reduction and Cortisol Levels:

Studies examining the physiological effects of meditation reveal a reduction in cortisol levels, the hormone associated with stress. Mindfulness practices, such as Mindfulness-Based Stress Reduction (MBSR), have been particularly effective in promoting stress resilience.

Improved Attention and Cognitive Function:

Meditation has been associated with improvements in attention and cognitive function. Mindfulness meditation, in particular, has shown promise in enhancing sustained attention, cognitive flexibility, and working memory.

Enhanced Emotional Regulation:

Regular meditation has been linked to enhanced emotional regulation. Practitioners often report increased emotional resilience, a greater capacity to respond thoughtfully to emotions, and a reduction in emotional reactivity.

Clinical Applications:

Incorporation into Psychotherapy:

Mindfulness-based interventions have been integrated into psychotherapeutic approaches, such as Mindfulness-Based Cognitive Therapy (MBCT) and Mindfulness-Based Relapse Prevention (MBRP). These interventions aim to prevent relapse in individuals with recurrent depression and support those dealing with substance use disorders.

Mindfulness in Schools:

Research in educational settings suggests that incorporating mindfulness practices into school curricula can contribute to improved emotional well-being, attention, and social skills among students. Mindfulness programs have shown promise in reducing symptoms of anxiety and improving overall psychological health in young populations.

Corporate Wellness Programs:

Corporations are increasingly adopting mindfulness programs to enhance employee well-being and productivity. Studies indicate that workplace mindfulness interventions can lead to reduced stress, improved job satisfaction, and better overall mental health in employees.

The studies on meditation, neuroplasticity, and mental health converge to paint a compelling picture of the transformative potential of contemplative practices. From structural changes in the brain to tangible improvements in mental health outcomes, the research underscores the adaptability of the brain and its responsiveness to intentional mental training through meditation. As this field continues to evolve, the integration of meditation into mainstream mental health interventions holds promise for a more holistic and personalized approach to well-being.

The Growing Recognition of Meditation in Mainstream Healthcare

In recent years, there has been a notable shift in mainstream healthcare towards recognizing and integrating meditation as a valuable and evidence-based tool for promoting overall well-being. This transformation reflects a deeper understanding of the mind-body connection and the potential of meditation to complement conventional medical interventions. This exploration delves into the factors driving the growing recognition of meditation in mainstream healthcare and the evolving landscape of its integration.

Mind-Body Connection and Holistic Health:

Acknowledgment of the Mind-Body Connection:

Mainstream healthcare has increasingly acknowledged the intricate connection between mental and physical health. The recognition that mental well-being profoundly influences physical health has led to a more holistic approach that considers the interplay between mind and body.

Holistic Health Paradigm:

The shift towards a holistic health paradigm emphasizes the importance of addressing not only physical symptoms but also the psychological and emotional aspects of well-being. Meditation, with its emphasis on mental clarity and emotional balance, aligns with this holistic approach to healthcare.

Scientific Validation and Research:

Growing Body of Scientific Evidence:

The expanding body of scientific research on meditation has provided robust evidence supporting its efficacy in various health domains. Rigorous studies on mindfulness-based interventions, TM, and other contemplative practices have demonstrated positive outcomes in managing stress, anxiety, depression, and even certain physical conditions.

Neuroscientific Findings:

Advances in neuroscience have contributed to the understanding of how meditation induces structural and functional changes in the brain. Neuroplasticity, the brain's ability to reorganize itself, is now recognized as a mechanism through which meditation influences mental and emotional well-being.

Integration into Clinical Practice:

Mindfulness-Based Interventions (MBIs):

Mindfulness-based interventions, such as Mindfulness-Based Stress Reduction (MBSR) and Mindfulness-Based Cognitive Therapy (MBCT), have gained acceptance as adjunctive therapies in clinical settings. These structured programs incorporate mindfulness meditation to address conditions like chronic pain, anxiety disorders, and recurrent depression.

Psychotherapeutic Integration:

Psychotherapists are increasingly integrating mindfulness techniques into traditional therapeutic modalities. Mindfulness helps individuals cultivate present-moment awareness, promoting emotional regulation and resilience. Therapeutic approaches like Dialectical Behavior Therapy (DBT) and Acceptance and Commitment Therapy (ACT) actively incorporate mindfulness principles.

Mental Health and Stress Reduction:

Stress Reduction Programs:

Recognizing the pervasive impact of stress on health, many healthcare institutions now offer stress reduction programs that include meditation components. Employees, patients, and the general population are provided with tools to manage stress through mindfulness and meditation.

Employee Well-Being Initiatives:

Corporations are integrating meditation into employee well-being initiatives. Workplace mindfulness programs aim to reduce stress, enhance focus, and improve overall job satisfaction. Such initiatives align with a preventive healthcare approach, acknowledging the importance of mental health in the workplace.

Patient-Centered Care:

Patient Demand and Preferences:

The increasing demand for patient-centered care has led healthcare providers to consider holistic and patient-preferred interventions. Many patients express an interest in complementary and alternative approaches, including meditation, leading to its incorporation into treatment plans.

Inclusion in Chronic Disease Management:

Meditation is finding a place in chronic disease management. Patients with conditions like hypertension, diabetes, and chronic pain are encouraged to explore meditation as part of their self-management strategies. The integrative approach considers both the physiological and psychological aspects of these conditions.

A Paradigm Shift in Healthcare:

The growing recognition of meditation in mainstream healthcare marks a paradigm shift towards a more integrative and patient-centered approach. As healthcare professionals increasingly acknowledge the mind's impact on overall health, meditation has emerged as a versatile and accessible tool.

Whether integrated into psychotherapeutic practices, stress reduction programs, or chronic disease management, meditation is fostering a more comprehensive understanding of health that transcends the conventional boundaries of medical care. As this trajectory continues, the synergy between ancient contemplative practices and modern healthcare reflects a holistic vision that places the well-being of the individual at its core.

Chapter 8:
Environmental Wisdom

Vedic Teachings on Nature

The Interconnectedness of Humanity and the Environment

The interconnectedness of humanity and the environment is a central theme in Vedic philosophy, which emphasizes a holistic and harmonious relationship between humans and the natural world. The Vedas, ancient Indian scriptures, provide a profound perspective on the symbiotic connection between humanity and the environment. Here are key aspects detailing the Vedic perspective on the interconnectedness of humanity and the environment.

The interconnectedness of humanity and the environment in the Vedic perspective is rooted in a holistic worldview that recognizes the intrinsic unity of all existence. This worldview goes beyond viewing humans as separate from nature; instead, it emphasizes a symbiotic relationship where the well-being of one is intricately tied to the well-being of the other.

The Vedic perspective encourages individuals to approach nature with reverence, acknowledging its sacredness and divinity. This recognition fosters a sense of responsibility and stewardship, prompting ethical and sustainable practices. By living in harmony with the environment and recognizing the interconnected web of life, individuals can contribute to the well-being of the planet and future generations, aligning their actions with the timeless wisdom embedded in Vedic philosophy.

1. Unity of Existence (Rigveda 1.164):

The Rigveda, one of the oldest Vedic scriptures, contemplates the concept of the unity of existence. It transcends the boundaries of individual identities and recognizes a singular truth that is expressed in various ways. The hymn emphasizes that despite the diversity in how this truth is named or understood, it ultimately points to a unified reality. This perspective underscores the interconnectedness of all aspects of existence, including humanity and the environment.

The Vedic understanding of unity doesn't merely apply to the human realm but extends to the entire cosmos. It suggests that every element of creation, from the smallest particle to the vast cosmic forces, is interconnected. This interconnectedness forms the basis for a harmonious relationship between humanity and the environment.

2. Sacredness of Nature:

In Vedic philosophy, nature is not merely a resource to be exploited but is considered sacred and divine. The rivers, mountains, forests, and animals are seen as manifestations of cosmic divinity. The personification of these elements as deities reflects a reverence for the natural world. Such a perception encourages humans to approach nature with respect, recognizing its intrinsic value beyond its utility.

The sacredness of nature is often expressed through rituals and ceremonies conducted in natural settings. Pilgrimages to sacred rivers, mountains, and forests highlight the belief that connecting with nature enhances one's spiritual journey. This sacred view of the environment fosters a sense of responsibility and stewardship among individuals.

3. Balance and Harmony (Rigveda 10.85):

The concept of Rita, often translated as cosmic order or eternal law, emphasizes the importance of maintaining balance and harmony in the universe. Humans are encouraged to align their lives with this cosmic order, recognizing that their well-being is intricately connected to the well-being of the entire cosmos. This holistic perspective discourages actions that disrupt the natural balance and encourages sustainable practices.

The Vedic emphasis on harmony extends to human relationships as well. Just as the cosmos operates in a harmonious rhythm, human communities are encouraged to live in harmony with each other and with nature. This interconnected worldview reinforces the idea that disruptions in one aspect of existence can have cascading effects on the entire system.

4. Environmental Stewardship:

Vedic philosophy places a significant emphasis on environmental stewardship. Humans are regarded as custodians of the Earth, entrusted with the responsibility to protect and preserve the environment. This stewardship involves not only avoiding harm to nature but actively contributing to its well-being. Sustainable living practices, conservation efforts, and ethical treatment of animals are integral aspects of this environmental stewardship.

The Vedic emphasis on responsible environmental conduct encourages individuals to consider the impact of their actions on the ecosystem. This sense of responsibility goes beyond immediate concerns and considers the long-term effects of human activities on the environment and future generations.

5. Ahimsa (Non-violence) and Respect for Life:

Ahimsa, the principle of non-violence, is a cornerstone of Vedic ethics. This principle extends beyond human interactions to encompass all living beings. The interconnectedness of life is recognized, promoting compassion and respect for every creature. This perspective aligns with the understanding that all life forms are interconnected in the grand orchestra of existence.

In practicing ahimsa, individuals are encouraged to minimize harm to living beings, including animals and plants. The Vedic perspective underscores the interconnectedness of the web of life, emphasizing the interdependence between different species and the role each one plays in maintaining the ecological balance.

6. Rituals and Nature:

Vedic rituals often involve elements from nature, reinforcing the connection between humans and the environment. Whether it's performing ceremonies near rivers, under specific trees, or in natural settings, these rituals symbolize the acknowledgment of the sacredness of the environment. The choice of natural locations for rituals is a deliberate act to strengthen the bond between humanity and the natural world.

The inclusion of nature in rituals serves as a reminder that the divine is not confined to temples but is omnipresent in the natural elements. This acknowledgment reinforces the idea that humans are an integral part of the broader ecological system, and their spiritual practices should reflect a deep respect for the environment.

7. Vedic Cosmology:

Vedic cosmology, as portrayed in the scriptures, provides a comprehensive view of the interconnectedness of the universe. The cycles of creation, preservation, and destruction are seen as part of a cosmic dance where all aspects of existence are interwoven. The concept of cyclical time emphasizes the continuity of life and the eternal nature of the cosmic order.

This cosmological perspective encourages individuals to recognize that they are not isolated entities but integral components of a vast and intricate system. The interconnected web of existence, spanning both the material and spiritual realms, is portrayed as a harmonious dance where each element plays a crucial role in maintaining the balance of the cosmos.

8. Sustainable Living:

Sustainable living is embedded in Vedic teachings as individuals are encouraged to lead lives that strike a balance between material well-being and spiritual harmony. The emphasis is on simplicity, moderation, and mindfulness in consumption. The idea is to meet one's needs without excessive exploitation of natural resources, recognizing that overconsumption disrupts the delicate balance of the ecosystem.

The Vedic perspective discourages the exploitation of nature for purely material gains. Instead, it encourages individuals to live in harmony with the environment, using resources responsibly and minimizing their ecological footprint. This approach aligns with the understanding that the well-being of the individual is intricately linked to the health of the entire ecosystem.

Sacred Environmental Practices in Vedic Traditions

1. Agni Hotra (Fire Ritual):

Rationale:

Purification: Agni Hotra is a fire ritual performed at sunrise and sunset, invoking the sacred fire, Agni. The ritual is believed to purify the environment, both physically and spiritually.

Offerings to Deities: Ghee, grains, and medicinal herbs are offered to the fire, symbolizing a harmonious relationship with nature. The belief is that these offerings generate positive energy.

2. Yajna (Sacrificial Offering):

Rationale:

Balancing Cosmic Forces: Yajnas involve the offering of grains, ghee, and other items into the sacred fire, with mantras recited for specific deities. This is believed to create a harmonious balance in the cosmic forces, promoting environmental equilibrium.

Sustainable Agriculture: Yajnas are also associated with sustainable agriculture. The ashes from the sacrificial fire were traditionally used as fertilizers, promoting fertility in the soil.

3. Planting Sacred Trees:

Rationale:

Symbolism: Planting and protecting sacred trees, such as the Peepal and Banyan, are considered auspicious. These trees are believed to embody divine energy and are often associated with various deities. Protecting these trees reflects reverence for nature.

Environmental Benefits: Beyond the spiritual significance, these trees contribute to the environment by providing shade, improving air quality, and fostering biodiversity.

4. Rituals by Water Bodies:

Rationale:

Deity Worship: Many Vedic rituals are performed near rivers or other water bodies. This emphasizes the sacredness of water and its association with specific deities like Saraswati and Ganga.

Environmental Purification: The act of worship near water bodies signifies the importance of keeping water sources pure and clean. It reinforces the connection between spiritual practices and environmental stewardship.

5. Conservation of Cows:

Rationale:

Symbol of Purity: Cows are revered in Vedic traditions as symbols of purity. The protection and care of cows are considered virtuous acts.

Sustainable Agriculture: The use of cow dung as a natural fertilizer enhances soil fertility. The traditional practice of using cow dung for fuel also promotes sustainable energy usage.

6. Vratas (Fasting and Observances):

Rationale:

Environmental Detox: **Fasting during specific lunar phases or festivals is believed to detoxify the body and mind. This practice extends to reducing environmental impact by promoting simplicity and minimal consumption.**

Resource Conservation: Observing vratas involves abstaining from certain activities, contributing to resource conservation. The emphasis on moderation aligns with sustainable living.

7. Eco-friendly Celebrations:

Rationale:

Biodegradable Offerings: During festivals like Ganesh Chaturthi, eco-friendly idols made from clay are encouraged. This reduces environmental impact compared to non-biodegradable materials.

Water Conservation: Rituals involving immersion of idols in water bodies emphasize the importance of choosing materials that do not harm aquatic ecosystems.

8. Ahimsa (Non-violence):

Rationale:

Respect for Life: Ahimsa, a core principle in Vedic traditions, extends to compassion for all living beings. Vegetarianism is often practiced to avoid harm to animals.

Eco-friendly Diet: Choosing a vegetarian diet contributes to environmental sustainability by reducing the ecological footprint associated with meat production.

9. Vana Prastha (Forest Dwelling):

Rationale:

Communion with Nature: Vana Prastha is a stage of life where individuals withdraw to forests for contemplation. This practice highlights the importance of living in harmony with nature, appreciating the solitude and serenity of forests.

Conservation: The withdrawal to forests signifies a simple and sustainable lifestyle, minimizing impact on the environment.

10. **Dhanya Lakshmi Puja (Harvest Festival):**

Rationale:

Gratitude to Earth: This harvest festival involves expressing gratitude for the bounty of the earth. It emphasizes the cyclical nature of agriculture, recognizing the importance of sustainable farming practices.

Promotion of Agriculture: By celebrating the harvest and offering thanks, individuals are encouraged to respect the land and adopt sustainable agricultural methods.

Sacred environmental practices in Vedic traditions are rooted in a profound understanding of the interconnectedness between humanity and nature. These practices not only foster spiritual well-being but also promote ecological harmony and sustainable living. By aligning daily rituals and celebrations with environmental stewardship, Vedic traditions offer timeless wisdom for cultivating a harmonious relationship with the natural world.

Scientific Perspectives

Environmental Science and the Urgent Need for Sustainability

In the face of escalating environmental challenges, the field of environmental science plays a pivotal role in understanding, mitigating, and reversing the impact of human activities on the planet. This discourse delves into the urgent need for sustainability, emphasizing the crucial contributions of environmental science in addressing contemporary ecological issues.

Global Environmental Challenges:

Climate Change:

Climate change, driven primarily by human-induced activities such as burning fossil fuels and deforestation, poses a severe threat to the planet. Rising temperatures, extreme weather events, and disruptions to ecosystems underscore the urgency of addressing climate change.

Biodiversity Loss:

The unprecedented rate of species extinction, largely attributed to habitat destruction, pollution, and climate change, constitutes a biodiversity crisis. Preserving biodiversity is not only essential for ecosystems but is also integral to human well-being, as biodiversity supports essential ecosystem services.

Resource Depletion:

Overexploitation of natural resources, including water, forests, and fisheries, contributes to resource depletion. Unsustainable consumption patterns strain ecosystems and threaten the livelihoods of communities dependent on these resources.

Pollution:

Pollution, from air and water pollution to soil contamination, jeopardizes human health and ecosystem integrity. Chemical pollutants, plastics, and other contaminants have far-reaching consequences, necessitating comprehensive solutions to curb pollution.

The Role of Environmental Science:

Understanding Ecosystem Dynamics:

Environmental science provides a comprehensive understanding of ecosystem dynamics. By studying ecological processes, researchers can identify the intricate relationships between species, the role of biodiversity, and the factors influencing ecosystem stability.

Climate Science and Mitigation:

Climate science, a core component of environmental science, contributes to understanding climate patterns and the impacts of human activities. Environmental scientists play a crucial role in developing and advocating for mitigation strategies to reduce greenhouse gas emissions and adapt to a changing climate.

Conservation Biology:

Conservation biology, an interdisciplinary branch of environmental science, focuses on preserving biodiversity. Through habitat conservation, restoration efforts, and species management, conservation biologists work to mitigate the effects of biodiversity loss.

Resource Management and Sustainable Practices:

Environmental scientists contribute to sustainable resource management by evaluating the impact of human activities on ecosystems. They propose and implement strategies for sustainable agriculture, fisheries management, and responsible forestry practices to ensure resource longevity.

Pollution Control and Remediation:

Studying the sources and effects of pollution, environmental scientists develop strategies for pollution control and remediation. This includes designing technologies for cleaner energy, waste management practices, and remediation techniques to restore polluted environments.

The Urgent Need for Sustainability:

Preserving Ecosystem Services:

Ecosystem services, such as clean water, air purification, and pollination, are essential for human survival. Embracing sustainability ensures that ecosystems can continue providing these services, maintaining a delicate balance between human needs and environmental health.

Promoting Global Equity:

Sustainable practices promote global equity by ensuring that resource consumption and environmental impacts are distributed more equitably. This includes addressing issues of environmental justice and acknowledging the global interconnectedness of environmental challenges.

Mitigating the Impact on Vulnerable Communities:

Environmental degradation often disproportionately affects vulnerable communities. Pursuing sustainability involves not only mitigating environmental harm but also addressing social and economic disparities to build resilient communities in the face of environmental changes.

Transitioning to Renewable Energy:

Sustainability requires a shift towards renewable energy sources to reduce reliance on fossil fuels. Environmental scientists play a crucial role in advocating for and developing technologies that harness clean, renewable energy to mitigate climate change.

A Call to Action:

In conclusion, the urgent need for sustainability is paramount in addressing the multifaceted environmental challenges facing our planet. Environmental science serves as a guiding force in understanding these challenges and proposing solutions rooted in sustainability. Embracing a holistic and interdisciplinary approach, grounded in scientific research, is essential for fostering a harmonious relationship between human activities and the environment. The call to action is clear: prioritize sustainability to safeguard the planet for current and future generations.

The Alignment of Vedic Principles with Modern Ecological Concerns

The intersection of Vedic principles and modern ecological concerns unveils a harmonious relationship between ancient wisdom and contemporary environmental challenges. This discourse explores the profound alignment of Vedic principles with the urgent need for ecological sustainability, emphasizing the timeless relevance of Vedic insights in fostering a balanced coexistence with the natural world.

Vedic Principles as Ecological Guides:

Ahimsa (Non-Violence):

Ahimsa, a foundational principle in Vedic philosophy, emphasizes non-violence and compassion towards all living beings. This principle aligns with modern ecological concerns by advocating for the ethical treatment of animals, the preservation of biodiversity, and sustainable agricultural practices that minimize harm to living organisms.

Prakriti and Purusha (Nature and Consciousness):

Vedic philosophy recognizes the intrinsic connection between Prakriti (nature) and Purusha (consciousness). This holistic perspective aligns with modern ecological thinking, emphasizing the interconnectedness of all living entities and the recognition that human well-being is intricately linked to the health of the environment.

Yajna (Sacrifice and Balance):

Yajna, the Vedic ritual of sacrificial offerings, symbolizes the cyclical relationship between humans and nature. The concept of Yajna aligns with modern ecological concerns by highlighting the importance of sustainable resource use, recognizing that a balance must be maintained to ensure the well-being of both humans and the environment.

Dharma (Righteous Duty):

Dharma, the righteous duty prescribed in Vedic texts, extends to environmental stewardship. Aligning with modern ecological concerns, Dharma encourages responsible and ethical conduct in the use of natural resources, emphasizing the importance of preserving the environment for future generations.

Vedic Insights on Sustainable Living:

Simple and Sustainable Lifestyle:

Vedic principles advocate for a simple and sustainable lifestyle, emphasizing contentment over excessive materialism. This aligns with modern ecological concerns by promoting minimalism and responsible consumption, reducing the ecological footprint of individuals and communities.

Respect for All Life Forms:

The Vedic perspective instills a deep respect for all life forms, acknowledging the inherent value of every living being. This aligns with modern ecological concerns by fostering a sense of environmental ethics that transcends anthropocentrism, recognizing the intrinsic value of biodiversity.

Cyclical Understanding of Time (Yugas):

The Vedic concept of Yugas, representing cycles of creation and destruction, encourages a cyclical understanding of time and existence. This aligns with modern ecological concerns by emphasizing the importance of regenerative practices and acknowledging the finite nature of resources.

Vedic Rituals and Environmental Harmony: Sacredness of Natural Elements:

Vedic rituals often involve the worship of natural elements such as fire, water, air, and earth. This sacred connection with the elements aligns with modern ecological concerns by fostering a sense of reverence for the environment and highlighting the need to protect these essential components of life.

Tree Worship and Afforestation:

Vedic traditions include rituals like tree worship, emphasizing the sacredness of trees. This aligns with modern ecological concerns by promoting afforestation and recognizing the crucial role of trees in carbon sequestration, biodiversity conservation, and overall ecological balance.

Bridging Ancient Wisdom with Modern Challenges:

The alignment of Vedic principles with modern ecological concerns serves as a beacon for sustainable living and environmental harmony. The timeless wisdom embedded in Vedic philosophy offers a holistic perspective that resonates with the urgency of addressing contemporary environmental challenges. By bridging ancient insights with modern challenges, humanity has the opportunity to forge a path towards ecological sustainability, guided by the profound principles encapsulated in Vedic wisdom.

Chapter 9:
Common Threads and Divergences

Identifying Commonalities

Overlapping Principles in Vedic and Scientific Thought

The confluence of Vedic wisdom and scientific thought reveals a fascinating overlap in principles that transcend cultural and temporal boundaries. This exploration delves into the shared tenets between Vedic and scientific perspectives, demonstrating that both traditions, despite their distinct methodologies, converge on fundamental principles that contribute to a holistic understanding of the universe.

1. Interconnectedness and Unity:

Vedic Perspective:

The concept of "Vasudhaiva Kutumbakam" from Vedic literature emphasizes the idea that the world is one family. This interconnected worldview promotes a sense of unity among all living beings.

Scientific Correlation:

In contemporary science, ecological and systems thinking acknowledges the interconnectedness of ecosystems and the interdependence of various components. The Gaia hypothesis, for example, views the Earth as a self-regulating system where living organisms and their environments are intricately linked.

2. Cyclical Nature of Time:

Vedic Perspective:

The Vedic understanding of time, characterized by the concept of Yugas, recognizes the cyclical nature of cosmic and human existence. Time is seen as a series of repeating epochs.

Scientific Correlation:

Scientifically, certain theories propose cyclic models of the universe, suggesting that the cosmos undergoes cycles of expansion and contraction. Concepts like the Big Bang and the oscillating universe hypothesis align with this cyclical understanding.

3. Holistic Approach to Health:

Vedic Perspective:

Ayurveda, rooted in Vedic principles, takes a holistic approach to health, considering the interconnectedness of the mind, body, and spirit. Balance is a key concept in maintaining well-being.

Scientific Correlation:

Modern integrative medicine acknowledges the importance of a holistic approach, recognizing the influence of psychological, social, and environmental factors on health. The mind-body connection is a focal point in understanding overall well-being.

4. Inquiry and Exploration:

Vedic Perspective:

The Rigveda, one of the oldest Vedic texts, encourages inquiry and exploration. The pursuit of knowledge and a deep understanding of the cosmos are celebrated.

Scientific Correlation:

Scientific inquiry is foundational to the scientific method. The curiosity to understand the fundamental principles governing the universe and the relentless pursuit of knowledge drive scientific exploration.

5. Consciousness and Self-Realization:

Vedic Perspective:

Vedic philosophy delves into the nature of consciousness, asserting the existence of a universal consciousness (Brahman) and the journey of self-realization (Atman).

Scientific Correlation:

Neuroscience and cognitive science are exploring the nature of consciousness and self-awareness. While scientific methodologies differ, both traditions share an interest in understanding the intricacies of the mind.

6. Ethics and Moral Values:

Vedic Perspective:

Vedic teachings emphasize ethical conduct and moral values as integral to leading a righteous life. Dharma, or righteous duty, guides actions and decisions.

Scientific Correlation:

Ethical considerations are essential in scientific research and practice. Scientific integrity, transparency, and the responsible use of knowledge are ethical principles upheld in the scientific community.

7. Respect for Nature:

Vedic Perspective:

Vedic traditions emphasize reverence for nature and consider elements like rivers, mountains, and trees as sacred. The environment is viewed with deep respect.

Scientific Correlation:

Environmental science and conservation biology align with the idea of respecting and preserving nature. The recognition of ecosystems' intrinsic value and the importance of biodiversity conservation reflect shared principles.

A Convergence of Wisdom:

The overlap in principles between Vedic and scientific thought underscores a convergence of wisdom that transcends cultural and historical contexts. Both traditions, though distinct in their methods, share foundational principles that contribute to a comprehensive understanding of the universe. By recognizing these commonalities, humanity has the opportunity to integrate diverse perspectives for a more holistic and enriched worldview.

Shared Goals and Values in Understanding the World

The exploration of shared goals and values in understanding the world illuminates the harmonious confluence between Vedic wisdom and scientific principles. Despite their diverse origins and methodologies, both traditions converge on overarching objectives and values that transcend cultural and temporal boundaries. This discourse delves into the common goals and values that bind Vedic and scientific thought in their pursuit of comprehending the intricacies of the world.

1. Unraveling the Mysteries of Existence:

Vedic Perspective:

Vedic wisdom seeks to unravel the mysteries of existence by delving into the profound nature of consciousness, the cyclical patterns of time, and the interconnectedness of all living beings.

Scientific Correlation:

Scientific inquiry shares the goal of unraveling the mysteries of existence through empirical observation, experimentation, and the formulation of theories that explain the fundamental principles governing the universe.

2. Promoting Human Well-Being:

Vedic Perspective:

Vedic principles, as encapsulated in Ayurveda, prioritize a holistic approach to health, promoting physical, mental, and spiritual well-being for individuals and communities.

Scientific Correlation:

Scientific and medical endeavors also share the goal of enhancing human well-being, with research and innovations aimed at understanding health, preventing diseases, and improving overall quality of life.

3. Cultivating Ethical Conduct:

Vedic Perspective:

Vedic teachings emphasize ethical conduct and righteous living, fostering a sense of responsibility and duty (Dharma) towards oneself, others, and the environment.

Scientific Correlation:

The scientific community upholds ethical standards in research and practice, emphasizing integrity, transparency, and responsible use of knowledge for the betterment of society.

4. Preserving the Environment:

Vedic Perspective:

Vedic traditions highlight the sacredness of nature and advocate for the preservation of natural elements, recognizing the environment as integral to human well-being.

Scientific Correlation:

Environmental science aligns with the goal of preserving the environment by studying ecosystems, advocating for sustainable practices, and addressing issues such as climate change and biodiversity loss.

5. Understanding Interconnectedness:

Vedic Perspective:

Vedic wisdom underscores the interconnectedness of all living beings, fostering a sense of unity and oneness in the cosmic fabric (Vasudhaiva Kutumbakam).

Scientific Correlation:

Modern scientific understanding acknowledges the interconnectedness of ecosystems, species, and even at a quantum level, reflecting a shared recognition of the interdependence of elements in the natural world.

6. Promoting Knowledge and Wisdom:

Vedic Perspective:

The Rigveda encourages the pursuit of knowledge, celebrating the value of wisdom and the quest for a deeper understanding of the cosmos.

Scientific Correlation:

Scientific inquiry embodies the pursuit of knowledge, with scientists dedicated to expanding the boundaries of understanding through research, experimentation, and the dissemination of knowledge.

7. Harmony with Nature:

Vedic Perspective:

Vedic principles advocate for a harmonious relationship with nature, emphasizing sustainable living, responsible resource use, and a deep respect for the Earth.

Scientific Correlation:

Sustainability, a key focus in scientific and environmental discourse, also emphasizes a harmonious relationship with nature, promoting practices that ensure the well-being of ecosystems and future generations.

Converging Paths towards Wisdom:

The shared goals and values in understanding the world illustrate a convergence of paths between Vedic and scientific principles. Both traditions, driven by a quest for wisdom, ethical conduct, and the well-being of humanity, contribute to a holistic comprehension of the universe. Embracing these shared goals fosters a symbiotic relationship between ancient wisdom and modern scientific endeavors, offering a rich insight that can guide humanity towards a more enlightened and sustainable future.

Exploring Divergences

Areas Where Vedic Insights and Scientific Discoveries May Differ

While there are areas of convergence between Vedic insights and scientific discoveries, it's important to acknowledge that these two realms of knowledge have distinct methodologies, scopes, and approaches. Here are areas where differences may arise:

1. Methodology:

Vedic Insights:

Vedic wisdom often relies on ancient scriptures, meditation, and philosophical contemplation. It involves subjective experiences, intuitive understanding, and interpretations of ancient texts.

Scientific Discoveries:

Science relies on empirical evidence, systematic observation, experimentation, and the scientific method. It demands replicable and testable results to establish theories and conclusions.

2. Approach to Truth:

Vedic Insights:

Truth in Vedic philosophy is often considered eternal and timeless, rooted in spiritual and metaphysical realities. It can be based on intuitive or divine revelations.

Scientific Discoveries:

Science views truth as provisional and subject to change based on new evidence. Scientific truths are based on the best available explanations supported by empirical data.

3. Explanation of Natural Phenomena:

Vedic Insights:

Vedic explanations often involve metaphysical and spiritual elements. Natural phenomena are sometimes attributed to cosmic forces, deities, or transcendental principles.

Scientific Discoveries:

Science seeks naturalistic explanations for phenomena, relying on principles like causality, laws of physics, chemistry, and biology. Supernatural explanations are not within the purview of scientific inquiry.

4. Concept of Time:

Vedic Insights:

Vedic cosmology includes cyclical time concepts like Yugas, suggesting repeating epochs. Time is often seen as part of cosmic rhythms and divine order.

Scientific Discoveries:

Scientific models often conceptualize time linearly, especially in the context of cosmological theories like the Big Bang. While some scientific theories involve cyclic models, these are distinct from traditional Vedic concepts.

5. Understanding Consciousness:

Vedic Insights:

Vedic philosophy explores consciousness as an essential and eternal aspect of existence. The nature of the self (Atman) and its connection to a universal consciousness (Brahman) is a central theme.

Scientific Discoveries:

Science investigates consciousness primarily from a neuroscientific standpoint, exploring the brain's role in generating consciousness. While progress is made, the nature of subjective experience remains a challenge for scientific inquiry.

6. Purpose and Meaning:

Vedic Insights:

Vedic teachings often emphasize spiritual purposes, the pursuit of self-realization, and understanding the purpose of life in a cosmic context.

Scientific Discoveries:

Science, by design, doesn't address questions of ultimate purpose or meaning. It focuses on understanding the mechanisms and processes underlying natural phenomena.

7. Morality and Ethics:

Vedic Insights:

Moral and ethical guidelines in Vedic traditions are often derived from religious scriptures, emphasizing duties (Dharma) and righteous conduct.

Scientific Discoveries:

Science itself doesn't prescribe moral values or ethics. Ethical considerations in scientific research are determined by societal and institutional guidelines rather than intrinsic scientific principles.

While Vedic insights and scientific discoveries can complement each other in certain aspects, they operate within different paradigms. Recognizing and respecting these differences allows for a nuanced understanding of the diverse ways in which humans seek to comprehend the world.

Steering Through Conflicting Perspectives and Fostering Dialogue

The coexistence of Vedic insights and scientific discoveries often gives rise to conflicting perspectives rooted in distinct methodologies and worldviews. Understanding these conflicts requires a nuanced approach that acknowledges the strengths of both traditions while fostering open dialogue. This chapter explores strategies for understanding, appreciating, and reconciling conflicting perspectives between Vedic insights and scientific discoveries.

1. Recognition of Complementary Roles:

Vedic Insights:

Acknowledge the role of Vedic insights in addressing existential, spiritual, and metaphysical questions that may lie beyond the scope of scientific inquiry.

Scientific Discoveries:

Recognize the strengths of science in explaining natural phenomena and generating empirical knowledge, providing valuable insights into the workings of the physical world.

2. Cultural and Contextual Understanding:

Vedic Insights:

Appreciate the cultural and historical context of Vedic wisdom, understanding its metaphorical and symbolic nature in addition to its spiritual significance.

Scientific Discoveries:

Emphasize the importance of understanding the evolving nature of scientific knowledge and how cultural biases may influence the framing of scientific questions.

3. Promotion of Interdisciplinary Studies:

Vedic Insights:

Encourage interdisciplinary studies that integrate Vedic perspectives with fields such as philosophy, psychology, and consciousness studies.

Scientific Discoveries:

Support interdisciplinary collaborations that explore the intersection of scientific findings with philosophical and spiritual dimensions, fostering a holistic understanding.

4. Dialogue Platforms:

Vedic Insights:

Facilitate platforms for dialogues that allow scholars, spiritual leaders, and scientists to share insights, fostering mutual understanding and appreciation.

Scientific Discoveries:

Engage in open dialogues with representatives from Vedic traditions to build bridges between scientific communities and those grounded in ancient wisdom.

5. Emphasis on Education:

Vedic Insights:

Integrate Vedic perspectives into educational curricula, ensuring that students are exposed to a diverse range of philosophical and spiritual traditions.

Scientific Discoveries:

Promote scientific literacy and critical thinking skills, enabling individuals to appreciate the scientific method while respecting other ways of seeking knowledge.

6. Ethical Considerations:

Vedic Insights:

Emphasize the ethical and moral values embedded in Vedic teachings, providing a foundation for ethical decision-making and responsible conduct.

Scientific Discoveries:

Prioritize ethical considerations in scientific research, ensuring transparency, integrity, and responsible use of knowledge for the betterment of society.

7. Integration of Mind and Body Practices:

Vedic Insights:

Integrate practices such as meditation and yoga from Vedic traditions into healthcare and well-being initiatives, acknowledging their potential benefits.

Scientific Discoveries:

Conduct rigorous scientific studies on mind-body practices to validate their efficacy and contribute to evidence-based approaches to health and wellness.

Bridging Wisdom for a Harmonious World:

Going through conflicting perspectives between Vedic insights and scientific discoveries requires a balanced and inclusive approach. By recognizing the strengths of both traditions, fostering interdisciplinary collaboration, and promoting open dialogue, we can cultivate a harmonious worldview that honors diverse ways of seeking understanding and wisdom.

Ultimately, the integration of Vedic insights and scientific discoveries has the potential to enrich our collective understanding of the universe and our place within it.

Chapter 10:
Future Directions

Integration Opportunities

Possibilities for Blending Vedic Wisdom with Future Scientific Advancements

The exploration of blending Vedic wisdom with future scientific advancements holds promise for a holistic approach to understanding the universe. This critical appraisal examines the possibilities, challenges, and potential benefits of integrating ancient Vedic insights with cutting-edge scientific discoveries, considering the implications for knowledge, well-being, and the evolution of human consciousness.

1. Integration of Mind-Body Practices:

Possibilities:

Vedic wisdom offers rich traditions of mind-body practices like meditation and yoga.

Scientific research supports the positive effects of these practices on mental health, stress reduction, and overall well-being.

Challenges:

Scientific validation of subjective experiences in meditation remains a challenge.

Standardization of practices for research purposes may conflict with the diversity of Vedic contemplative techniques.

Critical Appraisal:

While challenges exist, the potential synergy between Vedic mind-body practices and scientific studies holds promise for enhancing mental and physical health.

2. Holistic Health and Ayurveda:

Possibilities:

Ayurveda, rooted in Vedic principles, emphasizes holistic well-being and personalized healthcare. Integrating Ayurvedic principles with genomic medicine and personalized healthcare aligns with emerging trends in scientific medicine.

Challenges:

Ensuring scientific rigor in validating Ayurvedic treatments poses challenges.

Bridging the gap between traditional diagnostics and modern medical standards requires careful consideration.

Critical Appraisal:

The synthesis of Ayurveda with evidence-based medicine could lead to personalized and holistic healthcare approaches, but robust scientific validation is imperative.

3. Consciousness Studies:

Possibilities:

Vedic philosophy delves into the nature of consciousness and the self. advancements in neuroscience and quantum physics provide avenues for scientific exploration of consciousness.

Challenges:

The subjective nature of consciousness poses challenges for empirical study.

Bridging the gap between spiritual experiences and scientific inquiry is complex.

Critical Appraisal:

While challenges persist, collaborative efforts could lead to a deeper understanding of consciousness, enriching both spiritual and scientific perspectives.

4. Environmental Sustainability:

Possibilities:

Vedic traditions emphasize ecological consciousness and respect for nature.

Integrating Vedic principles with modern environmental science aligns with the global pursuit of sustainability.

Challenges:

Balancing ancient wisdom with contemporary ecological knowledge requires careful consideration.

Implementing sustainable practices may clash with modern economic and industrial systems.

Critical Appraisal:

Striking a balance between traditional ecological wisdom and scientific advancements is crucial for fostering sustainable practices.

5. Quantum Physics and Metaphysics:

Possibilities:

Vedic metaphysics aligns with certain aspects of quantum physics, such as interconnectedness.

Exploring the philosophical implications of quantum phenomena resonates with Vedic concepts.

Challenges:

Drawing parallels between metaphysical concepts and quantum phenomena requires caution.

Ensuring a nuanced understanding of both traditions is essential to avoid misinterpretation.

Critical Appraisal:

The intersection of quantum physics and Vedic metaphysics offers intriguing possibilities but demands careful scholarly examination to avoid oversimplification.

Striking a Delicate Balance:

Blending Vedic wisdom with future scientific advancements offers a host of possibilities and challenges. A critical appraisal calls for careful consideration, interdisciplinary collaboration, and a nuanced understanding of both traditions. While the integration of ancient insights with modern discoveries holds the potential for a more comprehensive understanding of existence, a balanced and critical approach is indispensable for steering the complexities of this harmonious synthesis.

The Potential for Interdisciplinary Collaboration

Interdisciplinary collaboration holds the key to unlocking the synergies between Vedic wisdom and scientific inquiry. This exploration delves into the potential of fostering collaboration across disciplines, facilitating a shared journey towards a more holistic understanding of the universe, human existence, and the mysteries that lie beyond.

1. Synergy in Mind-Body Practices:

Potential:

Integrating Vedic mind-body practices with fields like psychology, neuroscience, and medicine could yield comprehensive insights into mental health, stress management, and overall well-being.

Interdisciplinary Challenges:

Balancing subjective experiences with objective scientific measurements.

Establishing common frameworks for research and analysis.

Way Forward:

Establish collaborative research centers that bring together spiritual leaders, meditation practitioners, and scientists to explore the intersection of contemplative practices and mental health.

2. Holistic Healthcare Integration:

Potential:

Combining Ayurvedic principles with modern medical practices could offer personalized and holistic healthcare solutions.

Interdisciplinary Challenges:

Ensuring scientific rigor in studying traditional treatments.

Bridging the gap between ancient diagnostics and contemporary medical standards.

Way Forward:

Establish collaborative projects involving Ayurvedic practitioners, medical researchers, and genomic scientists to validate traditional treatments and develop personalized healthcare approaches.

3. Consciousness Studies Dialogue:

Potential:

Bringing together philosophers, neuroscientists, and physicists could lead to a deeper understanding of consciousness, incorporating both spiritual and scientific perspectives.

Interdisciplinary Challenges:

Navigating the subjective nature of consciousness in empirical studies. Balancing spiritual interpretations with empirical evidence.

Way Forward:

Organize interdisciplinary conferences and seminars that encourage open dialogue between scholars of consciousness studies, neuroscience, and philosophy.

4. Environmental Sustainability Integration:

Potential:

Aligning Vedic ecological principles with modern environmental science could contribute to sustainable practices and policies.

Interdisciplinary Challenges:

Balancing traditional wisdom with contemporary ecological knowledge.

Addressing economic and industrial conflicts with sustainable practices.

Way Forward:

Facilitate collaborative projects involving environmental scientists, policymakers, and scholars of Vedic traditions to develop sustainable solutions.

5. Quantum Physics and Metaphysics Exploration:

Potential:

Creating a space for physicists, philosophers, and scholars of Vedic metaphysics to explore parallels between quantum phenomena and ancient wisdom.

Interdisciplinary Challenges:

Ensuring accurate representation of both quantum concepts and Vedic metaphysical principles.

Promoting mutual understanding and respect for each discipline's unique contributions.

Way Forward:

Establish collaborative research initiatives that encourage cross-disciplinary exploration and understanding, fostering a nuanced interpretation of both quantum physics and Vedic metaphysics.

Fostering a New Era of Understanding:

Interdisciplinary collaboration presents a pathway to synergize the richness of Vedic wisdom with the precision of scientific inquiry. By overcoming challenges through open dialogue, shared projects, and mutual respect, interdisciplinary efforts can usher in a new era of understanding, where diverse perspectives contribute to a more comprehensive grasp of the complexities inherent in the universe and human existence.

Embracing this potential for collaboration holds the promise of creating a thoughtful pool of knowledge that transcends disciplinary boundaries, enriching our collective exploration of the mysteries that lie ahead.

As we navigate the intersection of Vedic wisdom and scientific inquiry, the potential for interdisciplinary collaboration emerges as a transformative force. This expansion delves deeper into the realms where these two traditions can converge, creating a synergistic tapestry that enriches our understanding of the universe, human existence, and the intricate threads that bind them together.

1. Synergy in Mind-Body Practices:

Unlocking Potential:

The integration of Vedic mind-body practices with scientific disciplines, such as psychology, neuroscience, and medicine, has the potential to unveil the intricate connections between consciousness, well-being, and the physiological responses to contemplative practices.

Interdisciplinary Challenges and Solutions:

Balancing Subjectivity and Objectivity: Establishing methodologies that respect the subjective nature of spiritual experiences while incorporating rigorous scientific measurements.

Common Frameworks: Forming collaborative research centers that provide a space for spiritual leaders, meditation practitioners, and scientists to collectively shape methodologies and share findings.

2. Holistic Healthcare Integration:

Unlocking Potential:

Harmonizing Ayurvedic principles with modern medical practices creates an opportunity for personalized and holistic healthcare solutions, blending ancient wisdom with evidence-based medicine.

Interdisciplinary Challenges and Solutions:

Scientific Validation: Ensuring the scientific rigor of Ayurvedic treatments by conducting robust research studies and clinical trials.

Bridging Diagnostics: Establishing collaborative projects involving Ayurvedic practitioners, medical researchers, and genomic scientists to bridge the gap between traditional diagnostics and contemporary medical standards.

3. Consciousness Studies Dialogue:

Unlocking Potential:

The collaboration between philosophers, neuroscientists, and physicists offers a promising avenue for unraveling the mysteries of consciousness, fostering a dialogue that integrates both spiritual and scientific perspectives.

Interdisciplinary Challenges and Solutions:

Handling Subjectivity: Developing research methodologies that honor the subjective nature of consciousness while striving for empirical validation.

Balancing Interpretations: Organizing interdisciplinary conferences that promote open dialogue, encouraging scholars from various fields to explore and appreciate diverse interpretations.

4. Environmental Sustainability Integration:

Unlocking Potential:

Aligning Vedic ecological principles with modern environmental science holds the promise of shaping sustainable practices and policies that respect both traditional wisdom and contemporary knowledge.

Interdisciplinary Challenges and Solutions:

Balancing Traditions: Establishing collaborative projects that seek to balance traditional ecological wisdom with modern environmental science, recognizing the strengths of both.

Addressing Conflicts: Engaging environmental scientists, policymakers, and scholars of Vedic traditions in joint initiatives to address economic and industrial conflicts with sustainable practices.

5. Quantum Physics and Metaphysics Exploration:

Unlocking Potential:

Creating a space for physicists, philosophers, and scholars of Vedic metaphysics to explore parallels between quantum phenomena and ancient wisdom can lead to profound insights into the nature of reality.

Interdisciplinary Challenges and Solutions:

Accurate Representation: Ensuring accurate representation of both quantum concepts and Vedic metaphysical principles in collaborative research initiatives.

Promoting Mutual Understanding: Establishing forums that facilitate mutual understanding and respect, fostering a nuanced interpretation of both quantum physics and Vedic metaphysics.

Embracing a New Era of Wisdom:

The expanded horizons of interdisciplinary collaboration offer a transformative journey towards a more profound understanding of existence. By wading through challenges with openness, dialogue, and shared objectives, this collaborative endeavor holds the promise of not only unraveling the mysteries that lie at the confluence of Vedic wisdom and scientific inquiry but also fostering a harmonious integration that transcends disciplinary boundaries. Embracing this new era of wisdom is an invitation to collectively explore the vast potential that unfolds when diverse perspectives converge in the pursuit of universal truths.

Encouraging Dialogue

Building Bridges Between Traditional Wisdom and Cutting-edge Science

The imperative to build bridges between traditional wisdom and cutting-edge science stems from the recognition that these two domains hold unique insights into the nature of reality, human existence, and the universe. This imperative is not merely a philosophical pursuit but a pragmatic approach necessary for addressing the complexities of our world and fostering a harmonious future.

1. Holistic Understanding:

Importance:

Traditional wisdom often provides holistic perspectives on life, encompassing spiritual, ethical, and moral dimensions.

Cutting-edge science excels in dissecting and understanding the material aspects of reality.

Harmony Through Integration:

By building bridges, a harmonious synthesis of holistic understanding and empirical exploration becomes possible.

This integration can lead to a more comprehensive worldview that addresses both the seen and the unseen dimensions of existence.

2. Cultural Preservation:

Importance:

Traditional wisdom is often deeply embedded in cultural narratives, practices, and rituals.

The erosion of cultural identity can lead to the loss of valuable insights passed down through generations.

Harmony Through Integration:

Bridging traditional wisdom with science ensures the preservation of cultural richness and prevents the loss of ancient knowledge.

Integrating cultural perspectives into scientific discourse fosters a more inclusive and diverse scientific community.

3. Ethical Guidance:

Importance:

Traditional wisdom provides ethical frameworks rooted in values, compassion, and interconnectedness.

Scientific advancements, while powerful, raise ethical questions and dilemmas that require thoughtful consideration.

Harmony Through Integration:

By building bridges, ethical guidance from traditional wisdom can inform scientific endeavors, ensuring responsible and humane applications of knowledge.

Ethical considerations rooted in ancient wisdom can act as a moral compass, guiding scientific progress towards the betterment of humanity.

4. Ecosystemic Balance:

Importance:

Traditional ecological knowledge often emphasizes the interconnectedness of all living beings with nature.

Scientific understanding of ecosystems aids in addressing environmental challenges.

Harmony Through Integration:

Bridging these perspectives allows for a more holistic approach to environmental conservation, balancing scientific interventions with traditional practices.

Collaboration ensures that technological solutions consider the delicate balance of ecosystems as understood by traditional wisdom.

5. Human Well-being:

Importance:

Traditional healing practices focus on holistic well-being, incorporating mental, emotional, and spiritual dimensions.

Modern medicine excels in understanding physiological aspects and developing targeted interventions.

Harmony Through Integration:

Integrating traditional healing practices with modern medicine provides a more comprehensive healthcare approach.

Patients benefit from a harmonious blend of treatments that address the multi-faceted nature of human well-being.

A Unified Path Forward:

Building bridges between traditional wisdom and cutting-edge science is not just an intellectual pursuit; it is a necessity for a harmonious and sustainable future. Recognizing the strengths of each domain and fostering collaboration ensures that humanity navigates the complexities of the present and future with wisdom, compassion, and a holistic understanding. In this unity of diverse perspectives, lies the potential for addressing global challenges and creating a world that embraces the richness of both ancient wisdom and modern knowledge.

The Role of Open-minded Exploration in Shaping the Future

Open-minded exploration stands as a cornerstone for shaping the future, offering a dynamic approach to diving through the unknown. This exploration is not merely a scientific or philosophical endeavor but a holistic and inclusive mindset that fosters innovation, understanding, and the harmonious integration of diverse perspectives.

1. Embracing Diversity of Thought:

Importance:

Open-minded exploration encourages the inclusion of diverse perspectives, experiences, and worldviews.

Diversity of thought is a catalyst for creativity, innovation, and the emergence of novel solutions to complex challenges.

Empowering the Future:

By embracing a diversity of thought, we empower future generations to approach problems with a broader, more inclusive mindset.

This mindset contributes to a more resilient and adaptable society capable of handling the uncertainties that the future holds.

2. Fostering Interdisciplinary Collaboration:

Importance:

Complex issues often require interdisciplinary solutions that draw on insights from various fields.

Open-minded exploration breaks down disciplinary boundaries, fostering collaboration between seemingly disparate domains.

Empowering the Future:

Interdisciplinary collaboration is vital for addressing multifaceted challenges, from climate change to healthcare.

Future endeavors benefit from the synthesis of knowledge, leading to innovative solutions that emerge at the intersection of different disciplines.

3. Adaptability in the Face of Uncertainty:

Importance:

The future is inherently uncertain, marked by unforeseen challenges and opportunities.

Open-minded exploration cultivates adaptability, enabling individuals and societies to navigate uncertainties with resilience.

Empowering the Future:

An adaptable mindset fosters a culture of continuous learning and evolution.

Future generations equipped with adaptability are better prepared to respond creatively to the dynamic and unpredictable nature of the world.

4. Integration of Tradition and Innovation:

Importance:

Open-minded exploration involves the respectful integration of traditional wisdom with contemporary knowledge.

Balancing tradition and innovation provides a holistic approach to societal progress.

Empowering the Future:

Future societies benefit from the wisdom of the past while leveraging the innovation of the present.

Integrating tradition and innovation fosters a balanced and sustainable trajectory for societal development.

5. Cultivating Lifelong Learning:

Importance:

The pace of change in the modern world demands continuous learning and adaptation.

Open-minded exploration instills a culture of lifelong learning, valuing curiosity and the pursuit of knowledge.

Empowering the Future:

Lifelong learners are equipped to embrace new technologies, adapt to evolving job markets, and contribute to a knowledge-based economy.

Cultivating a mindset of continual exploration ensures that future generations remain dynamic and engaged with the ever-changing landscape.

Shaping a Future of Wisdom and Discovery:

Open-minded exploration is the compass that guides humanity through the uncharted territories of the future. By embracing diverse perspectives, fostering interdisciplinary collaboration, cultivating adaptability, integrating tradition and innovation, and promoting lifelong learning, we empower ourselves to shape a future marked by wisdom, discovery, and the harmonious coexistence of tradition and progress. In the spirit of open-minded exploration, the future becomes a canvas where the strokes of innovation and understanding paint a tapestry that reflects the collective endeavors and aspirations of a thriving global society.

Chapter 11:
Case Studies: Vedic Wisdom in Modern Context

Real-World Examples of Vedic Principles Influencing Scientific Practices

The intersection of Vedic principles and scientific practices has manifested in various ways, demonstrating the potential harmony between ancient wisdom and modern inquiry. Below are real-world examples where Vedic principles have influenced scientific endeavors:

1. Mind-Body Connection and Meditation:

Vedic Principle:

The Vedas emphasize the interconnectedness of the mind and body and advocate practices like meditation for holistic well-being.

Scientific Influence:

Scientific research on meditation has flourished, exploring its impact on mental health, stress reduction, and physiological well-being.

Studies have shown that meditation practices rooted in Vedic principles can lead to changes in brain structure and function, influencing cognitive abilities and emotional regulation.

2. Ayurveda and Integrative Medicine:

Vedic Principle:

Ayurveda, an ancient Vedic system of medicine, emphasizes personalized and holistic healthcare, considering the mind, body, and spirit.

Scientific Influence:

Integrative medicine incorporates Ayurvedic principles into contemporary healthcare, aiming for a comprehensive and patient-centered approach.

Research explores Ayurvedic treatments for conditions like arthritis and digestive disorders, integrating traditional wisdom with evidence-based medical practices.

3. Yoga and Stress Reduction:

Vedic Principle:

Yoga, originating from Vedic traditions, encompasses physical postures, breath control, and meditation to achieve harmony and balance.

Scientific Influence:

Numerous scientific studies have demonstrated the effectiveness of yoga in reducing stress, anxiety, and improving mental well-being.

The integration of yogic principles into therapeutic interventions is recognized for its positive impact on mental health.

4. Environmental Sustainability and Vedic Ecology:

Vedic Principle:

Vedic literature emphasizes the interconnectedness between humanity and the environment, advocating for sustainable practices and reverence for nature.

Scientific Influence:

Concepts from Vedic ecology have influenced discussions on sustainable development and environmental conservation.

Scientific research increasingly acknowledges the importance of traditional ecological knowledge, aligning with Vedic principles, in maintaining ecosystem balance.

5. Consciousness Studies and Eastern Philosophy:

Vedic Principle:

Vedic philosophy delves into the nature of consciousness, positing an interconnected and transcendent understanding of self-awareness.

Scientific Influence:

Interdisciplinary studies at the intersection of neuroscience, psychology, and philosophy explore consciousness from Eastern perspectives.

Researchers draw inspiration from Vedic ideas to frame questions about subjective experiences and the nature of consciousness.

6. Vedic Mathematics and Computational Efficiency:

Vedic Principle:

Vedic mathematics, with its ancient mathematical techniques, promotes mental calculations and efficient problem-solving methods.

Scientific Influence:

Some computational researchers and educators integrate Vedic mathematical principles into modern mathematics education.

Vedic mathematics techniques are explored for their potential applications in improving computational efficiency and problem-solving skills.

Bridging Ancient Wisdom with Modern Inquiry:

These real-world examples showcase the tangible influence of Vedic principles on diverse scientific practices. The integration of ancient wisdom with modern scientific inquiry offers a harmonious approach, fostering a deeper understanding of the world and enriching the scientific landscape. As these influences continue to unfold, they exemplify the potential for collaboration between traditional knowledge systems and contemporary scientific methodologies.

Instances of Successfully Applying Ancient Insights in Contemporary Settings

Ancient insights, often rooted in wisdom and experience, continue to find practical applications in contemporary contexts. Here are instances where ancient wisdom has been successfully applied in various fields:

1. Traditional Agricultural Practices:

Ancient Insight:

Indigenous and traditional farming practices often emphasize sustainable and organic methods, respecting the natural rhythms of the environment.

Contemporary Application:

Modern organic farming and permaculture draw inspiration from traditional agricultural wisdom to promote sustainability and reduce environmental impact.

Agroecology principles incorporate ancient knowledge to enhance soil fertility and biodiversity, fostering resilient and sustainable agriculture.

2. Mindfulness and Stress Reduction:

Ancient Insight:

Mindfulness practices, rooted in ancient contemplative traditions like Buddhism, advocate for present-moment awareness and mental well-being.

Contemporary Application:

Mindfulness-based stress reduction (MBSR) programs have been successfully implemented in clinical settings to alleviate stress, anxiety, and improve overall mental health.

Corporate wellness programs incorporate mindfulness techniques to enhance employee well-being and productivity.

3. Traditional Medicine and Integrative Healthcare:

Ancient Insight:

Traditional systems of medicine, such as Ayurveda and Traditional Chinese Medicine, view health holistically, considering the mind, body, and spirit.

Contemporary Application:

Integrative medicine combines conventional healthcare with traditional practices, offering a holistic approach to patient care.

Herbal remedies from traditional medicine are researched for their therapeutic properties, leading to the development of new pharmaceuticals.

4. Community-Based Decision-Making:

Ancient Insight:

Indigenous cultures often rely on communal decision-making processes, valuing collective wisdom and consensus.

Contemporary Application:

Collaborative decision-making models in modern organizations draw inspiration from indigenous practices, fostering inclusivity and employee engagement.

Participatory approaches in urban planning involve communities in decision-making for sustainable and culturally sensitive development.

5. Cultural Sustainability and Conservation:

Ancient Insight:

Indigenous cultures prioritize the preservation of traditional practices, languages, and knowledge as integral components of cultural identity.

Contemporary Application:

Cultural heritage conservation initiatives recognize the importance of preserving traditional knowledge and practices for sustainable development.

Indigenous-led conservation projects integrate ancient insights into modern strategies, ensuring both ecological and cultural sustainability.

6. Holistic Wellness Resorts:

Ancient Insight:

Ancient cultures often integrated natural healing methods, spa rituals, and mindfulness practices for overall well-being.

Contemporary Application:

Wellness resorts draw inspiration from ancient spa traditions, offering holistic experiences that encompass physical, mental, and spiritual well-being.

Integrative wellness programs combine modern health practices with ancient wisdom, providing guests with a comprehensive approach to self-care.

A Timeless Relevance:

These instances illustrate that ancient insights possess timeless relevance and can offer valuable guidance in addressing contemporary challenges. By integrating traditional wisdom with modern practices, societies can create a harmonious blend that honors the wisdom of the past while adapting to the evolving needs of the present and future. The successful applications of ancient insights serve as a testament to the enduring wisdom embedded in diverse cultural traditions.

Chapter 12: Conclusion

As we come to the conclusion of our journey through the realms of knowledge and wisdom, it is fitting to reflect on the relevance of ancient Vedic wisdom in modern explorations. Throughout this book, we have traversed the landscapes of science and spirituality, guided by the timeless insights of the ancients. In this final chapter, we advocate for the importance of embracing ancient wisdom as a complementary force in our quest for understanding, rather than viewing it as a competing force against modern inquiry.

Ancient Vedic wisdom offers a treasure trove of insights that resonate with the explorations of modern science. From the enigmatic realms of quantum mechanics to the mysteries of consciousness, we have seen how the echoes of Vedic philosophy reverberate through the corridors of time, offering profound parallels and insights into the nature of reality. In this age of rapid technological advancement and scientific discovery, it is more important than ever to heed the wisdom of the ancients and recognize the value of integrating ancient knowledge with modern explorations.

One of the key lessons we have learned on this journey is the importance of being inquisitive – of asking questions and seeking answers beyond the confines of our current understanding. Ancient Vedic texts, written ages ago, contain profound insights that have stood the test of time, leading to many parallels in modern explorations. By delving deeper into these ancient texts and traditions, we have the opportunity to uncover hidden gems of wisdom that can enrich our lives and contribute to the betterment of humanity.

It is important to recognize that ancient Vedic wisdom and modern science are not opposing forces, but rather complementary aspects of the human quest for knowledge. While modern science offers us tools and methodologies for exploring the physical world, ancient wisdom provides us with a holistic framework for understanding the deeper mysteries of existence. By embracing both perspectives, we open ourselves up to a richer and more nuanced understanding of reality.

In our exploration of the parallels between ancient Vedic wisdom and modern science, we have seen how these two traditions converge on fundamental truths about the nature of reality. Concepts such as the interconnectedness of all existence, the illusory nature of the material world, and the importance of consciousness in shaping our experience of reality are central to both Vedic philosophy and modern scientific inquiry. By recognizing these parallels, we can bridge the gap between science and spirituality and cultivate a more holistic approach to knowledge.

Furthermore, by delving deeper into ancient Vedic wisdom, we have the opportunity to uncover new insights and avenues for exploration that can benefit humanity as a whole. The profound wisdom contained within these ancient texts has the potential to inspire new scientific discoveries, technological innovations, and spiritual insights that can lead to a more harmonious and sustainable world.

The journey we have undertaken in this book has been a testament to the enduring relevance of ancient Vedic wisdom in modern explorations. By embracing the insights of the ancients and integrating them with the discoveries of modern science, we can unlock new dimensions of understanding and usher in a new era of enlightenment and discovery. Let us continue to be inquisitive, to ask questions, and to seek answers that lead us ever closer to the truth. As we embark on the next phase of our journey, let us do so with open hearts and open minds, ready to embrace the wisdom of the ages and chart a course towards a brighter future for all of humanity.

In future, it would also be of great interest to find out how, till date, does the Vedic Indian period stand as a beacon of intellectual and spiritual enlightenment, wherein sages and scholars delved into the mysteries of existence with unparalleled depth and insight. It is truly remarkable to consider how a civilization thousands of years ago could document such profound wisdom that finds relevance even today in almost all subjects of human interest, notably the human mind, cosmology, mathematics, and health. Of further interest to find more would be the following.

The Human Mind:

Ancient Vedic texts provide profound insights into the nature of consciousness and the workings of the human mind. Concepts such as the nature of the self (Atman), the interconnectedness of all beings (Brahman), and the illusory nature of the material world (Maya) are central tenets of Vedic philosophy that continue to resonate with modern explorations of consciousness and cognitive science. The Upanishads, for example, delve into deep philosophical inquiries about the nature of reality and the self, offering profound insights into the nature of consciousness that are increasingly being corroborated by modern neuroscience and psychology.

Cosmology:

Vedic cosmology offers a holistic framework for understanding the universe and our place within it. The Rigveda contains hymns that describe the celestial bodies, the cycles of the sun and moon, and the interconnectedness of all existence. The concept of Lokas, or different realms of existence, parallels modern cosmological theories of parallel universes and multiple dimensions. By studying Vedic cosmology, we gain valuable insights into the interconnected nature of the cosmos and our role within it, insights that continue to inform modern explorations of the universe and our place within it.

Mathematics:

The Vedic period also saw significant advancements in mathematics, with the development of sophisticated mathematical techniques and concepts that continue to influence modern mathematics. The Sulba Sutras, for example, contain geometric principles and mathematical formulas for constructing altars and fire pits that demonstrate a remarkable understanding of geometry and algebra. The concept of zero, which originated in ancient India, has had a profound impact on mathematics and science and is a testament to the mathematical sophistication of the Vedic period.

Health and Medicine:

Ayurveda, the ancient Indian system of medicine, is another area where Vedic wisdom continues to offer valuable insights into human health and well-being. Ayurvedic texts contain detailed descriptions of medicinal herbs, dietary guidelines, and therapeutic practices that have been used for thousands of years to promote health and treat disease. The holistic approach of Ayurveda, which emphasizes the interconnectedness of mind, body, and spirit, resonates with modern integrative medicine approaches and offers valuable insights into the promotion of holistic health and wellness.

In conclusion, the profound wisdom of the Vedic Indian period stands as a testament to the intellectual and spiritual achievements of ancient Indian civilization. By embracing the insights of the ancients and integrating them with the discoveries of modern science, we can unlock new dimensions of understanding and usher in a new era of enlightenment and discovery. Let us continue to be inquisitive, to ask questions, and to seek answers that lead us ever closer to the truth. As we embark on the next phase of our journey, let us do so with open hearts and open minds, ready to embrace the wisdom of the ages and chart a course towards a brighter future for all of humanity.

> असतो मा सद्गमय ।
> तमसो मा ज्योतिर्गमय ।
> मृत्योर्मा अमृतं गमय ॥"

(Asato mā sadgamaya,
Tamaso mā jyotirgamaya,
Mṛtyor mā amṛtaṁ gamaya.)

Lead me from untruth to truth,
Lead me from darkness to light,
Lead me from death to immortality.

— *The Rig Veda*

www.ingramcontent.com/pod-product-compliance
Lightning Source LLC
LaVergne TN
LVHW091718070526
838199LV00050B/2450